Acknowledgements

I would like to thank my wonderful publisher and dear friend Paula Campbell for first giving me the opportunity to become a published author, back in 2002. It really did change my life for the better and there's nothing else in the world I'd rather be. Thanks also to Paula for giving me such a gorgeous cover this time, and in my favourite colour, too!

I'd like to thank all the team at Poolbeg, and all the booksellers in the country, for their tireless work behind the scenes. It's amazing how much attention to detail, and dedication, goes into the production of each and every book. Until I became a writer myself, I never gave a second thought to just how much hard work it takes to fill the shelves of our favourite bookstores.

Special mention has to go to my brilliant editor Gaye Shortland who misses nothing but at the same time always understands what I'm trying to say. Thank you, Gaye. And to all the lovely people in the media who have supported me from the very beginning, even though I am hopelessly camera-shy, a huge thank you. To everyone at Penguin Books especially Clare Ledingham, and to my other publishers throughout the world, and to all the Irish authors, a massive thank you. I am extremely proud to be part of such an amazing team.

Once again, this book could not have been written without the support of my beloved husband Dermot, who is not only my IT-expert and my constant chauffeur, but also my best friend. And to Alice: you make the world a special place just by being in it. I love you both.

To readers everywhere, a heartfelt thank-you for buying my books and for keeping the art of reading alive. Without you there wouldn't be a need for writers and I would have to go out there and find myself a much less interesting job. And thank you for all your lovely messages of support: each and every one is most welcome and deeply appreciated. I sincerely hope you enjoy this story.

With lots of love, Sharon.

For Dermot

1

Big Mouth Strikes Again

It was eight thirty on a frosty Friday night in December. The air outside the Tube station was bitterly cold and the end of Sarah's nose was soon bright red and nearly numb. The sudden drop in temperature always caught her by surprise at this time of year. She hurried down the street and into the smartly decorated foyer of her building. A quick dash up four flights of stairs (her only exercise, usually) and she was almost there. Now, where had she put her green-apple key-chain?

"Honey, I'm home!" Sarah said brightly, even though she knew most nights there was no one there to answer her.

Her fiancé, Mackenzie, lived near a tiny village called Glenallon (on the east coast of Scotland, about forty minutes' drive from Edinburgh) all year round, taking care of his country estate. It'd been romantically titled Thistledown in 1776 though in reality it was an austere and draughty place. A four-storey Gothic mansion complete with three turrets, four

1

gargoyles and an ancient, nail-studded, black-painted front door. Perched right on the edge of the cliffs, it was a bit foreboding for Sarah. But Mackenzie was very proud of the manor house and he enjoyed country life. And Sarah loved him with all her heart, and after the wedding she knew she would grow as fond of Thistledown as he was.

In the meantime, this prestigious address in London was a much nicer spot in which to live and the furniture was a lot more comfortable, too. There was a small M&S at the end of the street and two gorgeous boutiques just round the corner. The apartment had formed part of Mackenzie's inheritance after his father died. And Sarah had been living here for the last three years – ever since getting engaged to him, in fact. (They'd been together for five years.) He came down to London to see her as often as he could and she went up to Thistledown most Fridays after work. Still, it was lonely sometimes, this long-distance love. It was nice to pretend, therefore, when she was coming home from work, that Mackenzie was pottering in the kitchen or singing in the shower or sitting in his favourite wingback chair reading the evening paper.

Sarah set her large black-patent handbag down on the hall table and switched on one or two of the electric radiators. The only downside to having such high ceilings, she admitted glumly, was having to shiver in the winter, in permanently freezing rooms.

She was exhausted after a long day spent taking photographs of a duck-egg-blue soup tureen full of lamb casserole and floury dumplings. And then a fantastically tall sponge cake, studded with silver balls and topped with sugar rose-petals. Sarah was a professional photographer by trade, currently working for a glossy cookery magazine. 'Gastro-porn' her best friend Abigail called it. Dishes that most people weren't able to make, displayed in houses most people weren't able to afford or weren't talented enough to decorate for themselves, even if they could be bothered to gather up the typically long list of ingredients.

"An entire bottle of expensive sherry?" Abigail had once remarked. "Just to add one teaspoon of it to the recipe? Madness. Who drinks sherry anyway? And who's got a long-handled serving spoon going spare? I mean, a silver spoon, for heaven's sake?"

"Don't blame me," Sarah had replied indignantly. "I only take the pictures for them. I only follow orders."

"That's what Colonel Paul Tibbets used to say."

"Who?"

"The pilot of *Enola Gay*, the man who dropped the atomic bomb on Hiroshima."

"Swot!"

Abigail had always been the clever one. She worked as a clinical psychologist in a top London clinic, counselling the depressed, the bewildered and the broken-hearted. Sarah knew Abigail didn't have to justify her work to anybody. Nobody went around making fun of clinical psychologists.

Well, she wouldn't be working in the gastro-porn industry for much longer, Sarah thought happily. Because on Christmas Eve, Sarah Quinn, thirty years old, professional photographer and dedicated fashionista, would be giving up her glamorous career in publishing, moving to Scotland and marrying Mackenzie Campbell, gentleman farmer and gorgeous older man. She was going to wear her Grandmother Ruby's cream satin wedding dress with the long line of covered buttons up the back and carry a huge bouquet of cream roses and trailing ivy. And for once in her life, she'd willingly be swapping her comfy ankle boots for a pair of cream satin shoes. She was counting down the days, the very hours, until the ceremony.

Ever since she'd first met Mackenzie on a location-shoot at Thistledown Manor (featuring Thistledown Fine Foods, his small cheese-and-jam-making business), she'd been hopelessly in love with him. He was tall and broad shouldered, gorgeous looking with tousled grey-blonde hair and bright blue eyes. He'd been married before, to the beautiful Jane, but she'd died in a car accident years earlier. Jane had been expecting their first child at the time. So that was all incredibly poignant and tragic, of course, but he didn't talk about it much. And Sarah respected his privacy and never asked him anything about Jane. But she wanted to look after Mackenzie when they were married, the way he'd always looked after her. And have at least one child with him. Hopefully two or maybe even three. Then Mackenzie wouldn't be the last of the Campbells of Glenallon to live at Thistledown. (seven hundred years, they'd been there.) She'd have the nursery walls painted with a delicate pastel mural of interlocking trees; she'd have a huge crib with warm curtains around it to keep out the draughts. She would be the best mother of all time.

Speaking of which, Mackenzie's mother, Millicent, was a bit of a dragon, it had to be said. And she lived with him at Thistledown Manor. Relentless in her daily routine, she was always doing something. Never sitting down, never relaxing. And Sarah was a London girl who didn't really know how to sew or cook or handle dogs, and Mackenzie had six prize-winning German Pointers. In truth, she still knew next-to-nothing about running a country estate with a big house and a dairy herd and a small business attached. But these were minor things. She would learn the ropes soon enough.

"Soon enough," she said to herself now, slipping off her boots. "Okay, first a drink and then I'll order pizza."

The flat was dark and humming with silence as she sloped through to the grand sitting room, took off her trench coat and polka-dot scarf and selected a large glass and a screw-top bottle of Merlot from the walnut cabinet. She'd forgotten to open the blinds before going to work that morning and now the room was cold and had a forlorn feeling, the way rooms do when they haven't been aired all day. The walls of the sitting room were painted a dark grey-blue and a huge resin-cast mirror from Italy hung above the mantelpiece. Far below on the street outside she could hear the evening traffic trundling past, some impatient tooting of horns and the occasional angry shout at those drivers still determined to double-park outside their favourite shops despite the stricter parking laws that had recently been introduced. Sarah blew a kiss to the back of Mackenzie's wingback chair and sank onto the sofa. She opened the wine and poured some very carefully into her glass. She didn't want to spill any on the red brocade cushions.

"I'm getting married," she said as she raised a glass to her reflection in the beautiful, silvery mirror. "I'm actually getting married. Little old me, who'd have thought it?"

It was so exciting. She had to talk to someone, she had to go over all the girly details one more time. She decided to give Abigail a call. Fridays were Abigail's "admin" days at work and hopefully she wouldn't be too tired for a good, long chat about personalized books of matches and tiny pink boxes of sugared almonds. But there was no answer at Abigail's house – a sleek and modernized two-bed maisonette in Chelsea. She could have moved further out and got something bigger, she said. But she valued her privacy more than anything and her neighbourhood was quietly exclusive with its established trees and close-knit community of long-term residents. Sarah hung up and dialled her friend's mobile number.

"Hello? Sarah? Sorry, I must have nodded off," Abigail mumbled, yawning. "God, this thing has a loud ring on it. I must work out how to turn it down one of these days."

"Hi there," Sarah replied, immediately feeling guilty for waking her friend. "Didn't mean to wake you up."

"It's fine, I'll go to bed soon. How are you?"

"Oh, I'm good. Just fancied an old chinwag. I'm home alone tonight. Are you busy?"

"Not at the moment, obviously! I was lying on the sofa with my feet up, waiting for something decent to come on the telly. Are you not on your way to Mackenzie's by now? Don't tell me you've mislaid your tiara again?" That was Abigail, always teasing Sarah about her posh boyfriend and his landed-gentry lifestyle.

"Ha, ha. No, I was too tired to go this weekend – we were way behind on the latest shoot. It was nothing in particular I wanted, only a chat with you about the wedding. I know I'm completely obsessed with it all but indulge me, please. Did you ever get around to buying that nice diamante clasp for your hair? You know, the one you saw in the antique shop in Notting Hill?"

"Not yet, no. But I will. I'll go tomorrow morning, first thing."

"Yes, well, the wedding's only three weeks away and you *are* my chief bridesmaid. And you haven't bought any shoes yet either. I'll have to get Big Millie onto your case."

"Very funny."

"Yes, Big Millie will sort you out. I'll get her to slither under your bedroom door at midnight and scare the living daylights out of you."

And they both dissolved into fits of girlish laughter. For Millicent Campbell stood six foot two in her sock soles and was very, very skinny. Sarah and Abigail secretly called her Big Millie when they were feeling mischievous. In fact, Sarah used to joke privately to Abigail that if they ever lost the knives at Thistledown Fine Foods, they could use Big Millie as a cheese wire.

"She's not fattened up then on the Christmas fare?" laughed Abigail.

"No, tweeds and all, she'd still be thin enough to slice through that cheddar like a dream," Sarah spluttered.

"Can't wait to see her in the flesh, so to speak!"

(Abigail hadn't met Millie yet but she'd seen the photographs.)

"I'm only sorry it's too late to get her a walk-on part in *Harry Potter*," said Sarah, giggling. "With that long white hair of hers and those long coats, she'd be a natural. Not to mention she knows her way around old castles. Up and down the stairs she goes like a panther, completely silent. You never know where she is, you just turn a corner and there's Big Millie, dusting away at the antlers like nobody's business. So watch what you say when you come to Thistledown, won't you?"

7

"I will. I'll be on my best behaviour, I promise."

"Honestly, Abigail, when you meet Big Millie, you'll be terrified. She's even scarier in real life than she is in pictures. And when she looks at you, it's as if she can read your mind."

"Oh, you're mean!"

"Yes, I know. I'm a bit giddy tonight but I'm just so excited. I wish the wedding was tomorrow morning. I wish I was in the church right this minute. I wish Big Millie was flying off into the sunset on her broomstick so Mackenzie and I had the house to ourselves for a while."

"Wow, go easy on the poor guy, won't you? He's pushing fifty, remember. We don't want him croaking it before you've got the heir and the spare safely in their cradles."

"Now who's being mean? Mackenzie is in great shape. Oh, wait till you hear what happened today at work. I forgot to tell you, but at the end of the shoot when I was out of the room switching things off, Eliza dropped a chocolate penis into the casserole. And then she took a picture of my face when I came back and clocked it sticking up between the dumplings. She said she was going to post it on MySpace tonight. I'm going to look beyond ridiculous – my eyes were out on stalks."

"Oh wow, I've got to see that."

"It was disgustingly vulgar really, but we were falling about the place. Eliza is priceless, isn't she? I know she only joined the magazine last year but I'm glad I asked her to be my second bridesmaid. We'll have great craic in Thistledown on the hen night."

"Would you listen to Miss London Irish 2007! We'll have great *craic*, indeed. Our parents might be Irish but you and I were born and bred here in London town, m'lady!"

"I *know* that. For your information, I am getting into the Celtic spirit. In preparation for my imminent move to Scotland."

"Fair enough. But in Scotland they don't say *craic*, they say something else – oh, what was it again?"

All in all, a very enjoyable chat. Just two best friends having a laugh on a quiet Friday night in.

It was only a pity that Mackenzie himself was merely a few feet away from Sarah and heard almost every word. Well, it wasn't his fault he'd fallen asleep in the wingback chair, was it? And then woken up just in time to hear his mother being ridiculed. He'd come to London on a whim to take Sarah out to dinner. But he'd been awake since dawn working on the farm, and then she'd been late home from work. And then he'd had a few drinks while he was waiting and dozed off in the chair. Now he was going to have to let her know he was in the flat. She'd probably have a heart attack. Coughing gently, he leaned round the edge of the chair and waved at Sarah with an apologetic hand.

Predictably, she nearly collapsed with fright. Her wineglass leapt from her hand and splattered dark red Merlot all across the carpet. She quickly hung up the phone without even saying cheerio to Abigail.

"What's going on?" she gasped, both hands over her mouth in shock and acute embarrassment.

"Hello, Sarah."

"Mackenzie, oh my God, what are you doing here?"

"I came to see you – why else would I be in town? With the wedding so close, I didn't want us to spend a weekend apart, that's all. And I didn't mean to overhear your conversation. It was just, well, I couldn't help it. It was so interesting."

"Look, I'm sorry," said Sarah. "I'm sorry for what I said about Big Millie. I mean, Millicent. I was joking, Mackenzie. I didn't mean any of it. You didn't think I was serious, did you? We were only having a bit of a laugh."

"It doesn't matter," he said, smiling fondly at her.

But it did.

2

There's a Ghost in my House

Abigail flicked her blonde bob out of her eyes and smoothed a crease out of her red velvet dress – the one that showed her ample cleavage off to perfection while skimming over the rest of her voluptuous figure.

"Girls, girls, could someone possibly turn that music down for two ticks?" she said loudly, as she handed out the sparkling champagne in seven tall glasses. "Thanks, Eliza. There's only so much of Slade we can take. Now, can I have your attention for a moment? Thank you. Ahem. I propose a toast to Sarah Quinn, the luckiest girl of all time! Raise your glasses, please!"

"Cheers!" the women chorused loudly.

"Cheers! Yes, here's to our jammy mate Sarah," Abigail said, winking at the bride-to-be, to show her how happy they all were for her. "And congratulations to her for bagging Scotland's most eligible, and might I add best-looking, bachelor, Mackenzie

Campbell! May she never forget her dearest friends, that's us lot by the way, when she's the reigning Queen of Thistledown Manor. And good luck to Sarah and Mackenzie on the day itself: here's to Christmas Eve! Hip hip, hooray!"

"Yay!" they all shouted, clapping as best they could whilst holding cut-glass champagne flutes.

"Thank you, you mad things," Sarah smiled, blinking back tears of gratitude. "Thanks so much for coming here from London with me today, and thanks for sharing this lovely time with us both. Cheers!"

"Yay!" they all shouted again and the music was turned up once more.

There were three days to go until Christmas Eve and a bitterly cold wind was blowing in over the cliffs. It made strange moaning sounds in the gaps of the sash windows, and the small wooden gate that led down the steps to the beach had worked itself loose and banged open and shut relentlessly. On the evening news weather forecast they said there'd be snow, falling most heavily along the coast, and that some of the least accessible villages and hamlets in the area could be cut off for days if the snow froze over. But Sarah didn't care. Her heart was soaring on wings of happiness because everything she needed was in this house. Right here in Thistledown Manor. Well, except for her parents, of course, but they'd get here: she'd no doubts on that score. No mere snowstorm would stop Mr and Mrs Quinn from being at their only daughter's wedding. So everything was in place – even the minister, the very sweet and gentle Reverend James Alexander. He was downstairs with his lovely wife, Susan, and their two adorable little Scottie dogs. They'd popped in earlier in the day for a pre-wedding chat with Mackenzie and herself, and Millicent

12

had invited them to stay for dinner. The reverend and his wife were in the formal sitting room now, having a hot port and mince pies with Millicent before going home.

Meanwhile, Mackenzie and his friends were having their stag party in the massive kitchen at the back of the house. And Sarah had commandeered the upstairs drawing room for her hen party. The girls had been due to drive into the village pub for some karaoke but, with heavy snow predicted, they were staying at home and making the best of it.

Sarah looked again at the beautiful plain gold bracelet Mackenzie had given her as a wedding present. It sat snugly on her wrist, glowing with a thousand starry pinpricks of warm, yellow light. He had told her, only the week before, that he would love her forever. And even Big Millie, who doted on her only child and was very protective of him, was being extra nice to her at the moment, after keeping her distance for quite a long time at the beginning of their relationship. Perhaps she had doubted Sarah's commitment to Mackenzie and to Thistledown, but that was all in the past now.

And Mackenzie would be close to her all day long from now on – that was the best bit. They'd be running the estate and the family business together. Thistledown Fine Foods even had its own logo: a wreath of purple thistles curled around a silhouetted stag. And they exported their produce all over the globe in tartan-lined wicker baskets. (Ex-pats were mad for it.) But yes, he'd be able to nip home to the house any time he wanted for a mug of coffee and a cuddle by the Aga. It was all so utterly perfect. She hugged herself with pure joy. Abigail saw her smiling into the flickering flames (of a cosy log fire) and nudged her playfully.

"Come on, now," she said, pretending to be cross with the girl she had known since their first day together in primary school. "Leave some happiness in the tin for the rest of us. Stop grinning to yourself there and spare a thought for the lonely old spinsters of this world."

"That's right," agreed Sarah's second bridesmaid, and award-winning stylist, Eliza McKenna. "It's cold and dusty up here on the singles shelf. Have pity, kind lady!" Eliza held out her hand and wobbled towards Sarah in a woeful display of infirmity. The seven women in the room dissolved into fits of uncontrollable laughter. Eliza McKenna had never been, and never would be, sitting lonely on any shelf. Her only problem was trying to remember which guy she was supposed to be going out with at any one time, so she wouldn't use the wrong name when she answered the phone. And she was a comedian to boot – all the guys in their set adored her. But the girls were madly jealous of Sarah and her great catch and there was no point denying it. So they didn't bother trying.

"I'll tell you this much for nothing," said Eliza, topping up her glass before sitting down again. "Mackenzie Campbell better have some fit mates or there'll be trouble at the reception. I wonder are there any more like the reverend around? He's not bad-looking for a man of the cloth."

"Never mind," Sarah giggled. "You can always make do with one of your little chocolate friends if nothing else turns up. And I'll get you back for putting that picture on MySpace, by the way. Just you wait and see."

But Eliza only laughed so much she accidentally slipped off her spot on the edge of the sofa and collapsed onto the sheepskin rug, luckily without spilling a single drop from her glass.

"Eliza McKenna, you watch yourself!" warned Abigail, who was indisputably the sensible one of the group.

"Oh yes, you count those drinks, Eliza," said one of the other women. "And don't be carrying on like this the night before the wedding! We can't have the second bridesmaid chucking up over her own dress."

"Or over the reverend," added Sarah, giggling. "She's done that before, haven't you, Lizzy?"

And the laughter exploded again.

"I hope Mackenzie and his friends can't hear us," laughed Abigail, patting Sarah's arm tenderly. "We don't want to frighten them off."

The groom-to-be and his circle of friends were enjoying glasses of fine whisky, plates of roast venison and a video of some major football match on the television. Millicent had ruled out the idea of anything more saucy as completely unacceptable, and for once Sarah was delighted that her future mother-in-law had a piercing stare that tolerated no arguments. And nobody wanted to say it straight out but Mackenzie was a mature man of forty-nine who had lost his first wife in tragic circumstances. So anything racy wouldn't have been in good taste. He wouldn't have wanted that type of thing anyway, Sarah knew. Mackenzie was a true gentleman, kind and wise and the sort of person who could always be relied upon to do the right thing. Yes, Sarah's life was just too good to be true. She looked again at her beautiful bracelet.

And then she remembered the watch.

The watch she'd bought for Mackenzie for his birthday. Which was today, the 21st of December. She'd forgotten to give it to him! What a complete airhead – how could she have forgotten something as important as that? For heaven's sake, he'd think she'd forgotten his birthday altogether. What sort of start was that to their fairytale wedding? (The theme for the wedding was black and white, and the girls were comparing dresses now and sighing over each others's glittery shoes and feathery fascinators.) Or would it be bad luck to see Mackenzie on his stag night?

But no, Sarah wasn't superstitious. And today was Mackenzie's birthday. She couldn't let his birthday pass without kissing him tenderly and giving him her lovely gift. So she didn't stay in the drawing room drinking champagne with her little clutch of giggling, cackling hens. She checked that her mid-length, black hair was glossy and straight in the mirror above the fireplace, and she added some powder to her face to lessen the effects of four glasses of sparkling wine and one tall flute of Krug. Then she slipped the watch from her handbag and stepped out of the room just as Eliza was starting up a sing-song.

There was no one around as she hurried down the main staircase.

Such a silly thing to be bothering with but she really wanted to give him the watch. She'd had it engraved too, with the message *All my love, Sarah*. She would give it to him now and then she'd have another glass of Krug and say goodnight to the girls. Go and get some beauty sleep. She didn't look too bad, considering she was tired from the journey here from London and more tipsy than she'd been in ages. Then again, she was secretly longing to wriggle her bare feet under those warm flannel sheets in the best guest-room, the one she was sharing with Abigail until the wedding night (when she could legally go back to sleeping in Mackenzie's bed!) With any luck, she'd be able to summon him out of the kitchen for a minute and no one would be any the wiser. She tiptoed past the dazzling array of multicoloured lights on the enormous Nordman Fir Christmas tree in the hall and down the corridor to the kitchen. Every picture along the way had lavish sprigs of fresh holly tucked in behind it, and there was a woven basket of cinnamon-scented pine-cones beside the fireplace in the smallest sitting room, the one Mackenzie used for smoking the occasional cigar. She could smell the delicious spicy scent of the pine-cones wafting out of the open door now and filling the house with Christmas promise.

And then she heard Mackenzie sighing and saw him standing by the fireplace, rubbing his eyes with the back of his hand as if he'd been crying. Sarah froze for a second, then gently drew back.

"It's okay, Mackenzie," said a man's voice gently. (She thought it might be Mackenzie's best friend, Dougal, though he was just out of her line of vision.) "It's only the whisky, that's all it is. You've had far too much to drink. Heaven knows I've done it enough times myself to know what I'm talking about."

"I'm sorry, Dougal," Mackenzie said, between soft, defeated gasps.

And that was the strangest thing of all, because in their five years together Sarah had never heard him cry. And he'd told her that not even when his beloved father, William, had been killed twenty years ago, falling off a horse, had he been able to weep. He'd been devastated at the time but he wasn't the crying type. He'd just set his jaw into a stiff line, according to Millicent, and the sparkle had faded from his sky-blue eyes for a long time. Even when Jane had died he hadn't cried. When he was upset about something he would usually go quiet for a day or two. But cry? No. That wasn't how the Campbells of Glenallon had become one of the most respected families in the country, she supposed.

So Sarah was stumped now as to what to do. She waited outside the door, torn between wanting to listen and not wanting to get caught. Anyone could come along, maybe even Big Millie to heat some more mince pies for her guests or replenish their hot ports.

"Now listen to me, Mackenzie Campbell," Dougal said firmly. "Let's go for a quick stroll up the drive. Walk it off, yeah? Sarah might see you, pal. She might get the wrong idea."

"She won't see me – she'll be upstairs with the girls all night."

"Well, fair enough, but seriously, Jane wouldn't have wanted you to spend the rest of your life alone – she'd have wanted you to be happy. Brrr, the temperature seems to be dropping – I'll close these curtains. Look, there's some snowflakes! Good job we parked the cars in the barn."

"I hope she doesn't mind, if she's up there watching over me, I hope she doesn't mind that I'm getting married again," Mackenzie said then. "I still can't believe she's gone. Two years we were together, just two short years."

"Aye, well, they say God works in mysterious ways."

"Sometimes when I visit her grave after church it's like a punch to my chest. I feel it all over again, the shock of it."

"Of course, mate, you would do. Anyone in your shoes would feel that way."

"And I hate leaving her there, alone, and coming home to a good dinner and a warm bed. The day they told me, I just shut down. I couldn't form a proper sentence for weeks after.

I still miss her every day, Dougal. I never let myself cry at the time because I was afraid that if I did start, I might never be able to stop."

"We all miss Jane, Mackie, God rest her soul. It was an awful blow to everyone – she was the heart of the village. She looked after us all, got everyone working together that time to stop the bypass. Come on, let's cancel that walk – it's freezing out there – and get you to bed. You'll look a right state in the morning. Aren't you going to let everyone try some shooting or fishing or something?"

"Yeah, that's right. If we're not knee-deep in snow, that is."

"Looks like we will be. Come on, let's go. Listen, you'll be fine, man. You care for Sarah now, you know you do. The two of you are great together. She's a warm-hearted girl and steady as they come, just what you need. What this house needs is a family of young children in it. Sarah will take care of everything. she'll make everything all right again."

"Yes, I know that. She's a great girl, isn't she?"

"She is."

"Too young and beautiful for an old misery like me, I suppose. I don't deserve her, you know. Giving up her amazing job to be a farmer's wife – she's far too talented to be sticking the labels onto pots of jam."

"She loves you, you fool. And you're only forty-nine, Mackie: you're not exactly ancient. I'm forty-eight and I'm certainly not ready to sit in the corner with a picnic rug over my knees. Come on, we'll go in to the kitchen and say goodnight to that lot, then I'll put you to bed."

"Okay, I'm okay now," Mackenzie said. "Sorry about that little display. I don't know what came over me."

"That's all right. I understand, I do. First love cuts the deepest, hey? As far as I'm concerned, this conversation never took place."

"You're a good friend, Dougal, do you know that?" Mackenzie had stopped crying now and he just sounded sad and deflated. "As Mum always says, my father and Jane have gone to a better place and we've just got to keep going, haven't we?"

"Aye, we have."

"I heard Sarah making fun of Mum on the phone, you know. In London, a couple of weeks ago. It was funny, I suppose, and I made nothing of it at the time. But all I could think to myself was, Jane would never have said anything like that. The two of them were best friends. Jane knew Mum was all bark and no bite. It's just she's been so lonely here without my father all these years. She's a lost soul, like I am. I mean, like I *was*, before I met Sarah."

"Don't be too hard on her, Mackie, nobody's perfect."

"Jane was perfect. She was everything I wanted and more. And I let her down, Dougal. Nothing can take all that away."

Silence.

Sarah could hardly stand up straight, she was that shocked and hurt. She never expected Mackenzie would stop loving Jane entirely, of course she didn't think he would ever forget her. And anyway she couldn't exactly miss Jane's well-tended grave in the Glenallon churchyard. It was the only one with a carved stone angel above it – all the other headstones were quite plain. But Mackenzie had never spoken of his first wife with such tenderness and devotion before. And tonight it seemed as if there was only room in Mackenzie's heart for one woman. And that woman was definitely not Sarah Quinn.

3

Fairy Tale of New York

"Come on, we should get back."

Sarah suddenly found enough energy to dodge into a nearby room just before the two men came out of the room and went to rejoin the party in the kitchen. She could hear a chorus of shouts and teasing as Mackenzie's friends assumed he'd been sick from drinking too much whisky.

"Ah, would you look at the state of him and his eyes all red! Are you getting too old to take your drink any more? Oh, the shame of it! He'll need a sick note from his mammy the next time we're having a party, bless him!"

And then Dougal's calm voice telling them they were a bunch of overgrown teenagers and he was taking Mackenzie upstairs to put him to bed. At which point there was another round of raucous laughter and good-humoured teasing.

"Hey, what happens on the stag-do is your business, Mackenzie! Our lips are sealed. What Sarah doesn't know won't hurt her!"

Sarah felt like she was having an out-of-body experience. She was having hot and cold flushes at the same time. Yes, Mackenzie was hammered drunk and understandably remembering with affection the good times he'd shared with his first wife. Any man his age was bound to have some serious romantic history, for heaven's sake. Sarah understood that. But now she knew the reason he didn't talk about Jane very often was because he was still in love with her. And that she was merely the one who would be his trusted companion, who would hold his hand on gentle walks through the countryside, who would bring some semblance of life and colour back to the house, who would try to fill the huge void that Jane had left behind. And suddenly it all seemed like such an awful lot of work. Maybe more work than she had the energy for? Sarah had always thought of her move to the village of Glenallon as marking the beginning of a period of great peace and tranquillity in her life. Now she feared that all eyes would be on her, waiting to see if she could dig Mackenzie out from under his avalanche of grief. And how could she even begin to do that when he'd never even told her just how heartbroken he was? The walls of Thistledown seemed, irrevocably, to have become the bars of a maximum-security prison.

Leaving her hiding place she darted off upstairs.

Shaking with the effort of running in high heels, and also with despair, she reached the drawing room and plonked herself down on a chair by the window. Abigail noticed at once the drawn look on her friend's face and the small leather box clasped tightly in her hand. Mackenzie's watch, which Sarah had forgotten all about.

"Where did you get to?" Abigail whispered, as she perched

on the edge of the window seat. The snow was falling steadily by now. It was quite light at the moment but they guessed it would soon get heavier.

"Mackenzie's still in love with Jane," Sarah said flatly. "I heard him talking in the cigar room."

Abigail instantly understood what had happened.

"Oh dear, Sarah, listen to me for a minute, you poor sweetheart. Whatever you heard, I can see it's upset you terribly. But it's merely guilt on Mackenzie's part. It's only guilt that he's getting married again and moving on with his life. And Jane is being left behind. It's a normal thing to do, really it is. He's letting go of the past. Was it Dougal he was talking to?"

Sarah nodded.

"I thought so. Look, Mackenzie's just feeling very emotional tonight, I daresay. The beginning of the celebrations and all. And his mates probably poured enough whisky into him to floor five people."

"No, he still loves her – you didn't hear his voice. He sounded so sad. I've never heard him speak like that, Abigail. He's heart-broken still. I don't know if I can go ahead with the wedding now. I'd feel like an impostor."

"Don't go there, girlfriend! Don't even think about it."

"You know, Jane was tall and dark-haired, too. With narrow green eyes like mine."

"Oh Sarah, please don't go making comparisons. It's just a shame you heard him. I'm sure he didn't mean he would rather have Jane back. He loves you so much, you know he does."

"He sounded crushed though, so utterly bereft. He sounded like he would leave me in a heartbeat and go back to her, if he only could," Sarah said quietly and she began to weep fat, silent tears. "How could I have not known this, Abigail? How could I have been so blind?"

"Sarah, are you okay over there?" asked Eliza, suddenly aware that the party was faltering somehow.

"Yes, I'm fine. I'm just a little bit tired," Sarah smiled back, waving at them to show she was all right.

"Look, let's go to our room and get you tucked up into bed. Yes?" said Abigail. "We've had plenty of booze ourselves, to be perfectly honest. I'll nip down to the kitchen and fetch you some tea and toast. Nothing like some tea and toast to put things in perspective, I always say. Or would you like to talk to Mackenzie about this – would you like to talk to him tonight? Would that help at all? Wait a minute, it's gone midnight now and he's obviously sozzled. Talk to him tomorrow morning when you're both feeling better. Yes?"

"No way, Abigail. Promise me you won't say anything to him or to Dougal. I need some peace and quiet right now, I need to think." Sarah stood up and prepared to bid goodnight to her friends. She took a deep breath and said cheerfully, "I'm off to bed, you lot. Try not to party all night."

"Righty-ho!" they chorused and began to sing something that sounded vaguely like "Fairytale of New York". Possibly because Mackenzie and Sarah were going to New York on their honeymoon.

"See you lot in the morning," said Abigail gently, expertly shepherding Sarah past the little group of tipsy, tone-deaf females. Eliza had made a feather boa for herself out of some fat strands of reflective tinsel and she was twirling it above her head in time to the music.

But once they were in the relative stillness of their bedroom, Sarah began to sink even deeper into her despairing mood.

"I'll get us that tea and toast," Abigail announced, trying to cheer them both up. "I don't know about you but I'm starving. We can get cosied up in bed and talk it all through," she added, throwing on a warm sweater. And hoping that Sarah would eat some supper and then fall asleep. And that she might be better able to deal with her feelings in the morning.

"I'm not hungry," Sarah muttered, going into the bathroom to lock the door, sit on the loo-seat and sob like a lost child.

"Are you all right in there?" Abigail asked her. "I'll stay here if you want me to? Are you crying? Come out and give me a hug. Sarah?"

"I'm fine, go and get some tea for us. I'm not hungry, though."

"Okay. I'll get you something to nibble anyway in case you change your mind." With that, Abigail left the room and set off down the hall at a cracking pace.

Meanwhile, Sarah wept until her eyes hurt.

How could Mackenzie have shared something as intimate as that with Dougal, she thought bitterly, tearing off a long strip of loo-roll and dabbing at her eyes with it. With Dougal Patterson, of all people? The best man! Who would now have to look Sarah in the face all through the ceremony on Christmas Eve and know that Mackenzie still loved Jane. The unfairness of it all! For how could she ever compete with Jane Campbell? And why had Mackenzie made her wait three years for this wedding if it didn't really matter to him, one way or another? When it was obvious Sarah was eager to move to Thistledown

25

and take on her responsibilities as lady of the manor? Was it because his heart wasn't really in it, she wondered? Did it matter what Mackenzie said or what he didn't say about Jane, or if he spoke to Dougal or to herself about it? He still loved Jane. That was the truth, pure and simple. Sarah had read somewhere that the truth was so final sometimes it could feel like a death in the family. And that's exactly how she felt tonight, empty and cold inside.

Bereaved, almost.

Numb.

The dream was over.

She took off her dangly earrings and threw them into her make-up bag on the bathroom shelf, wiped off her glittery make-up and collapsed into bed. Still fully dressed except for her metallic-blue shoes.

When Abigail came back ten minutes later with a tray of piping-hot tea and a plate of toasted, buttery muffins, Sarah put one arm across her face and pretended to be asleep. She didn't want to talk about it any more. And especially not to dear, sweet Abigail who was such a mother-figure to everyone and who always insisted on seeing the best in people. She would only advise her to respect the residual feelings Mackenzie still had for Jane. And that he was entitled to feel some guilt in the final days before his second wedding. And that everyone had some little part of themselves that they needed to keep separate from their partner, some life-changing experience or moment that was private and precious to them. And that Mackenzie did love Sarah now, as much as any man could love a woman. And that she should decide to be happy and enjoy her fabulous wedding day, and the dream honeymoon in New York. Flying

26

to New York on Christmas Eve! Honeymoons didn't come any better than that, she would say.

And maybe Abigail was right. But Sarah couldn't forget what Mackenzie had said to Dougal tonight as the first snow of winter began to fall. And she didn't think she ever would.

4

I Know It's Over

When Abigail opened her eyes next morning she was almost afraid to turn her head towards Sarah's bed in case she found it empty. But the suspense was taken away from her when she spied the tell-tale note propped up on the dressing table. Oh sweet Lord! Abigail's heart sank like a stone being dropped down a well. Yes, Sarah's bed was indeed empty. Her bags were gone from beside the wardrobe; her pointy-toed ankle boots were not under the bed.

Fucking hell's bells!

"Sarah's done a runner," Abigail said out loud, her heart jolting again and missing a beat with the realization of it. Or maybe she's just tidied up her stuff and gone out for a walk, she thought, clutching at straws. Getting out from under her warm covers, Abigail crossed the room in a few short steps and unfolded the small slip of paper torn from one of Sarah's trademark spiral-bound notebooks. Yes, Sarah had indeed left

Thistledown in the middle of the night. Oh dear God, what now?

Abigail went to the bedroom window and opened the curtains as if that might somehow bring Sarah back. But all she saw was a thick blanket of pristine, virgin snow covering the courtyard and the various farm buildings, and the fields behind the house with their pretty stone walls, and all the bare branches of the Silver Birch trees. The Christmas tree plantation in the distance was a mass of white and so was the village of Glenallon and the dark purple hills beyond.

Abigail's hands, clutching the note, almost shook with frustration. She sighed loudly and sat down on her bed to read the note again. The gist of it was an apology from Sarah to everyone concerned for her sudden departure and could Abigail please explain to them all what had happened.

Abigail closed her eyes.

God, but it was hard at times, being the wise old owl. Think, she commanded herself. Think about this logically. Right. She couldn't possibly "explain" to everyone. Explain what, exactly? That Sarah had left her fiancé in the middle of the night because it'd suddenly dawned on her that Mackenzie still had feelings for his first wife? That was between him and Sarah, at the end of the day. Abigail also knew she'd only humiliate Mackenzie if she even attempted to take control of this situation. No, she couldn't do that to him. Anyway, Sarah was hurting now but she would see sense eventually. Oh God! Abigail could have slapped Sarah for ruining her own dream wedding like this. Just because she was a pampered only child, and was super-sensitive to criticism, and incredibly stubborn to boot. And Mackenzie was entitled to his feelings, wasn't he,

Abigail told herself, her heart aching for them both already. Mackenzie wouldn't want all his friends and family to know he'd been caught sobbing his heart out over Jane. After keeping up such a show of strength his whole life. Poor Mackenzie! And Big Millie would be devastated too. And so would Sarah's devoted parents, who were a very shy and nervous little couple. They'd have to be contacted and told to cancel their travel plans. That's if they weren't already on their way to try and beat the snow. And what about the girls? Poor Eliza, as excited as a small child the night before Santa comes, despite her laddette persona. The girls were all here, expecting a few days of traditional country-house entertainment before the fabulous Christmas Eve wedding. Not to mention all the other guests who'd be arriving on the day itself, some of them flying in from abroad.

Oh, Sarah!

"You really do pick your moments," Abigail said furiously.

Then she noticed Sarah's wedding dress hanging on the back of the bedroom door, covered with a protective plastic sheet. She must have been so desperate to get away she'd forgotten all about it. Wearing that vintage dress had meant so much to Sarah. Abigail knew her friend would die if anything happened to it. Sarah really must have been at her wit's end, she realized. Abigail then wondered briefly why she'd never heard a taxi pulling up or the front door closing, but then again, she'd been drinking the night before. And maybe the sound of the sea had covered Sarah's escape with its crashing and slapping against the rocks.

"Phone her!" Abigail said suddenly, springing up again. "I'll phone her right now, maybe it's not too late!" She retrieved her mobile phone from her bulky white-leather handbag and selected Sarah's number from the address book. "You'd better not have your phone switched off, lady," she whispered, getting more and more worried by the second. She couldn't even bear to contemplate what Sarah might be feeling, setting out by herself like that when she was so tired and emotional. "Oh, please answer!"

Mercifully, Sarah accepted her call almost at once.

"I thought I'd be hearing from you around now. I'll be back in the flat in a few minutes," said Sarah, yawning loudly. "I'm just off the Tube. Thank goodness I didn't have to wait too long for the flight from Edinburgh this morning. They had one seat left. Just the one, imagine that! I got the taxi to pick me up at the gates, Abigail. It must have been about half past four when I left the house and walked down the drive – it was really spooky in the dark. I'm so sorry I didn't tell you but I didn't want a scene – I didn't want to wake anyone else."

"Oh Sarah, why did you run away? Why? You didn't have to do this."

"Yes, I did. Have you told Mackenzie yet?"

"No, not yet. I just woke up and got your note, for heaven's sake. I'm barely awake, Sarah. I'm still whacked from last night. What time is it?"

"Eight thirty."

"I don't think anyone is awake yet."

"Okay. Knowing Millie, though, she'll be out walking the dogs or baking bread or shovelling the paths clear – you know what she's like," Sarah sighed. "I have no idea where she gets her energy from."

"She gets it from Thistledown, that's where. She told me

yesterday at dinner: the house is in her blood. She couldn't function without it. Neither could Mackenzie."

"She told you that? Jesus, she must be very fond of you."

"I only said the house was absolutely breathtaking, which it is," Abigail said wearily.

"Suck-up!" said Sarah.

"Look, never mind that – are you going to come back here? When you've calmed down? I mean, couldn't you just come back, please, and one of us can pick you up?"

"Abigail, I'm not coming back. Not ever," Sarah said firmly, another deluge of silent tears running down her face. "Mackenzie doesn't love me. How can I share the rest of my life with him, how can I sleep with him again, knowing that? I wanted this wedding to be perfect. Now I know I'm just second-best."

"Sarah, I told you already, Mackenzie was drunk last night, staggering drunk. Weren't we all? It's normal to feel a sense of loss at important times in your life, and crying is a very good release-mechanism. If anything, it shows that he was coming to terms with it all." Abigail began to perspire underneath her warm fleecy pyjamas. Things really would get out of hand if Sarah couldn't be persuaded to return to Thistledown immediately.

No, logic wouldn't work, she decided.

Better try flattery instead.

"He does love you," she pleaded. "He adores you, Sarah, it's so plain to see. We're all worn out with jealousy, just looking at the pair of you, him gazing down the table at you at dinner last night. I'm telling you, everything will be fabulous on the day of the wedding. Please don't hurt him like this, please don't leave him like this, without even saying goodbye. Don't hurt yourself either. This was supposed to be your dream wedding, remember? Sarah, are you listening to me?"

"You know, you'll think this is weird but all the time Mackenzie and I were together, I used to look up at the façade of Thistledown, and at Mackenzie heading out to walk the dogs, and I used to think to myself, this is just too good to be true. This is a dream I'm living in. I'm never going to have my portrait hanging in the library and all that upper-crust stuff. I'm never really going to be Mrs Mackenzie Campbell. And now I know why. Because it was always Jane that he wanted."

"Of course he wanted her, and yes, he loved her. She was his wife! Sarah, I'm begging you, can you please stop being so emotional and just do what I say? It's not too late to fix this, okay?"

"It is too late."

"You really are some kid, you know, taking off like this. You've landed me right in it, too, thanks a million. Not!"

"Abigail, you've been my best friend for twenty-five years. Do you remember when we used to sit on the swings in the park for hours and talk about nothing at all, just pass the time cloud-watching and dreaming of what we were going to be when we grew up? And we hadn't even the money for sweets or ice-creams?"

"Yes, I remember."

"Well, I've been thinking how those days were really, well, real. You know? Even though we did nothing in particular. It felt so immediate. Like we were living in the right lives, in the right moment. I know it sounds daft but being engaged to Mackenzie never felt like that. Even when he was showing me round the estate and when we were strolling on the beach and through the village, I felt a bit detached. And when he was giving me the tour of the workshops behind the house, I felt like a visitor. And when he was telling me the names of the animals and the dogs and everything, I thought, why do I need to know what the cows are called? Even showing me the antiques and stuff, it was always like it was happening to someone else and I was only watching it on television. I was kidding myself from the start."

"No, you weren't, silly. Why would he even do all those things in the first place if he didn't love you? My God, Sarah Quinn, but you have a really annoying habit of interpreting things in a very peculiar way."

"But going along the roads early this morning, in the taxi to the airport, with the snow swirling into the windscreen and the air so frosty and the radio playing awful Christmas jingles: all of that felt *real*. And I didn't freak out or have second thoughts, not once." Sarah sighed and wiped her tears away with the back of her hand. "Look, it's simply got to be perfect for me or I don't want it. I'm sorry but that's the way it is. I don't believe in the sort of love that two people have to work at: it should just be there. I'll give you a call tonight when I've had a rest, okay? I've got to pack my stuff, too."

"What do you mean, pack? Where are you going?"

"Well, the flat belongs to Mackenzie, doesn't it? To the Campbell estate, if you want to get pedantic about it. And he paid for my gorgeous car, too, when he couldn't really afford it. He only sells gourmet cheese, Abigail, not diamonds. I'm leaving him. And I'm giving up the lifestyle I had with him. I don't want to keep anything that isn't truly my own. I'm serious about this, heaven help me. It's over."

"Oh Sarah, fucking hell, please don't do this! Look, I know

I'm not supposed to tell anyone what to do with their lives but in my opinion Mackenzie needs you a lot more than you think. You can learn to live with Jane's memory, can't you? I think it's incredibly romantic he still cares for her. Doesn't that show he's got real depth and respect for the women in his life? What do you want him to do? Just dismiss Jane out-of-hand, like she meant nothing to him. Sarah, are you listening to me?"

"No. I mean, yes, I'm listening. But no, it's too late."

Privately, Abigail thought Sarah was behaving like a little girl who'd just spilt red lemonade down the front of her brand new princess outfit and wanted to leave the party because she wasn't having fun any more. On the other hand, she didn't want to start making accusations of immaturity when what Sarah really needed at this moment was a friend, not a therapist. Diplomacy was called for now, as never before.

"Right, I'll tell you what I'm going to do. I will explain the situation, but only to Mackenzie himself. And I'll leave it up to him to decide what to do about the wedding arrangements. I don't want to wade in there shouting 'cancel everything!', only for you to come to your senses and get your ass back here. I mean, the church isn't going anywhere and neither is Mackenzie. You've got a few days to change your mind. Though you might have to walk back to Thistledown if the roads ice over. Have you called your parents yet? I'm worried about them – they might be on their way already."

"No, not yet. I didn't want to wake them. I'll call them now. Actually, maybe you could break it to them for me? You know what they're like when they get bad news. I'm sure they're still at home, fussing with their tickets and bickering over whether to close the blinds or leave a light on."

"Okay. And you should get some sleep."

"Thanks, I will. Well, it's up to you, what you tell Mackenzie. But I know in my heart, it's over. I'm doing the right thing. Love you, Abigail. I'll talk to you soon. Bye." The line went dead.

"Bye," said Abigail sadly, clicking off her phone and looking at it for a few seconds. Praying against hope it would ring again and this nightmare would come to an end. But no, the phone stayed resolutely silent.

"Sarah, you silly girl," she said softly. "Well, this is going to be absolutely brilliant fun for me. Thanks a bunch, Sarah Quinn. You might be running away to nurse your wounded pride but what am I supposed to do? And here was me thinking I was going to have a few days off from counselling. Better tell Mr and Mrs Quinn first, I suppose. And then I'll break the happy news to the groom. Oh, joy!"

Abigail hurried into the bathroom for a super-quick shower and to brush her teeth. She might not have time to do either later on, she told herself, especially if anyone got hysterical. She blow-dried her blonde bob, put on the merest trace of make-up to cover her own rather tired-looking skin and donned a pair of black wide-leg trousers and a smart black polo top. Counselling clothes.

Predictably, Sarah's mother was very upset as Abigail did her best to explain the situation. But Mr Quinn seemed to grasp the situation fairly quickly.

"Well, I don't blame her for leaving Mackenzie. What was he thinking of, saying something like that when he knows how sensitive she is? She should have rung and told us last night when it happened. We could have come to Thistledown and fetched her. She must be gutted."

"I suppose that would have been better, yes. But I was hoping they could sort it out, you see. I blame myself for not doing more last night, as it happens," said Abigail wearily. "I didn't think she'd take off like that, really I didn't."

"It's a disgrace, that's what it is. I'm going to phone her right this minute," said Sarah's father suddenly. "Make sure she's all right."

"Oh my word," gasped Mrs Quinn, getting all worked up again. "Do you think she might have a breakdown or something? Should we phone our GP?"

(Easy to spot where Sarah got her drama-queen streak from, Abigail thought sagely.)

"Look, don't worry, she'll be in touch with you, I'm sure," she said hastily. "Just as soon as she gets some rest. She sounded very tired on the phone."

"Ah, yes, we'll wait then. I think that would be best," said Sarah's father. "I'm very disappointed in Mackenzie for upsetting Sarah like this. Actually, she'll probably want to move back in, now I come to think of it."

"Oh yes," said Sarah's shell-shocked mother. "We'd better get sorted. I'll have to move my sewing-machine and the exercise bike out of Sarah's room. Air some sheets and buy extra milk and bread and so on."

That was the way to go, Abigail knew then. Give Sarah's parents something practical to focus on.

"That's a great idea," she told them. "Sarah did say something about moving out of Mackenzie's flat."

"Bless you for phoning, Abigail. You're such a good girl," Sarah's mother said, sniffling sadly. "Honestly, I don't know what's hit me. And there was me with a lovely Belleek clock to give them as a wedding present!"

5

Boys Don't Cry

Minutes later, on the landing above the main guest rooms Abigail took several deep breaths and knocked firmly on Mackenzie's door.

"This should be interesting," she whispered breathlessly.

Mackenzie opened the door in his bedroom slippers, wearing yesterday's trousers and shirt and with one hand clasped to his forehead. Obviously he was suffering from a blinding hangover.

"Abigail? What's wrong?"

"You're quick on the uptake," she said, grimacing. "Can I come in for a moment?"

He stood back to reveal a crumpled four-poster bed and a massive antique desk and chair.

"Oh, my head's lifting. Had a bit too much of the old amber nectar last night," he said sheepishly, ruffling his grey-blond hair, yawning and stretching.

Sarah must be out of her mind to let this lovely man go so easily, Abigail thought suddenly. They'd looked so good together, too. Sarah, so tall and slim, with her high cheekbones and piercing green eyes. Mackenzie, strong and handsome and just a perfect three inches taller than Sarah. Abigail herself was only an average five foot six.

"I'm surprised you're still standing," she smiled.

"Yeah, I suppose I did overdo it. Still, it's not every day a man gets married."

"True," she said nervously, sitting down on the blanket box at the foot of the bed. "Mackenzie, em, I've got a bit of bad news for you. I'm sorry, there's no easy way to tell you, but last night you were talking to Dougal about Jane. And Sarah overheard you."

Mackenzie's face dropped. "How? I thought she was upstairs with the girls all evening!"

"Not quite. She came down to give you a new watch. This watch – here, you might as well have it." Abigail took the box from her pocket and set it on the bed. It was the only thing Sarah had left behind when she'd packed her bags and done a midnight flit. Well, apart from her precious wedding dress, which she must have forgotten to take with her. "She's got it into her head that you don't love her, I'm afraid."

"Oh, Jesus! But why are you giving the watch to me? Where's Sarah? I've got to go and speak to her about this. Of course I love her, of course I do."

"Please, Mackenzie, I'm giving you the watch because Sarah has left the house and gone back to London. Mackenzie, I've just spoken to her on the phone and she told me she's not going to marry you on Christmas Eve."

"Ah, no! No way! I'll call her right now."

He darted over to the telephone by his bed.

"No, wait!" said Abigail. "She's exhausted and emotional. Let's give her a little time. I tried to talk to her but she's very stubborn. Her pride has taken a bit of a hammer-blow. She said to tell you it was, em, it was over."

"I don't believe this. I've done it again, haven't I? I've messed up for a second time. Oh God, what the hell am I playing at? I must be cursed. God, I should have listened to Dougal. I can't believe I was so bloody stupid. Crying like that."

"You were drunk, Mackenzie."

"I shouldn't have been drinking at all, then! I'm an idiot! I'm never drinking again!"

"Look, don't panic. I'm sure she's only sulking – she's a terrible sulk, you know she is. Even when we were kids, she'd go storming off in a huff if I beat her at tennis or a spelling test. She's hurting like hell, Mackenzie. She's terribly sensitive, that's all."

"I don't know what to do," he said huskily. "What can I do? I should have kept my big mouth shut but sometimes I can't get Jane out of my head. I keep asking myself, was she too tired to drive that day? Should I have spotted something bad was going to happen? Should I have sensed it? Is it my fault she died? My fault the baby died? She would never have driven carelessly on purpose – maybe some animal ran out in front of her? You know, maybe there was nothing anyone could have done. I just keep going over and over what happened."

"Tell me about it," said Abigail automatically. She heard these exact same words every day from her patients.

Mackenzie sighed and walked across to the window to stare out at the snow. The rooftops of the farm buildings were covered with a thick layer of sparkling white, like a Christmas cake. The estate itself had never looked prettier. They'd even put outdoor lights on the tallest fir tree and it was nicely decorated with old-fashioned twirly baubles.

"Will we go after her?" Abigail asked gently.

"What's the point?" he said sadly. "There's nothing I can do. There's nothing anyone can do. It's hopeless. Nobody understands."

"I might," Abigail said softly. "I'm no stranger to bereavement myself."

6

Will Never Marry

"So you're not going to even try and rescue this?" Abigail asked again after they'd been talking for twenty minutes.

"What's the point? I know Sarah wouldn't give me another chance anyway," Mackenzie said in a low voice.

His face was hollow with disappointment but at the same time he looked solidly determined, Abigail thought to herself. He certainly sounded very sure.

"I could bang your two heads together, I really could," she sighed.

"Sarah's right, in a way. There's no going back now, don't you see? What I said about Jane, I can never erase it," he said quietly. "I care too much for Sarah to start giving her a lot of guff, and I don't think she'd fall for it even if I did."

"But you were drunk, Mackenzie. People say all kinds of things when they're drunk."

"I don't. And Sarah knows I don't," he said simply. "It would always be there, between us, mocking us."

"So you're going to cancel the wedding? That's the end of it?"

"Looks like it."

"Mackenzie Campbell, I don't believe this. You were so good together." Abigail was nearly in tears herself by this time. "This is such a waste."

"Abigail, please don't think I'm just being stubborn because Sarah caught me out, blubbing to Dougal. I know what cancelling the wedding means, how bad this is going to make me look. But there's no point in running after Sarah because this has ruined everything between us. She knows now why I don't talk about Jane. It's because I can't talk about her without breaking down in tears; she knows now that I can't forget Jane. Every time Sarah and I have an argument about something, anything at all, she'll throw it in my face. She might even leave me somewhere down the line."

"She wouldn't leave you, Mackenzie."

"She just has! And I'd always be expecting her to leave me again."

He looked so hurt, Abigail could see that. He had lost Jane, and now because he was still trying to come to terms with that pain, he had lost Sarah too. But the famous Campbell determination was not going to let him down, it seemed. He might have been crying last night but he certainly wasn't crying now. There was only a resigned look in his eyes that told her he would weather this storm, as he had weathered the loss of Jane. Sort of. She tried again to make him go after Sarah, convinced that Mackenzie and Sarah would both regret this day of stubborn posturing for the rest of their lives. But he wouldn't budge. His male pride wouldn't let him, it seemed.

44

"Well, what happens now?" she sighed. "I've told Mr and Mrs Quinn but nobody else. Sorry I had to mention to them what happened, by the way. I thought they had a right to know."

"I agree, I understand. Right, I'll ask Dougal to take care of things, to start phoning people. He'll be very disappointed because he did tell me to shut up last night. I'll just get him to say we've had a change of heart, no need to give out any more details. He'll cancel the reception and the honeymoon on my behalf, I daresay. I'll speak to Mum, though, as soon as I've tidied myself up. I mean, I've slept in these clothes – I'm a total mess. I take it you can sort the girls out with transport and so on? I'll pay for new plane tickets if you need them."

"That's very decent of you but hopefully we can arrange something. Most of the passengers will be coming this way, to Edinburgh."

"Thank you, Abigail." Mackenzie rubbed his eyes, stopped pacing and sat down on the bed. He looked at the watch-box and eventually picked it up and opened the lid.

"Oh Sarah," he whispered, "we could have been so happy."

"I'm really sorry, Mackenzie. This is such a shock. How're you feeling?"

"I'll be all right. I hope Sarah will too."

"Okay, I'll get on then," she said, shrugging her shoulders. "Leave you be."

"You said you lost someone, before – your boyfriend, yes?" he asked suddenly as Abigail made to leave. "I mean, Sarah told me about it ages ago. He died in an accident, too?"

"Yes, his name was Donal. He was London Irish, like

Sarah and myself. Our parents all knew each other from an Irish club in Kilburn. He was knocked off his motorbike by a lorry. On the way home from work. The driver said he never saw him coming. It was dark, he said. Donal was wearing black leathers and a black helmet, he said. He didn't seem to notice all the bloody lights Donal had put on that stupid bike, though."

"That's terrible. When did it happen exactly?"

"Seven years ago, last November."

"Is that why you're not married, yourself?"

"Who wants to know?" she said, trying to smile. She was used to fending off questions from her patients. Some of them would do anything to avoid talking about their own issues.

"Sorry, Abigail, you don't have to talk about it if you don't want to."

"I never got over him, if that's what you mean. There was another guy I was seeing last year but it didn't feel the same. So I ended it. I mean, I did have feelings for the man but I knew it wouldn't work in the long term. Donal was very special to me. He made me feel, well, he made me feel special, too. True love, you might say."

"At least it wasn't your fault, hey? The accident, I mean?" Mackenzie asked, looking intently at her. "At least you haven't got that on your conscience. Like I have."

"No, that's not true. Jane's accident was not your fault. Don't look so shocked, Mackenzie. I'm a professional in these matters. She chose to drive that car when maybe she wasn't alert enough to drive. She could have called a taxi or asked you for a lift. But she wanted to drive herself. That was her choice. Just as your father loved riding horses. Just as Donal knew that owning a bike was dangerous. I mean, the statistics are appalling for motorbike accidents. His father was always begging him to trade it in for some big, boring car with a good safety record but he wouldn't listen. We were talking on the phone thirty minutes before the accident happened. Then I got the phone call."

"Oh, Abigail, that's awful. How long did it take you to stop grieving?"

"*You're* asking *me* about grief? You never stop hurting, do you? It becomes a part of your personality. You change, toughen up a little and keep plodding on. I don't laugh as much as I used to, I daresay. And yet, there's no point in tip-toeing through life because these things happen, don't they? You pray they won't happen to you but sometimes they just do."

"True."

"I have dozens of patients who can't accept the way their lives have turned out, you know. They're frozen in the moment when it all went wrong. The first time their husband hit them or the year they asked Santa for a new bicycle and he only brought a cowboy hat and a toy pistol. I don't want to end up like that, Mackenzie. Even half a life is better than getting stuck in one wrong moment."

"Like me, you mean? Why didn't you stay with that guy you were seeing last year then, if that's how you feel?"

"Because I don't really mind being alone: it suits me. I don't think I'll ever marry, to tell you the truth. He was too high-maintenance anyway, the extravagant type. He would have got on my nerves eventually with his little surprise gifts: the helium balloons and the cuddly teddy bears and the padded hearts with soppy messages written on them. He rented a white limo for my birthday. God love him for trying but I hate all that stuff. I can't take it seriously. I mean, toys are for kids. And white limos are for American teenagers on prom night, not for sitting at red lights in London traffic in the pouring rain."

"Poor guy, though, at least he made the effort. You've got to give him marks for trying!"

"He met another girl about five minutes later, don't worry about him. She gets the helium balloons nowadays."

"Fair enough."

Abigail checked the time and then stood up.

"Okay, I'd better get on. Everyone will be wondering where we are. I'll send Dougal up to you, shall I? Or will you come downstairs and have breakfast? You should eat something – it'll absorb the shock."

"I'll come down, thanks, have a cuppa. Go for a walk in the snow, maybe. I'll take the dogs out again. Mum's walked them already, I'm sure, but they love the snow."

"Mackenzie, listen, far be it from me to lecture anyone about love. But when you find love, I don't think you should let it go without putting up a fight. If I had Donal back I'd never let anything come between us. Maybe you should swallow your pride and try talking to Sarah? I'm sure you could convince her to give it another go. She's crazy about you."

But he just shook his head and smiled.

"You're quite a girl, Miss Halloran. Thank you for talking to me this morning."

Abigail nodded goodbye to him as she went out the door.

Later that morning, Abigail folded Sarah's wedding dress back into its tissue-paper cover and laid it reverently in the suitcase on top of her own clothes. She'd return the dress when she got back to London. The girls had decided to strike out for the airport in a rented minibus. More snow was predicted to start falling at lunchtime and they didn't want to get marooned here for the entire Christmas holidays. At least, not now they didn't, with this bombshell hanging over them. The mood was sombre as they said goodbye to a stony-faced Millicent and piled their bags into the boot. Poor Eliza was crying a little bit, her dreams of finding romance at the grand Christmas wedding now in tatters. Abigail saw Mackenzie watching them from the upstairs hall window as the minibus crunched away from the front gates. She waved up at him from the passenger seat and he nodded a greeting down to her but he did not smile or wave back.

7

Heaven Knows I'm Miserable Now

Sarah was bone-tired as she walked past her gorgeous, silver-coloured Saab in the car-park and in through the door of her building. Mackenzie had given her the car for her twenty-seventh birthday, along with a solitaire diamond engagement ring. Both of which she would now have to return to him. She wasn't tempted to hang on to either of these beautiful gifts. She knew they'd only break her heart. Every time she looked at the diamond glittering in sunlight or went cruising along in the car with her favourite music playing, her heart would crumble into ever-more-tiny fragments, into powdery dust. She would not cry now, she decided. She would not cry all day because she had a lot to do. When she'd found a new place to live and cleared her things out of the flat, then she would cry her eyes out.

Her pulse racing, Sarah walked slowly towards the lift. She wouldn't bother with the stairs today, she decided. The security guard was sitting at his little marble desk as usual, beside a rather lovely, huge, fresh Christmas tree decorated with cute Santa figurines and tiny glass reindeers; and there was a huge wreath with frosted-effect red berries on the wall opposite the lift.

"Hello Sarah," he said kindly. "Cold out, isn't it?"

"Hiya, Tim," Sarah said, as cheerfully as she could. "Gorgeous tree, very fancy! How are you?"

"Can't complain. You?"

"No, I can't complain either."

"Good," he said, indicating to Sarah to help herself to a candy cane from the goldfish bowl on his desk. "If I'm not careful, the new building manager will have me up on the roof with ten thousand fairy-lights and a staple-gun. She's just mad about Christmas. What's Santa bringing you this year?"

"A big surprise, he's already brought it," Sarah said sighing.

Then she noticed a small, tidy pile of folded plastic bags on the communal hall table, asking for donations of unwanted goods and clothes in aid of Help the Aged. Sarah stood rooted to the spot, staring at the little mound of yellow bags for a full ten seconds before collecting them into a bundle and going up to Mackenzie's apartment. Someone at Help the Aged had taken the time and trouble to deliver these bags, she thought, feeling extremely emotional. How sad that the welfare of Britain's poorest senior citizens should depend on people's unwanted bric-à-brac. She laid the bags out in a line on the kitchen table. There were nineteen of them. She reckoned that would be enough for her stuff.

First of all, though, she called her parents to tell them she was all right. They were delighted to hear from her, naturally.

"God bless us, Sarah pet," her father said tenderly, "it's good to hear your voice. We've been pacing the floor all morning here. Well, for the last half-hour. Abigail filled us in briefly on what happened and we're on your side, needless to say. He doesn't deserve you, love. I've never heard anything like it. He should have kept them silly auld thoughts to himself, so he should. I mean, it wasn't the right time. It was *your time* to be in the spotlight. I was going to have it out with him, of course I was, but in the end we decided to keep our gobs shut. Abigail didn't think it was any of our business. I mean, she said it was between himself and yourself. Shame on him, though. And Millicent was always so civil to us when we visited, too."

"Are you going to move back to ours today?" her mother wanted to know next, wrenching the phone out of her husband's hands. "Only your room's not quite ready. But don't worry, it will be. I have the heating on full blast and your duvet is in the airing cupboard. It'll be lovely to have you home for Christmas, my darling. Except, of course, that your engagement is off and the wedding is cancelled also. Oh, I didn't mean it to come out like that, sweetheart. But you know I meant well. What time will we see you? I'll make chicken and chips."

"Give me that phone, woman," her husband said impatiently. "Chicken and chips, at a time like this? We need to know is our daughter all right? I could thump that stupid man right now. Even though he's twice my size."

"A good meal will help Sarah get her strength back. It'll do a lot more good for our daughter than you getting yourself arrested, you bloody eejit!"

Sarah could hear them whispering furiously at each other.

They seemed to have forgotten she was on the other end of the phone.

"Oi! Stop it, you two! I haven't decided what I'm going to do yet. I'm having a lie-down first: I haven't slept all night. I need to rest."

"Well, you shouldn't have crept off like that in the middle of the night," her mother scolded. "Anything could have happened. Was the taxi from a proper taxi firm – did you even think to check? There could have been a fire at Thistledown or anything, and nobody would have known where you were."

"I wanted to be by myself, Mum. I'm sorry you were worried. I know it was a stupid thing to do."

"Yes, well, that's all right. It's done now, isn't it? We'll be here, pet, when you're ready to see us. We'll come and pick you up at the apartment, if you like. And don't you dare disappear like that ever again, do you hear me now? Poor Abigail was beside herself with worry when she got your note. Be strong, pet. We love you."

"We love you," her father repeated over his wife's shoulder.

"Yes, I know. I love you, too. Bye for now."

"Cheerio, darling. Keep in touch."

"Cheerio."

Then she lay down on the sofa and slept for several hours, not stirring once, not even dreaming.

* * *

Far away in Scotland, Mackenzie had walked both the dogs and himself to the point of exhaustion. He'd been on the verge of calling Sarah several times, just to say goodbye as friends, but then he'd bottled out. Eventually he'd lost his temper with the mobile phone and thrown it away down a steep hill. Which was a very foolish thing to have done because the weather was icy cold, and getting colder by the minute, and in the end he had to go digging in the snow with his bare hands to try to retrieve it. Hypothermia was setting in, and the dogs were shivering violently. Then he discovered the phone was broken and he began to panic. But not to worry, Millicent was out searching for him in the jeep. She'd brought blankets for the dogs and a flask of hot soup for her precious son, and she'd not bothered giving him one of her famous lectures on the way home, about always behaving sensibly in wintry conditions. Even Millicent knew when someone had suffered enough already.

Mackenzie was sleeping now, in an old armchair in front of the fire in the kitchen, with a thick blanket over him and the six Pointers also asleep on the rug at his feet. Millicent looked at them all fondly, her little family. Then she got on with running Thistledown as she always had. Making more soup, answering that day's mail, washing dishes and dusting shelves, checking the workshops and letting the staff leave early before the snow got any worse, saying a prayer for her beloved late husband and missing him as much as ever, bringing in more firewood, sweeping up crumbs. And also thinking she might have to intervene at this late stage in her son's love-life. Not that she approved of parental meddling or match-making, definitely not. But she decided she was going to have to do something to bring Mackenzie out of his shell for once and for all. Otherwise he was going to end up growing old and crotchety like herself.

* * *

Just as the afternoon sun was fading in the sky, Sarah was jolted awake by someone playing Christmas carols loudly in the flat next door. It would soon be Christmas Eve, she remembered suddenly. The day of the wedding. She would have been on her way to New York with Mackenzie by her side as Christmas Day dawned. Her gorgeous new husband and all their plans for the future: all gone now.

As if she were a robot, Sarah got up, went silently into the main bedroom of the flat and opened her wardrobes.

"I will only keep what I really, really need," she told herself sternly. For one thing in this entire fiasco was crystal clear to her: if she was going to leave Mackenzie Campbell, she was going to do it properly. A clean break with no coming back for this particular book or that favourite casserole dish or to return keys or collect letters. None of that co-dependent nonsense for the likes of Sarah Quinn! And so, she laid her two hard-shell, ponyskin-patterned suitcases open on the bed. She set her favourite shoes into the biggest case, the ones she had worn to her hen party: a pair of dark-blue, shiny snakeskin-effect high heels with scalloped edges and gold ankle straps. Next, she added three more pairs of ankle boots, her best work suit, two pairs of her most comfy jeans and two warm sweaters, socks and underwear, her photography portfolio and her document case of personal papers. Her best make-up and her favourite pyjamas she packed in the smaller case, as well as one winter coat, some vintage Stranglers T-shirts and CDs and two signed books on photography. All the rest of her clothes and shoes, all the rest of her lovely accessories she placed neatly in the yellow bags and took them down to the foyer in the lift.

"Are you moving out or what?" Tim asked, slightly alarmed

at the huge pile of stuff he was going to have to keep an eye on. For he couldn't be too careful about theft, even in a posh building full of wealthy people like this. And besides, the yellow sacks were clashing terribly with these fancy Christmas decorations. The manager would go spare! He wondered had he enough room in the cleaner's store to hide them away until they were collected.

"Yeah. I am."

"Really? Are you? I was only joking."

"Yes, I'm going today," Sarah smiled back, her whole body feeling like it was made out of painted glass (like the fragile, antique drop-baubles at Thistledown) and might shatter at any moment.

"Well, this is big news," he said, scanning down the pages of his log book. "I've got nothing written down here about anyone moving out."

"It's just me who's going, not Mackenzie," she said, fighting back a sob.

"Oh, right. I see. Well, that's a shame. I'm sorry to hear that. Oh, is that what you meant before? About the surprise that's come already?"

"Yes, I suppose I should have been more specific. Take care with these four bags here, will you? They've got breakables in. Cookware and tableware. Some good pieces, actually. I'd hate for them to get broken. I've a few more bags to bring down."

"Will do, Sarah. They'll be chuffed to bits when they see this lot."

"Thanks, Tim, you're very kind."

They smiled at each other, a sad sort of smile. She was leaving the building for the last time; he was probably trapped there forever since he hadn't worked harder at school and now had a wife and daughter to support.

Together they lined the sacks up tidily behind the desk though Tim knew he'd have to hide them all as soon as Sarah left. Her vast collection of coffee-table books went to the foyer too. Her precious photography props, including a pink glass cake-stand she'd bought in Venice, were wrapped in sheets of tissue paper and added to the charity pile. Her old make-up and other things not fit for donation she binned in the communal dumpster at the back of the building.

She went back upstairs feeling strangely blank, made a reviving cup of tea and called her old boss to say she wasn't getting married and moving to Scotland now after all and was there any chance she could have her old job back? He sympathized for a few minutes and said he'd keep her in mind if a vacancy came up but he was very sorry, he'd made other arrangements. Sarah thanked him anyway and wished them all a happy Christmas. She could hear the staff party going full swing in the background.

Then she took a deep breath and got on with the job of leaving Mackenzie. She changed the sheets on the bed and cleaned the bathroom until it shone. Her jars of decaf coffee, crunchy peanut-butter and some other foods she knew Mackenzie would not want, she threw away. She cleaned the fridge and even emptied the small bin under the sink, lining it with a fresh bag. For who knew when Mackenzie would be here again? He'd only kept this apartment on as an investment and in case he ever had children who needed it for college digs.

She deleted her phone messages and stored numbers from the telephone and closed her personal e-mail account on the computer after first arranging to have her snail-mail redirected to her parents' address in Islington. Then, still holding back the tears, she wrote a letter to Mackenzie on a pad of pale-blue notepaper, using her very best fountain pen.

Dear Mackenzie,

I know it was wrong of me to eavesdrop last night, and if I could turn back the clock, I would. But we know each other well enough by now to realize this is the end for you and me. You still love Jane, and I don't want to compete with her memory or live in her shadow. Or say I love you ever again, without judging the sincerity of your reply. Maybe some women could get past this, some women who are a lot more mature and forgiving than I am, but I can't get past it. So that's that. It's not your fault and I'm sorry I didn't understand sooner that you felt this way. I'm going to have a good rest and take stock for a while, and I hope you'll be okay too. I will miss you so much, and I'll always treasure the time we had together. But staying with you now would only be a pretence for both of us. I hope you understand. Please say goodbye to Millicent for me and I really didn't mean those things I said about her. And please take good care of yourself, and don't work too hard.

Love always,
Sarah. XXX

She held the envelope to her lips for a moment before addressing it and adding a stamp. She'd post it on her way out. There was a letterbox at the end of the street. She put the letter in her pocket. There was nothing else left to do now.

Rest and take stock, she'd said. Well, there wasn't much hope of that, was there? With her own mother fussing over her and her father quietly seething with impotent rage. They'd both be complaining about this cancelled wedding for the next ten years. Saying Mackenzie had been far too old for her anyway, that maybe it was a good thing Sarah had been eavesdropping like a spy that night. Convinced it was God's way of rescuing her from an unhappy marriage.

And she'd have to do the rounds of the magazines in the near future, too, looking for a new job in the cutthroat publishing industry. The one everybody else thought was such a doss-and-doddle. All launch parties and loads of lovely freebies and expensive cocktails. Chance would be a fine thing as far as photographers were concerned! Jade Goody was higher up the guest list than she'd ever be. And she'd have to manage without a car, too. Waiting on buses in the rain, squashed up against complete strangers on the Tube, knife-wielding hoodies eyeing her camera bag. Some hope of a rest.

If only she had someone to go on holiday with, she thought sadly. If only there was someone who would fly off with her to the Bahamas or some other sunny paradise for a fortnight. Mind you, the sight of the other honeymoon couples embracing beneath the coconut trees might tip her over the edge. Anyway, there was no one free to travel with her. Abigail was extra-busy at work each Christmas, and she couldn't bear to face the other girls for a while yet. And where could she go, on her own, at this time of year, without being stared at and treated like a freak?

The answer came to her like a Christmas wish.

Ireland.

8

Sometimes

Sometimes a girl just has to go with her instincts.

The Irish were a very tolerant bunch, Sarah thought, and they were well used to misery and despair, weren't they? They sang songs in the pub about how unhappy they were, they revelled in it, for goodness sake. Or they had in the past. Maybe they didn't sing sad songs any more? But anyway, they wouldn't think she was barmy if she popped over there by herself for a little holiday while everybody else was celebrating Christmas. She knew that for a fact. Because she'd been told by several of her Irish relatives that her own parents were "sound as a pound". Her parents – a couple so riddled with hang-ups and strange notions that they considered someone to be a runaway snob if they had a bottle of liquid soap in their bathroom. And if the colour of the soap actually matched their bathroom tiles or their towels or something, then that person was automatically upgraded to the Queen Mum (even now the dear lady was in the company of angels). And if someone had something really fancy like a power-shower with a curved glass door or a hardwood patio set, then they were pronounced the Queen of Sheba forevermore. On the other hand, her mother and father had a very, very long list of things that were indicative of "the sort of person you wouldn't want to get too friendly with", chief of which was an untidy front garden. So yes, if Sarah's parents could be described as "sound as a pound" by the Irish, then Ireland was definitely where she was going next. She would fit right in there hopefully. Hadn't Abigail told her lots of times she had a very peculiar way of looking at things?

So that was how Sarah decided she was going to go to Ireland for a while. To the tiny village (well, hamlet really) of Redstone on the west coast of Ireland, with its empty spaces and its much slower pace of life. Her parents were from Redstone and they'd spent some lovely holidays there when she was a small child. Peaceful holidays sitting on the beach or in a rented caravan, reading library books, eating salt-drenched fish suppers from the chippy. God, she had a sudden image of the young girl in the chippy liberally pouring the salt over their fish and chips from a bulky cardboard drum! Probably half a dozen spoonfuls of it, every time. Still, it'd tasted like heaven. This was because they used "the best of good lard" in the fryers, her father had told her proudly.

Sarah hadn't been back since she was little and even her parents didn't get back so much these days, as more and more of the people they knew there were replaced by "blow-ins and second-homers". (Never mind that they themselves had been blow-ins to London at one time. That was yet another of their complicated notions.)

But right now Redstone seemed the answer to Sarah's prayers. She was very tired in a general sort of way, she realized suddenly. She needed some time off the merry-go-round of life. Nobody would miss her, not really. Her parents always spent Christmas Day with relatives in Teddington, and they could still go there now the wedding was cancelled. They'd be okay without her. In fact, they'd be better off. She didn't want them to witness her weeping helplessly over the mushy parsnips and the HP sauce bottles. (They were all addicted to HP sauce in the Quinn family circle.) No, she really didn't feel up to a Chrimbo-hooley in Teddington this year. She smiled as she recalled how, by teatime, they'd have dug out their old vinyl showband records, pushed the furniture to one side and be jiving wildly to the "Hucklebuck". And she didn't want to spoil the day for them all. They'd have enough work to do, trying to recreate the working-class background they remembered from the 1970s, with a paper tablecloth and napkins, paper-concertina decorations on the ceiling and a paper hat on everyone's head. Setting fire to the Christmas pudding was nothing short of a nightmare. Her father always had to be standing by with the fire extinguisher when the blue flames went up.

Time to go.

She felt so emotional as she was wheeling her two bulky suitcases down the hall for the last time. She tried to slip her elegant, black fountain pen into her handbag but her hand was trembling too much to open the zip so she put it in her coat pocket instead. She took a final look round the flat to make sure she had not forgotten anything but no, it seemed she was all ready to go. She had her iPod and her passport and her mobile phone and her wallet. Her keys to the flat and the

Saab, and her engagement ring, she put in the small safe in the bedroom. They had nothing else in there, really. Just some insurance documents and a little bit of cash. The gold bracelet she toyed with for a moment and then decided to keep. Just to remember Mackenzie by. Just to remember the good times. She picked up her suitcases then, her handbag and her bulky camera rucksack, and almost whimpered with the finality of it all. She limped out the door, closed it behind her and made for the lift.

"Cheerio, love, and mind yourself," Tim said kindly from his little nest of retro decorations and striped candy canes.

She was barely able to nod goodbye to him.

All the way along the street, Sarah's heart was thumping like the bell that clangs when people hammer the pedal hard enough at fun-fairs. But she made it to the taxi-rank at the end of the road and somehow kept her wits about her long enough to catch the Heathrow Express at Paddington station and buy an airline ticket to Dublin.

Why didn't she simply go home to Islington, she mused in the airport café, sitting over a frothy cappuccino that was far too hot to drink. Why not go home again, where she had her old bedroom still waiting for her. Her shabby attic room with its textured floral wallpaper and the pop posters (clipped from music magazines) in coloured plastic frames. Her parents would be only too happy to have her back.

Well, she couldn't go to Islington precisely because her parents *were* lovely and her old bedroom *was* still there waiting for her with its aura of teenage innocence. She didn't want to have to sleep by herself in that little single bed under the skylight ever again. And she didn't want to have to explain everything

64

to her parents until she understood it all herself. She wanted to go somewhere new, to keep moving forward. She wanted to live a life that was perfect and not filled with compromises and "never minds" and "what-might-have-beens". Yes, she was idealistic to a fault, she knew that. They could have been happy enough together, despite what Mackenzie had revealed as she listened. But happy enough wasn't good enough for Sarah Quinn. She wanted to be blissfully happy. Abigail would say she needed counselling for her perfectionist leanings, she thought to herself as her flight was announced and she stood up to leave. Her cappuccino was untouched. Well, right or wrong, she had made up her mind.

"Never go back," she kept saying to herself as the plane gathered speed on the runway and pointed its bulbous nose to the darkening sky. "Never go back. I must never go back."

9

Pretty in Pink

Not surprisingly, Sarah dozed off for the fifty-minute evening flight to Dublin and the plane had already landed by the time she opened her eyes again. But the second she stepped off the shuttle-bus in Dublin city centre she began to feel wracked with guilt. She felt hot and panicky just imagining Mackenzie's reaction to her letter. Would he track her down and come to Ireland looking for a confrontation? She almost felt afraid of him then. He was always such a pillar of strength – he might not take this rejection lying down. However, he hadn't called her once or left a message. So probably he wasn't going to pursue her. She might never see him again. The thought left her feeling desolate. Reality was beginning to sink in. Maybe the compromisers of this world were onto something, she thought, terrified. But then she took some slow, controlled breaths and kept on walking.

She looked around the late-night shops for a little while,

inexplicably purchasing a Buddha's head made of stone in a tiny little giftshop called The Silver Birdcage. The statue was approximately two-thirds life-size and weighed an absolute ton, and she had more than enough to carry already. But for some reason she couldn't go past it. It made her feel relaxed just gazing at the Buddha's face, sitting there in a very ornate glass case surrounded by a host of other trinkets, lit by green and blue spotlights, the entire shop smelling of roses. The Buddha reminded Sarah that she was merely a speck in the cosmos. And therefore her problems must be mere specks also. It was a comforting thought. The woman who served her at the counter seemed to know she needed a friend, however. She was quite chatty, asking Sarah about her visit to Dublin and what she was doing for Christmas. Sarah tried to give away as little information about herself as possible, wishing this intuitive woman would simply wrap her statue quickly and shove it in a bag. She tried looking out the window, glancing at her watch, anything to make this person understand she was in a hurry. But she couldn't help noticing the shop-assistant's appearance because she had a raven-black bob and she was wearing a matt-black dress that looked antique, perhaps 1940s. She had dark smoky eyeshadow on her eyelids and she was incredibly beautiful. Her hands were long and slender with painted-black fingernails and she wore strong, spicy perfume. Sarah couldn't figure out what it was about her that was so compelling. Maybe she was a fortune-teller or something. She had that air about her.

"This'll bring you good luck," the mysterious woman said, smiling benevolently as she handed Sarah a thick, black paper carrier-bag. "Merry Christmas."

"Merry Christmas to you, too," laughed Sarah. "I guess it'll bring me massive biceps if it brings me nothing else. Bye now."

Clasping her belongings to her, for comfort as well as to prevent people bumping into her all the time, Sarah decided it was time to find a bed for the night.

Buying a cheap bottle of wine (just in case she felt like a nightcap), she booked into a small, friendly looking hotel near Saint Stephen's Green, took a long, hot shower and attempted to order coffee and something festive like turkey sandwiches from room service. But she was told they were ever so sorry, the kitchen had closed for the day. Whereupon she sank onto the bed in her surprisingly homely and old-fashioned hotel room, opened the wine and called her parents to say goodnight. There was an hour or so then when she forgot herself, sipping red wine from a teacup, laughing at the shambolic antics on *Most Haunted*, which she'd discovered by chance on the television. (The lot of them tripping over themselves, screaming with fright and floundering about like Laurel and Hardy in some harmless, dank cellar.) Soon, half of the bottle was gone. Then, exhausted to the bottom of her soul, she curled up on top of the covers and quietly cried herself to sleep. With relief as well as sadness, it had to be said. Relief that she had found out about the hold Jane still had over her fiancé before it was too late. And relief that she wouldn't have to spend the rest of her life winning over the hearts of everyone in the village. Although she did feel completely wretched for what she'd done to Mackenzie, abandoning him like that. And she hated him a little bit too, for not running after her and begging her to try again. (Which made no sense whatsoever, but then again she wasn't feeling very sensible at the moment.) And also, she missed his kisses. Mackenzie had been very tender and passionate in bed and now she'd never be able to press her soft body against his hard one any more and kiss him until she could feel her lips melting. But the main thing was, she had done the right thing. For both of them.

* * *

Sarah woke up at nine o'clock next morning feeling horribly hungover and with a stiff shoulder that she concluded she must have got by sleeping on her arm. She tried to cheer herself up by changing into her warmest pyjamas, getting into bed properly and lying there with her eyes closed, listening to the radio. But she couldn't help wondering what the hell she was going to do next. She was independent once again and she was terrified. She was living her new life but it looked pretty bleak at the moment.

Speaking of which, she needed to find somewhere else to live in London and also a well-paid job so she could afford the rent. Her savings barely added up to three thousand pounds. She'd ask her creative friends to be on the lookout for any possibilities or vacancies where they worked, she decided. And she still had Abigail to talk to, she mustn't forget that. She still had her best friend, though her phone seemed to be switched off most of yesterday. No doubt she was up to her eyes in unfaithful married men who were dithering over who to spend Christmas with, their long-suffering wives and children: or their pretty young mistresses. Abigail said a lot of playboys were troubled by their consciences when they saw adverts for toys on the television, though they were quite happy to compartmentalize their lives for the rest of the year. Come January, it'd be back to late-night "business meetings". Who'd be a counsellor?

Ten o'clock came and went and Sarah decided to get up and face her future. She'd spend a day or two pottering in Dublin until the Christmas rush was over. Maybe see if there was a show or something she could get a ticket for, to distract herself for a couple of hours. Meanwhile, she'd check out what accommodation was available in Redstone in the winter season. Maybe there would be a small hotel with an atmospheric (dimly lit) lounge, with a lone pianist playing sad songs for lonely hearts like herself? She had a long, soothing shower, dressed in her warm sweater and jeans and repacked her two suitcases until they were scientifically neat. Then she called her parents for a chat. They were just off to have tea and sandwiches at Aunty Jean's, they said, and then they were going to midday Mass and then they'd kneel and say a prayer at the outdoor crib. Which was funny because Sarah had always thought they sounded like they were heading off to pray on Mothercare's doorstep when they said that. (She wasn't really into religion herself.)

"Say one for me while you're at it," Sarah told them and this time she meant it most sincerely, imagining them stealing a little bit of the "holy straw" from beneath the ceramic Baby Jesus in the manger, like they did every year. It was one of the most precious of the Quinn family traditions, stealing holy straw.

"Are you sure you're all right, love?"

"Yes, really, I'm not too bad at all."

Once again, they were full of sympathy and sent her all

their love. And tried their best not to sound too bewildered that she was phoning them from a hotel in Dublin instead of having a lie-in in her own little bed upstairs. Sarah looked at her reflection in the bedroom mirror when the call ended. She looked a little older, she fancied. Older and wiser. Whatever, it was kind of nice to be in charge again, not just being swept along on a tide of routine and habit. All she had to do now was get through each hour and each day in little baby steps, until the days added up and became weeks and months and years. And then all of this sadness and shock would fade away and she'd emerge a much stronger individual. In theory at least.

By now she was very hungry. She went gingerly down to the shadowy basement dining room, which was decked out in silver foil bells and giant sparkly snowflakes. She found a small table in the corner where she attempted to eat a late breakfast of fried bread, pork sausages, scrambled eggs and grilled tomatoes. But without much success. For despite her gnawing hunger pangs, her throat seemed to rebel at the pungent smell of hot grease. Several times she pushed her plate away, then took it back and tried again. Make up your mind, she chided herself, aware that the waitress was eyeing her with concern. But no, she was still extremely nauseous from her four glasses of wine the night before, and the heady aroma of fat meaty sausages wafting around her nostrils did nothing to help. She managed to swallow a couple of spoonfuls of cornflakes with ice-cold milk before giving it up as too risky. Still, a nice cup of tea put a bit of lining on her stomach and Sarah made a mental note never to overdo the wine *ever* again in her entire life. She'd have two glasses at the very most from now on. The waitress seemed to understand Sarah's predicament and accepted her tip with a cheery and sympathetic smile.

"You watch yourself now and take care. Merry Christmas," she said in a very soothing voice and Sarah nodded in agreement, unable to even begin to account for what she was doing hungover and homeless in Dublin city centre. And wondering why she was so grateful for smiles and a kind word from security guards, shop-assistants and waitresses, when she'd just ditched a lovely man practically at the altar. Should she call him, she asked herself.

Should she?

No, she had hurt him enough.

She would keep going forward. She would ask at the hotel reception if they could recommend a good place to stay near Redstone. But when she walked past the desk a few moments later, there was no one in attendance. She could hear the few staff that were on duty having a laugh in the television room. Some chat show was on and they were in hysterics laughing at the presenter's baggy trousers, apparently.

"Aw, what? Nice threads, man. Pity you've no arse to put in them! Ha, would you look at the go of him! I don't know what's deserting him the fastest, his hair or his backside!"

Sarah went back to her room and sat on top of the covers for a little while, just thinking. After that she decided she needed some make-up on her face. A light dusting of blusher and a trace of bright-red lipstick would help her feel alive again, she decided. She brushed her glossy, black hair into a high bun and put a few glittery clips in it, for after all, it was Christmas. She added a slick of mascara to her eyelashes, too. Because even when a girl's heart is in turmoil she can still have voluminous eyelashes. She also tied her favourite polka-dot scarf in a big bow round her neck, just because she felt like it. Then she went out for a walk and did a lap of the streets close to the hotel, all the while telling herself she was a brave, independent woman setting out on a great adventure. She hoped she wouldn't have to go home to Mum and Dad when her adventure was over and throw herself on their mercy. It seemed she might have to, with property prices in London so impossibly high these days. And she really didn't want to house-share: oh hello, overflowing kitchen-bin and never any loo paper! Hell, she might be glad of that attic room in Islington if nothing else turned up in the near future. Mummy and Daddy and Sarah, all together again. The three of them plonked on the massive chintz sofa in the good room with cups of milky tea and almond slices on their laps, watching *Hetty Wainthrop Investigates*. Sarah could almost hear the mournful trumpet of the signature tune and she was afraid, very afraid.

Then, glancing into the window of a small letting agency on O'Connell Street, Sarah spied a little piece of property heaven. A tiny pink bungalow with a lopsided slate roof wedged in between two larger, more modern houses. Only one sash window and one Hansel-and-Gretel-style wooden door in the front of the house. A brown wicker basket filled with pretty pink and red flowers, hanging near the apex of the roof. And a pretty iron bench sitting snugly beneath the solitary window as if inviting passers-by to sit there and rest a while. The picture had been taken at the height of summer, she reminded herself. It probably didn't look quite so edible just now, in this dark and damp weather. But somehow the house seemed familiar to her and she was intrigued enough to read the details printed below the picture.

Rose Cottage, Redstone. Rent: 250 Euro per week.

Redstone?

Of course! She remembered now: the little pink house in Redstone!

Sarah almost collapsed where she stood. How weird was that? She was looking to spend a couple of weeks in Redstone and now here was the sweetest house in the entire world, available to rent. She couldn't believe it, her feet seemed to tremble with the effort of holding her upright. The rent was a bit steep, admittedly. But Redstone had become quite the artists' haven in recent years, according to her parents. Maybe that was why the fees were higher than in most London boroughs. One thousand Euro per month for that tiny little place? But the house seemed to be calling to her, and it was still cheaper than a hotel. It was the living embodiment of both delicate femininity and secure refuge. And the absolute opposite of Thistledown Manor, which was huge, imposing and built of charcoal-coloured stone. She wanted desperately to see Rose Cottage in real life, to stay there for a little while. Just to write a letter to someone (anyone, even a quick note to her bank manager) and sign her address as Rose Cottage, Redstone, Ireland. No postcode required. How absolutely wonderful! Dare she extend her holiday by a little while, she wondered idly. Three weeks? A month?

Then she remembered with a sudden jolt of frustration that she didn't have a lot of money at the moment. And that if she did rent the cottage for a month she would barely have enough cash left in her account for basic rations. Oh well. No need to mention to the letting agency that she was almost broke, she decided bravely. Before she could stop herself, she went in and asked the young man working there if Rose Cottage was still available. It was. Hallelujah! In Sarah's imagination, a choir of angels fluttered down from heaven and began to sing.

"That property just became vacant yesterday," he said proudly. "Aren't you the lucky one?"

"I'll take it for two months," Sarah said breathlessly, amazed at her own extravagance. To his credit, the young man didn't seem surprised that Sarah was renting a summer house for two months in the depths of winter. She'd need a survival suit to go swimming in the sea at this time of year. Still, that was none of his business.

"When would you be thinking of going?" he asked. "Would it be after the New Year?"

"Today, actually. I thought I might as well go today before the buses shut down for Christmas. If that's all right with you?"

"Oh, I didn't realize you were going as soon as that."

"Is there a problem?"

"No, not at all, it's your money!" He politely made out the receipt, swiped her debit card and handed her both items with a professional little flourish. "Right, so it's Redstone village for you, yeah? A lovely, quiet spot on the very edge of the Atlantic. Ten miles west of Galway City. Have you got a car? No? Well, you'll need to catch a bus from the main depot here in Dublin all the way to Galway, and then another bus to Redstone. I'm just not sure if the owner'll be around to help you settle in, that's all."

"I'll be fine, really. I can work most things out for myself, domestic-wise. And I've stayed in Redstone before."

"Okay, then. I hope you have a nice time there. Do you have family in the village that you're going to see?"

"Yes, lots," lied Sarah at once. She didn't want this guy to think she was unhinged or anything. Or sad and desperate, either.

He told her the address in the village where she could pick up the key to Rose Cottage.

Sarah was already lost in a daydream about her new home. No roses that she could ascertain but maybe the name meant the actual colour of the cottage, which was fair enough. Sarah couldn't bring herself to say the words "Rose Cottage" out loud because it sounded too good to be true. Like Thistledown, which had turned out to be an impossible dream. She thought, if I start thinking about this little pink house too much, it'll disappear. Just like my wedding plans.

"Miss, did you hear me?" the young man asked politely.

"Yes, that's it all sorted," she said, eager to be on her way. "I just turn up at number seven and ask for the key? But hang on – didn't you say the owner might be away? Haven't you got another key here in the office?"

"No. That's what I was trying to explain just now. You see, Mrs Casey lives two doors up from Rose Cottage, at number seven, and she has the *only* key, because the front-door lock is very old and the key to it is a bit of a family heirloom. I'll phone ahead to let her know you're coming, of course. If Mrs Casey isn't home when you arrive, for she usually spends Christmas with her sister in Spiddal, just ask at the grocery shop for the key. And if the shop is closed, ask in the pub. And if the pub is shut it'll be tucked into the hanging basket. Just stand on the bench and get it out. Okay, now?"

Sarah nodded wordlessly, fearing all this vagueness could mean a night for her spent sleeping out-of-doors on the dainty, iron bench.

"Is that okay?" he repeated. "Is there anything else you need to know?"

"Oh sorry, no, that's great. Thank you and Merry Christmas."

"Same to yourself. Cheerio then. Any problems, call this number." He gave her their business card.

"Thanks a lot. Bye."

Sarah was a bit worried now that Redstone sounded completely rustic and ramshackle. Not to mention Mrs Casey's foolhardy attitude to home-security. But she'd simply have to rely on the kindness of strangers, it seemed. She was on an adventure now, and adventures were full of surprises and uncertainty. Weren't they?

"Okay then, here we go," she said in a nervous, high-pitched voice that suddenly reminded her of her mother. She quickly made her way back to settle up at the hotel and catch a bus to Galway. She'd have liked to stay in Dublin for a day and explore the shops and maybe have afternoon tea in the Four Seasons but she knew it would take an entire day to travel to Rose Cottage on public transport so there was no time to delay.

She found the depot easily enough and bought her ticket. Unfortunately there were quite a lot of people going to Galway that day, what with so many festive souls going home for Christmas and everything. She could see a fleet of luxury express coaches lined up, and full of passengers already, in the depot yard. The bus company had put every vehicle they owned on the road today, the ticket-clerk told her. And even one or two private-hire coaches to ferry the extra passengers westward. The one Sarah was directed towards must have come from a transport museum. And it was making lots of extra stops along the way. It would take seven hours to cross the country, the clerk told her with a grimace of apology on his face.

Well, there was nothing else for it but to nip to the bathroom, buy some Tiffin chocolate bars and *Heat* magazine at the kiosk to keep her going and then climb on board.

As the bus chugged out of the depot ten minutes later and made its noisy progress towards the west, Sarah hugged the thought of Rose Cottage to herself and tried not to think of the day ahead. At least it wasn't snowing here in Ireland, she told herself, so that was one thing to be grateful for. Then, just as she was settling down to try to sleep for at least some of the gruelling journey, the sky clouded over and the first tiny flakes came down in a flurry and began to stick to the windows of the packed bus.

10

Weak in the Presence of Beauty

Sarah arrived in Redstone well after nightfall. And there was Rose Cottage, not merely a pretty picture on a brochure any longer but a real house made of bricks and mortar. Or maybe it was built of solid stone with a wooden roof. It was hard to tell in the dark. It was definitely smaller than she'd imagined but it was every bit as gorgeous, every bit as welcoming and homely, even though the hanging basket was currently empty. There was a police station a few doors up from the cottage and it was unbelievably tiny, even smaller than her own accommodation, if that were possible. It had a pretty window-box full of red Christmassy flowers and an old-fashioned blue police lamp glowing in the darkness. An elderly woman out walking her dog nodded hello to Sarah, and then a young couple dressed in scruffy denims went by, arms round each other's waists, deep in conversation about some gorgeous watercolour painting they'd just seen.

There was no answer at the door of number seven, Mrs Casey's house. And sadly, the grocery shop that had been described to her by the estate agent was firmly closed and shuttered too, with only a rusty HB Maxi Twist sign flapping slowly in the breeze.

"HB Maxi Twist," she said out loud, looking at the picture of the tall, fluted tubs of vanilla ice-cream shot through with lime and raspberry syrup. She hadn't had one of those for twenty years.

"I must remember to buy one tomorrow, if they're open. Oh my God, what if they're not open? I haven't brought any food with me. Just this stone Buddha, nice touch, girlfriend. I'll starve!" And then she reminded herself that people didn't really like seeing other people talking to themselves on the street. She was a woman on her own now and she must at least be seen to be coping.

The key to Rose Cottage? She needed to get her hands on it. She needed to feel that key in the palm of her hand to believe that her dream of independence was actually coming true. And more than anything, she needed a good night's sleep. She wanted to wake up in a place that wasn't a hotel or her parents' semi or Mackenzie's mansion. Just her own little space, however temporary. The pub, then, it had to be. The windows of the postcard-perfect tavern halfway down the street were glowing bright yellow in the smoky darkness, and snippets of lively conversation came drifting out from the open doorway towards her.

"Right," she said firmly, worn out by the trip, the last part of it over narrow, bumpy, winding roads, the slithering branches of hawthorn hedges lashing against the windows, making her fear they were going to break the glass and scratch her face at any moment. For all that, now she almost longed for the security of the bus. But the last bus of the evening was long gone and, anyway, there was nowhere else it could have taken her. Except maybe back to the airport. Home to Islington and the parental abode. And *Hetty Wainthrop Investigates*. An almond slice and her skylight window.

"Come on, you idiot. You've made it this far."

But again she hesitated.

All I have to do is go in there and ask the nice barman for the key, she thought to herself. Easy. Except then they'll see I'm all alone and that I wound up here in the middle of the night. I bet all the locals stop drinking and stare at me. But she couldn't hang about being shy and nervous because she was absolutely dying to use the bathroom. So, barely able to straighten her back after a day spent hunched up on two bone-shaking buses, she approached the open door and went in. Amazingly the locals didn't stare at her and they weren't dressed like extras from that film *The Field* either. The locals were all absolutely normal looking. Dressed in smart-casual clothing with up-to-date haircuts and even a set of laser-whitened teeth here and there, among the cloth caps.

And she noticed one rather interesting man standing on his own at the end of the bar. He was tall and lean and looked to be in his early thirties. His eyes were so dark brown and glittering he could have been Italian or Spanish. But his winter-pale skin betrayed his origins: he was definitely Irish. He had longish hair, worn in a deliberately shaggy style, which was very fashionable in London at the moment. He was wearing an old reefer jacket with the collar turned up and she could see his broad cheekbones casting shadows down his face from halfway across the bar. He was studying her intently. Which would have been quite flattering if she hadn't been so tired and hungry and if she hadn't just had her heart broken.

Sarah felt a wave of panic creeping across her chest. What the hell was she doing here in a village she hadn't set foot in for twenty years? With all her belongings in two suitcases, a Buddha's head in a carrier bag and her camera rucksack on her back.

She must be mad!

Stop it, she told herself crossly, before nodding a general hello to the company. She had to appear relatively normal, she told herself. She had to keep going forward, not back. She looked around her, noted how pretty the Christmas decorations were, all red and green gingham hearts, very cosy looking. Some of the men were drinking glasses of wine, she noted, much impressed. And not just from those small common-or-garden glasses either. But from proper fancy-restaurant ones. Some teenage girls were throwing darts and listening to a Snow Patrol CD on the stereo, and one or two older men were admiring a framed photograph on the wall of the most recent Grand National winner. They all smiled at Sarah politely and resumed their business. She wasn't going to be approached and interrogated after all, it seemed.

Her spirits picked up and she trailed her bags and cases into the Ladies'. Never was a woman so glad to see a lavatory. Even one with a concrete floor and an age-speckled mirror hanging above ancient, copper-stained sinks, and pervaded with a weird, nose-scorching smell that she slowly realized came from those solid cakes of air-freshener, the sort she assumed had gone out of production years ago.

"If it ain't broke, don't fix it, I suppose," she said, yawning widely, and then vowed not to talk to herself in public ever again. And she'd really try this time. It was such an embarrassing habit to fall into. She was on her own, that's all. She was not crazy.

"Repeat, I am not crazy," she told the mirror brightly as she stood at the sinks. "I am not even a little bit crazy. I have all my marbles accounted for and all my slates intact. I am not a sandwich short of the proverbial picnic. There is nothing to see here, as the policeman famously said. Show's over. Just move along, ladies and gentlemen. Move along there, please!"

A woman, probably in her early fifties, with long blonde hair scraped back into a French pleat, came out of one of the cubicles just then, glanced at Sarah, washed her hands quickly and practically sprinted out the door. Oh dear, Sarah hadn't noticed she had company. Sighing, she splashed some cool water on her face and neck and tidied her make-up. She looked quite awful. Which was fair enough considering the events of the last couple of days. Eventually she approached the bar and quickly explained her situation, showing her driving licence as proof of ID. Immediately the barman handed her a key. A large, brown, metal key. The kind usually found hanging on plate-sized key-rings in medieval castles. He also gave her a reusable carrier bag containing a loaf of unsliced white bread, a solid block of butter in waxy paper, four tins of tomato soup, a packet of teabags and a fancy box of oat biscuits. He fetched a carton of milk from one of the fridges and set it gently on top of the bag of groceries.

"Mrs Casey left these in for you on her way past, and welcome to Redstone," the barman said brightly. "Can I get you anything to drink?"

"A drink?" Sarah's liver immediately curled up in protest. Oh, no. She'd have loved a bowl of beef stew followed by a hot bubble bath at that point. "No! I mean, thanks but no thanks. Maybe tomorrow. And how lovely to get this bag of stuff," she said as she yawned again. "Thank you very much."

But as she staggered out again, practically asleep on her feet, she tripped over a loose tile and dropped the biggest suitcase on the floor. It burst wide open, scattering her things right and left. The embarrassment of this incident made her drop her sturdy carrier bag from The Silver Birdcage also. The Buddha rolled out and under a nearby table where it startled some of the customers for a second because they thought it was an actual human head. Sarah retrieved the Buddha immediately, fishing it out again with her right foot, apologizing profusely to the drinkers at the same time. And blushing all the way down to her waist with irritation and shame. Her hands were stiff and sore from grasping so many handles and straps and it took her a moment to set down everything else so she could start gathering up the stray items from her suitcase.

"Nice shoes."

Suddenly, the good-looking man with the dark eyes was at her side, offering to help. Up close, he was even better looking. Sarah felt rather weak, being so near to those gorgeous cheekbones. He had picked up her blue snakeskin shoes and offered them to her.

Sarah was very grateful and thanked him politely, but she

had almost got everything back in, she said, warming to him enormously.

"Let me carry something for you, then?" he said. "Have you a taxi coming or a lift?" He had very nice eyes indeed, she decided. Like a gypsy from a picture-book but without the hard-bitten edge. Like Johnny Depp's younger brother. He seemed kind and wise and ever so slightly, well, sexy. He was gorgeous, actually. Shockingly, Sarah felt a small spark of desire for him.

Well, you can forget about it, she told herself.

Forget about it, right now, lady!

Her heart was currently off work on a sick-note.

But he was so gorgeous, with those bee-stung lips. Just on the right side of pretty, for a man.

No, stop it: she wasn't so smitten that she was about to throw caution to the winds. She was still very reluctant to confide her business to a stranger, no matter how attractive he was. Then again, she did have an awful lot to carry. He *seemed* like a decent enough guy, she thought. Even though she wouldn't normally leave a bar with a man she didn't know. And besides, there were plenty of people in here tonight, local people. So he mustn't have a criminal record otherwise he wouldn't have spoken to her in front of them. At any rate, the barman seemed to know him.

"Ethan there's a good lad, he'll get you up the street, all right," the barman said, winking at her.

"Thank you," she said finally. "That would be great."

They went back up the street together. Sarah with the key, her handbag, her camera bag and the newly acquired haul of shopping. And him with the two suitcases and the statue.

She told him she'd decided to come to Ireland for a holiday but she didn't say why.

"I'm Ethan Reilly, by the way," he said when they reached Rose Cottage. "I'm the local mechanic. If you need any advice on buying a second-hand runabout, just give me a ring and I'll check it out for you. Works out cheaper than rental, sometimes."

"Thanks, I'll think about it. Oh, I'm Sarah Quinn. Thanks so much, Ethan. I really am worn out."

Her arms were killing her as she dropped her belongings on the doorstep and looked at the large key nestling in the palm of her hand before trying it. It fitted the lock like a dream and in she went, through the Hansel-and-Gretel door. Ethan set her cases inside and said goodnight.

"Hope to see you around, then?" he said, smiling again and walking backwards down the street. "And Merry Christmas to you!"

"Oh yes, I keep forgetting. I'll look out for you in the pub, Ethan, I owe you a pint," Sarah said, waving him off and closing the door. And wondering if he was a Romeo or a Good Samaritan, if he had spoken to her that night because he had felt some special connection to her? As if. Maybe he tried it on with every girl who came his way?

By this time it was pitch dark but Sarah felt euphoric that she'd managed to arrive in Redstone in one piece. She leaned against the door, the way people do in 1950s TV melodramas, and then she noticed how quiet the house was, a kind of quiet that simply didn't exist in London. She could almost feel the solitude sitting on her shoulders. There was not even a spider to be seen scuttling for cover. No hint of traffic noise, no distant motorway hum. Bliss.

However, Sarah did admit to feeling a physical pang of loneliness for Mackenzie (and his spacious luxury flat) when she switched on the overhead light and saw that she had rented the smallest house in the entire world. Really, it was shockingly small. Museum-small. Not-worth-the-rent small. Claustrophobic, really. Oh, what had she done?

The front door opened directly into the sitting room, which was surely no more than eight feet across at its widest point. There was a doll-sized sofa and a tiny cast-iron fireplace on one side and a pine table barely big enough for two plates and a teapot on the other. There were two oak chairs pushed in at the table and a white-painted coat-rack on the back wall. There was another door beside the sofa which she presumed led to the bedrooms, kitchen and bathroom but she was too tired to start making up a bed or looking for the rest of the light switches now.

"I'm pure crazy," she said. As luck would have it, she didn't have the energy for an anxiety attack. If she'd had the strength, she'd have yelled the house down, demanded her money back, cursed the Irish for being so poetic and beguiling and then renting her a cupboard with a chimney on it. She'd have abandoned her luggage and swum the long way home, spitting out jellyfish all the way across the Irish Sea.

Daylight robbery!

Then she switched off the light, sat down on the sofa and fell straight to sleep without looking round the house any further or even checking that the back door was locked.

She had the presence of mind to cover herself with a rug which was folded across the back of the sofa, but that was about it.

She woke once in the night to see the moon shining in through the sash window, highlighting the furniture in the room with a ghostly blue halo. But she thought she was dreaming and went back to sleep. Curled up in bed with Mackenzie, or so she thought, basking in the warmth of his powerful, muscular body. But it was only one of her suitcases that she had her arm draped over. Abigail did make a brief appearance in Sarah's dream, shaking her head slowly from side to side with professional disapproval.

"Avoidance, my dear," Sarah could almost hear her best friend saying. "You can't go on running away forever."

"Yes, I can," Sarah retorted in her sleep. "Watch me."

11

All Cried Out

Next morning, she woke slowly, stretched her arms and rubbed her eyes. She was almost too cold to move. Her breath was coming out in clouds of misty fog and her feet seemed to have turned into blocks of ice. It was Christmas Eve, her wedding day. This was the day she'd been dreading. If only she could fast-forward this day she'd be all right. Oh, wait a minute, something was bothering her . . . what was it? Something she'd forgotten to do, something she'd meant to do? Oh! She'd left her wedding dress hanging on the back of the door at Thistledown! Oh God, her Grandmother Ruby's beautiful wedding dress. Hand-made just before the war. How could she have been so bloody hopeless as to leave it behind?

Obviously, as soon as Sarah was able to process all this information, she had a thoroughly good sob. A good, long, crying-with-your-mouth-open, proper-bawling session. She frantically tried to call Abigail to check if she'd discovered the

SHARON OWENS

dress and taken it back to London with her but Abigail's various phone numbers were all switched to answer service. And the receptionist at the clinic said she was out of the office for a few days.

It was Sarah's lowest moment.

She had officially reached rock-bottom.

She literally felt sick to the bottom of her stomach.

And so alone in this little matchbox of a house it was scary.

However, because she was simply too weary to cry any more, Sarah decided she had to give this holiday a go. Or else she would have to go straight home to Islington before the airport got completely bunged, shovel some anti-depressants down her throat and join her parents at Aunty Jean's. Jive round the sitting room to the "Hucklebuck" and smother her dinner in HP sauce. Well, that vision was enough to rein in her mounting panic. As for her wedding dress, she would have to wait and see. She leapt off the sofa and began exploring the rest of the house.

The small pine door, which she assumed led to the kitchen and the other rooms, was beckoning to her and when she opened it she got the surprise of her life. For behind the door was a set of five stone steps which led down into a massive sitting room almost forty feet long. At the end of which was a big, square, 1960s picture-window with breathtaking views right out to sea past a row of bright yellow gorse bushes.

Between her window and the Atlantic Ocean (as well as the narrow beach, of course) was a small backyard with low walls painted white and miniature rose bushes planted around the place in ancient stone troughs. They were empty now of blooms but Sarah imagined they'd look heavenly in the summer months.

There was another curly bench and a small shed. It was idyllic. The rent she was paying to stay here immediately seemed laughably cheap and reasonable.

"Yippee!" she shouted, racing down the room as best she could on her sleep-stiffened legs for a closer look and feeling a strange bubbling sensation start up in her chest. She hadn't been this excited since getting a pink Triumph 20 bicycle for Christmas one year as a child. The view from over the backyard wall was beyond breathtaking. It had everything a person expected from the Irish seaside, right there in front of her. It was such an exhilarating feeling to be so close to nature, she felt quite giddy. Dark jagged rocks to the left, crashing jade-green waves out in front, bleached-white sand on the beach. Brooding purple hills in the distance to the right, and flocks of noisy seabirds in the sky. Everything that Glenallon had, in fact. Except maybe there were less clouds here. Oh, poor Mackenzie! She fervently hoped the landscape and the crashing seas around Glenallon would give him some crumbs of comfort now, the way the scenery here was beginning to lift her own spirits. The view was world-class, really. In spite of herself, she was delighted.

"Good old Mrs Casey, the little sweetheart! I knew she wouldn't rip me off!" Sarah almost shouted to the seagulls.

She hurried back to the other room to get her camera, laughing with sheer joy at what she now knew to be only the entrance hall of her holiday home. Perhaps it had been the only room in the house at one time but since the extension had been built onto the back, it was now simply a place for keeping coats and hats, and maybe opening the post at that sweet little table. Not that she'd have much post to open but it was nice to dream. And then she went to the picture-window again and just stood there, letting the sense of wide-open space wash over her, drinking it all in. Planning what pictures she would take. Not worrying for a few precious minutes about her future or her past. She pulled a mahogany rocking chair over to the window and sat there for a time, rocking softly, letting her thoughts wander, revelling in the silence of the house. Hearing only the soft whisper of timeless sea breezes. And imagining she could smell the stirring, sandy scent of ozone. She fell into a kind of trance, in fact, but it was a good feeling. Sometimes it was just what a person needed: to switch off and simply exist.

The sitting room was indeed sparsely furnished but there was a sturdy brick fireplace and a pair of comfortable (if slightly shabby) long, white sofas. Lots of scatter cushions. A dark wood bookcase on each side of the fireplace, though they were empty of books at the moment. Some brown, red and orange embroidered Indian rugs covered the floorboards and there were three large wicker baskets full of uneven lumps of turf. A smaller basket contained firelighters, small wooden sticks and boxes of matches. Sarah had never lit a fire in her life but there was one set up already in the fireplace, so she noted the structure of it for future reference. A tiny teepee of sticks, with two ultra-white firelighter blocks tucked underneath and about twenty pieces of fragrant brown turf on top. She darted around the house like a little bird, setting out her Buddha on one of the bookcases, moving the cushions into a more modern arrangement, even placing the baskets of turf in a better position. Then she sat down again and enjoyed her handiwork from the rocking chair.

A couple of hours later, Sarah's stomach decided it was starting to recover from all the alcohol she'd subjected it to in recent times and so she went to make something to eat. The kitchen was just off the enormous sitting room in a small but spotlessly clean annex.

Sarah spent the rest of the day putting away her few possessions and just settling in to her new home. She had a long soak in the bath and finally curled up to watch TV in front of a real turf fire. She was having such a lovely time, it was almost a wrench to have to go to bed and get some much-needed sleep.

* * *

On her second morning in Rose Cottage, Sarah was up bright and early. She'd intended lying in bed all of Christmas Day, hopefully asleep for most of it. But she didn't really fancy it now. The main bedroom was rather small and plain, as was the second one, and although they were clean and dry and freshly painted in brilliant white, they were just too empty to spend all day lounging in. Each contained a double bed, a wardrobe, a hard chair by the window and a pair of tiny bedside tables. No telly or even a radio to listen to, and the curtains were too thin to keep out the light. She decided that when she had the energy she would move her bed into the sitting room and place it facing out towards the sea, so she could open her eyes and gaze at the ocean first thing every morning of her holiday. She wasn't expecting to have many visitors here so what did it matter? Anyway, it was only a thought.

After getting to grips with the gas-powered grill, she made

some toast and a mug of tea, then put on some warm clothes and headed outside. Taking her camera with her, she struck out for a long walk on the beach, intending to get super fit or at least respectably fit, during her time here.

The beach was deserted at that early hour except for the seagulls wheeling and scolding overhead. The breeze was icy cold and there were patches of snow here and there but Sarah didn't mind, finding the experience spiritually uplifting. She would walk fast to warm herself up and then take some photos on the way back.

But she'd only been striding along the frozen sand for ten minutes when she spotted another early walker. A woman, crying her eyes out. She was dressed in very colourful clothes, Sarah noticed at once. A purple and green cardigan-coat with ruches and ruffles all over it, a green felt hat with purple crochet flowers on the side. Purple tights, brown leather shoe-boots, purple gloves. A big multi-coloured knitted handbag with a button on it the size of a saucer. And her plum-tinted hair was curled into pretty ringlets that framed her large grey eyes to perfection. Sarah reckoned she must be in her mid-thirties. She was wandering aimlessly along the water's edge, her shoulders moving with small, gasping sobs. Sarah's initial worry was that she didn't want to embarrass this poor distressed woman, who hadn't noticed her yet. She wondered if she should turn back or just pretend she hadn't seen her crying. But then the other woman noticed Sarah and spun round guiltily, as if she'd been caught doing something wrong.

"Hi there, I thought I'd go for an early walk," Sarah said hopelessly.

(Talk about stating the obvious.)

"Yes, yes, it's nice on the beach when there's no one else on it, isn't it? Peaceful."

"Yes, it's peaceful all right. Are you okay? Sorry for being nosy. But you seemed a bit upset," Sarah ventured, thinking it was just her luck to get caught up in a domestic drama or something but not wanting to leave this poor woman alone out here if she was in any kind of trouble.

"I'm fine, thanks. Just feeling a little bit emotional, you know? The time of year and everything. Christmas always seems to remind me of the things I've spent the rest of the year trying to ignore."

"Yes, I know what you mean," said Sarah sagely. "Look, I'm Sarah Quinn. I just got here from London. I mean, I'm staying at Rose Cottage on a winter break. Is there anything I can do to help? Can I call someone for you? I've got a phone with me."

"Oh dear, you must think I'm an awful eejit," the mystery woman smiled through her tears. "My name is Miriam. Miriam Gormley. I'm fine, honestly, there's no need to worry."

"Okay," said Sarah, feeling hugely relieved. "I'll see you around then. I'm staying in the village for a couple of months. Maybe we'll meet again sometime?" Now why had she made that offer, Sarah wondered regretfully. She wasn't running an advice centre, was she?

"Are you a friend of Mrs Casey's, by any chance?" Miriam asked timidly.

Sarah looked at Miriam's carefully co-ordinated finery and felt incredibly sorry for her for some reason. She looked like she was usually a happy and busy and upbeat sort of person. Judging by her clothes anyway. She was also very pale.

Although this probably was the typical Irish complexion at this time of year. No doubt the women in this village didn't go in for spray tans and a lot of make-up. But Miriam was so pale her skin had blue tones in it.

"The owner of the cottage? Well, I haven't met her yet – I just came here on impulse, you see. Sort of an impulse-holiday. I think she's gone away to her sister for Christmas. The guy I spoke to in Dublin said she would probably be away visiting for a day or two. I thought it was strange that they'd let me move in without being vetted first but there you are. I guess this Mrs Casey is very easy-going."

"Yes, she is," Miriam said, her tears starting to flow again and then she turned away from Sarah and walked on. "Bye now and take care."

But Sarah hurried after her.

"I'm sorry, em, Miriam, but can I ask what the matter is? You seem very upset. Has something happened? I don't mind staying with you until you're feeling a bit better. Can't I call someone for you, please?"

"No, really, I'm just feeling under the weather today. It's nothing. It's only disappointment. I thought I might be preggers but I'm not. That's all there is to it. Just another Christmas gone by with no thin blue line."

"Oh. Miriam, I'm sorry. I hope you have good news on that front very soon."

Miriam and Sarah smiled at each other, striking up an immediate bond, the way women do sometimes when they sense they have something in common.

"Do you have any kids, yourself?" Miriam asked.

"No, I'm not married. I mean, you don't have to be

married to have children, of course. But no, I haven't any kids. You see, I was supposed to be getting married yesterday but I changed my mind. Well, something happened to change it for me. A ghost came back to haunt me, you might say. Oh listen, I must sound bonkers to you."

"Far from it. You've had a worse time than me, it seems. Sarah, did you say your name was?"

"Yes, Sarah Quinn."

"It must have been a terrible experience for you, you poor thing."

"It *was* pretty terrible but I'll survive, I hope. That's why I came to Redstone. Keep my head down for a bit."

"Good idea, you've come to the right place. Well, Sarah, would you happen to have a tissue on you, by any chance? This bloody great bag of mine and it's got no tissues. I must have used them all up."

"I have some, yes."

Sarah swung her rucksack down off her shoulders and felt around for a pack of mentholated tissues she recalled buying in Dublin, eventually locating it beneath one of her camera lenses. She passed it across to Miriam, who took one gratefully and blew her nose as discreetly as she could.

"Thanks," Miriam said simply. "I needed that. Dig the menthol."

"Keep the rest of the pack," Sarah offered generously. "I've done enough crying recently. Not to mention drowning my sorrows. My head will be sore for a week. What are we like, eh? Us women! We complain when we don't have a husband and children, and we complain even more when we do."

"Would you like to have a bit of a stroll, and we can chat

about it?" Miriam asked, glancing down at the seashells round her feet.

"I couldn't impose," Sarah began, worried about getting too involved with anyone while she was here. But then she changed her mind. Some company might be nice this morning. "Oh, why not?" she said cheerfully. "But on one condition. I don't want to spend the rest of my life moaning and boring everyone with my tale of woe so I'll just tell you briefly what happened. I left my fiancé because I discovered he still had feelings for his first wife. And there wasn't a lot I could do about it because his first wife isn't with us any more. I mean, she died ten years ago. I couldn't handle it all so I fled. And that's me in a nutshell. So what about you? Have you been for fertility tests and all that sort of thing? I hear it's not as easy as people think."

They fell into line and progressed along together companionably, the waves lapping the beach only inches from their feet.

"I have, yes. He'd die if he heard me telling you this but the problem seems to be coming from him. I mean, my husband, Patrick."

"I see, and has he been for tests? Is it a low count or a motility thing?" Sarah asked matter-of-factly. She had no problems discussing such topics. IVF was a favourite water-cooler subject in her circle, all those Alpha females who'd left it too late.

"Oh, wow! You've not been in Redstone very long, have you, Sarah? The men here don't go rushing in for tests. Or at least, my husband doesn't. Don't get me wrong, he's a lovely man. But he doesn't like anything to do with hospitals."

"I see."

"You'd think I was asking him to go over Victoria Falls in a barrel instead of having a few simple tests."

"Men. They're such babies, aren't they?" said Sarah gently. "They can't get enough of war documentaries, V2 rockets and dangerous sports. But ask them to drop their shorts for the doctor and they break the three-minute mile. Or whatever the record is nowadays – I'm not very well up on my sporting trivia."

Miriam smiled. "You know, I can just see my Patrick in a tracksuit, running up the road with a squad of nurses after him!"

And for the first time in weeks, she began to laugh.

12

Getting Into Something

Sarah pulled the back door of Rose Cottage shut behind her and struck out for yet another long walk on the beach.

It was the day before New Year's Eve and she still hadn't been in touch with Abigail. She'd meant to call and catch up and ask about her dress. But it was hard to lift the phone when she had nothing interesting to say. Nothing much to report at all, really. Except that she'd walked along the beach every morning for hours until her thighs and ankles ached. And that she'd had about twenty Maxi Twists from the shop and maybe five fish suppers from the chippy and amazingly her jeans still fitted. Or that she'd simply sat each night in front of the television, on her own in that big empty sitting room. And she'd not even been listening to the programmes. The flickering screen had only served to keep her company. She'd been waiting for her heart to stop hurting and feeling guilty, and for it to start healing. That wasn't the kind of thing Abigail wanted to hear,

Sarah reckoned. Didn't she get enough of all that soul-searching at the clinic? Strangely, Abigail hadn't been in touch with her since either.

And neither had Mackenzie.

Sarah had sent her parents a chirpy postcard or two from the village, however, and they'd replied straight away to the first one, sending her ten twenty-pound notes wrapped up in a fluffy new tea-towel, with big, bold lettering on the front of the parcel, saying: *Contains Tea Towel*. That was her parents all over, she thought tenderly. Fussing constantly, and thank God for them! Sarah smiled with tears of love in her eyes. They could have sent a crossed cheque or an international money order. Or even asked their bank in Islington to do an e-transfer. Still, the cash had been very welcome indeed, given her newly reduced circumstances. She'd swapped the Sterling notes for Euro at the local bank and the money was now nestling safely in her smallest suitcase under the bed.

She took a deep breath and inhaled the clean, briny scent of the sea. The waves were sparkling white today and the sun was shining brightly, though it was still very cold. Her face was soon flushed and pink from both the walking and a sense of anticipation. For Sarah was just about to visit Miriam Gormley's house for the first time. She was also going to meet Miriam's friends, Aurora Blackstaff and Gemma Hayes. They had an informal little book-club thing going on, Miriam said. Nothing highbrow, she explained. It was Aurora's idea. Sarah was only going along to see them to be polite, really, because Miriam was such a lovely person. (She had no serious intentions of getting into something time-consuming like a book club.) And then she could go back to Rose Cottage, put her feet up and watch the flames flickering in the fireplace all evening, and surely nothing could be half as stimulating as the sound of the ocean beyond the yellow gorse bushes.

The sound of the waves was so soothing, she lost track of time and all too soon she had to turn back and start walking towards the hills in the other direction. Sarah found her second wind and got to Miriam's twenty minutes early. She was probably the first one to arrive, she thought nervously. But her worry that this visit to Miriam's house would be a bit of a chore vanished as soon as she saw the gorgeous lavender-painted house.

Miriam had told her to come straight round to the back door, so she circled the house.

And then the door opened.

"Oh my God!" Sarah couldn't stop herself from exclaiming when she saw Miriam's kitchen, even though she was still standing by the back doorstep and could only see part of the room and a small section of the sitting room beyond. Because the interior of Miriam Gormley's house was truly beyond gorgeous. A positive cache of homely treasures and trinkets, all perfectly displayed. The walls of the kitchen were painted a soft, chalky pink. Tea-rose pink. All the cupboards and shelves were painted white. There were round, white handles on all the drawers, on which were hanging (on loops of pink ribbon) pairs of sharp scissors, miniature salad baskets and floral-patterned oven gloves. There was a big, cream Aga draped with tea towels in bright candy stripes. There were some blue cups and saucers on the table and a pink wire cake-stand piled high with butterfly buns, dainty pale-blue meringues and chocolate éclairs in paper doily wrappers. All home-made cakes by the looks of it, Sarah noted greedily. It was so nice, she felt slightly overwhelmed.

"I would smother my granny for a house like this," Sarah heard someone say. And then realised it was herself speaking.

Miriam laughed heartily, hugged her guest and kissed her on both cheeks.

"Thank you very much for the compliment. I do hope you're not serious, though! Do come in and take a seat. Did you find the house without much bother?"

"Are you serious? Find the house? How could I miss it? A fabulous house like this? I mean, you did say it was painted lavender with a white picket fence and eight palm trees all along the front but I never dreamt it would be this amazing."

"Aw! I'm so glad you could come today, Sarah. Aurora and Gemma are dying to meet you."

"Well, I hope they aren't too disappointed!"

"Oh, now, they won't be! There's only the three of us in the book club so far because Aurora wants to keep it small and friendly. I mean that in a nice way, now. Don't be getting worried that we're a trio of stuffy old snobs or anything. But really, we want to keep the feeling cosy and relaxed without having any tedious debates about chick-lit versus Booker and all that rubbish. It's more of a friendship thing, not a serious book club as such. So it's women only, I'm afraid."

"That's fine by me. I'm totally off men at the moment."

"Enough said. And did I mention before, we like to eat rather a lot of cakes and ice-cream, I hope you aren't a health freak?"

"No way, Miriam. I'm the Queen of Ice-cream!" said Sarah at once. "Can't get enough of the stuff since I came to Redstone."

"Well, there's only so much you can do with raw carrots."

"Very true."

Today, Miriam had on a pair of skinny jeans, ballerina pumps and a long white sweater with pink snowflakes on it. She was the most feminine person Sarah had ever met. It was a huge shame her husband was so shy, Sarah thought. Miriam would have made a lovely mother.

"This house is just too much! I thought property prices would be moderate in Ireland but if anything they're higher than in London," Sarah said wistfully.

"The price of houses here is pure criminal," agreed Miriam thoughtfully, setting teaspoons delicately onto the blue saucers. "Really, I can't understand how it all happened so quickly. One year, the people were all emigrating as usual, and the next they were paying half a million Euro for a shoebox."

"Isn't it unbelievable?"

The kitchen was lovely and warm. Sarah was so distracted by the comfort of it all that she almost forgot her own life was in shreds.

"Would you like the guided tour?" Miriam asked suddenly, nodding towards the ceiling. "While we're waiting for the others?"

"Yes, I would indeed. Thank you very much," Sarah said immediately, standing up and peering into the sitting room beyond.

The rest of Miriam's house certainly lived up to Sarah's first impressions of it. An all-white sitting room filled with clear-glass candlesticks, enormous white sofas and abstract, textured paintings of the sea in shades of light blue and turquoise.

"I love it all," said Sarah, shaking her head in amazement.

"Especially those gorgeous seascapes. So serene and calming in a neutral white room like this."

"By a local artist, Brenda Brown," Miriam explained proudly. "She's the shining star of our little artistic community here, you know. She lives in Redstone all year round, has her own little gallery out by the headland. And Brenda's husband Sean's a bit of a looker, too. He's such a lovely guy and he always says hello to everyone. Some girls have all the luck! And he dotes on her. It would make your heart glad to see the pair of them walking about the place together. Love's young dream."

Sarah smiled but said nothing. She'd had enough of love's young dream to last her a lifetime.

"Brenda had a sell-out show at her gallery recently and I was lucky to get that painting over there." Miriam indicated a small canvas in a thick white frame. "I used to collect Brenda's work but it's going up in value and I almost can't afford it any more. She let me have that painting at the old rate because I supported her in the early days. Lovely girl, she is. Dresses down, you know, in raggy jeans and scruffy T-shirts."

"I'll keep an eye out for her. Scruffy, you say? Do you know, I think I might have seen her and her husband out walking the night I got here."

Meanwhile, the tour of Miriam's house continued. A cosy, lemon-coloured hall and a big dark-brown bookcase by the front door with lots of little seagrass baskets on it for shoes, tins of shoe-polish and brushes, letters and keys. The two women went up the stairs and again all was perfection. A cream master bedroom with heavy French-style furniture. A pristine peppermint-green bathroom with, yes, more baskets containing tubes of posh hand cream, shell-shaped soaps and powdery bath bombs. Oh how positively luxurious, Sarah thought to herself. These Redstoners certainly knew how to live. And then, they came to a small door at the end of the corridor, beside which Miriam hesitated for a second.

"This is my husband's study: it has the nicest window in the house." She opened the door and stood back to let her guest admire the porthole window.

"Oh wow, it's fabulous, isn't it?" Sarah sighed, by now weak at the knees with a terminal case of property-lust. The big, round window in Patrick's study was beautiful. The room itself was painted a soft blue and filled with hundreds of little wooden lighthouses, neatly arranged on dozens of white-painted shelves. There was a pine desk and chair and a blue, plaid armchair by the window.

"He collects lighthouses." Miriam laughed though the smile didn't quite reach her eyes.

They made their way back downstairs to the girly paradise of the kitchen and Miriam poured tea and told Sarah to help herself to cakes. Then a car pulled up and the other two ladies arrived. Aurora Blackstaff and Gemma Hayes. Sarah heard footsteps approaching the back door and held her breath. What if they didn't like her? What if she didn't like them? And then the door was open and the kitchen seemed to be full of women setting down bags and hanging up coats and hugging each other.

"I know you!" said Aurora.

Sarah was only too aware of that! It was Aurora who'd heard her declare she was not crazy in the bathroom of the pub, her first night in Redstone.

"Oh dear, I think we *have* met before," she said, looking rather embarrassed. "I had just got off the bus from Galway and was feeling a bit at sea. Pardon the pun. I came here on a whim, you see? Literally, on the spur of the moment. You must have thought I was a right oddball."

"Not at all. It's perfectly understandable: I did the same thing myself," Aurora trilled. A tall woman, she could have been in her early fifties but looked much younger, with her perfect bone-structure and jaunty manner. She wore her long blonde hair in a sleek bun. And she had a kind of authority about her, the posture of a natural leader. Sarah wondered if Aurora was a schoolteacher. (Miriam hadn't mentioned what the women did for a living yet.)

Gemma was also tall and very composed. She had a short peroxide crop and was wearing soft blue jeans and a long knitted cardigan. She looked super-cool and in control, the kind of woman who would cope well in a crisis. Sarah warmed to both of them at once. They all sat down at the table.

As Sarah predicted, Aurora took charge of the meeting.

"I'm absolutely parched! Miriam, is that tea still okay or should we make a fresh pot? Now, introductions! This is Gemma Hayes, Sarah. She's a tough old journalist so watch what you say. Anything you might reveal will be taken down and used in evidence. Or at the very least, it'll be recycled in her newspaper column."

"Stop it, Aurora!" said Gemma. "You'll upset the woman before the meeting even begins. I'm a novelist first and foremost, Sarah. You might have heard of me? But I also write an opinion-column for one of the tabloids. It's mostly ranty old nonsense but it pays the bills. And Aurora runs the little bookshop at the end of the promenade – it's called The Last Chapter – and before that she used to be a teacher. Miriam, on the other hand, is a lady of leisure. I'm only joking, Miriam. Don't look so offended. Actually, Sarah, Miriam does so much charity-work around the county she might as well be a full-time nurse or something. Old money, say no more! Aurora's from Belfast, and myself and Miriam are native Redstoners. So that's us for you."

"And what brings you to our humble village, Sarah Quinn?" Aurora purred. "Are you on a hippy-style career break? Scouting for a second home?"

"You see, she tells you to watch it and then she's straight into the questions herself," said Gemma sternly. "Ignore her, Sarah, she can't help it."

"It's okay," Sarah told them, laughing. "I have nothing to hide. I'm not doing anything in Redstone except having a long holiday. My parents were born here."

"Were they really? Tell us more!" Gemma wanted to know all the details.

"Yes, my dad's family ran the post office."

"Oh, those Quinns? Yes, I've heard of them. Of course, I would only have been a kid when they left the village."

"And Mum's name was Maguire – they '*had the drapery*', as she always puts it. So anyway, as I said to Miriam already, I've just left a long-term relationship."

"I'm sorry to hear that," said Gemma gently. But her big blue eyes were full of sympathy and Sarah immediately felt she had to defend Mackenzie to her new friends.

"He was a great guy, it wasn't his fault. He wasn't over this other person. I suddenly decided it wasn't the right path for me, that's all. So I left. And I wanted to get right away from London and do nothing but chill for a while. So I've rented Rose Cottage for two months – I've to meet Mrs Casey tomorrow, actually, she'll be back then. And in my working life, I'm a professional photographer. Mostly in publishing. I'm between jobs at the moment, though."

"How delightful, yes, Miriam did say," Aurora said. "A photographer! Well, I hope you enjoy our humble book club while you're here, Sarah. There's not a lot to do in the village sometimes except read. Especially in the wintertime. I always do well in the shop in winter."

"Speak for yourself," Gemma retorted. "I have a column to write each week not to mention a novel to deliver every eighteen months. Still, hanging out with this pair has given me no end of inspiration, Sarah, I can tell you."

"She's only kidding," soothed Aurora. "Will you have a refill of hot tea?" she asked, as Miriam set a fresh pot on the table.

"Oh yes, please," Sarah said, feeling she'd somehow ended up in an Enid Blyton story. All these pretty cakes with paper cases and a pink kitchen full of gorgeous bric-à-brac. Three chatty new friends who'd taken her straight to their bosoms without really knowing anything about her. And to cap it all, she was staying in a house called Rose Cottage with a huge secret room at the back, with spectacular sea views. It was all so wonderfully exciting after the sadness of recent days. She was enchanted. Totally enchanted, there was no other word for it.

"Is Patrick in?" whispered Gemma and the mood changed slightly.

Aurora raised her eyebrows and began to tidy away crumbs.

"No, he's gone fishing again," Miriam said quietly.

Aurora and Gemma exchanged meaningful glances. Then they all reached for and examined the books that Aurora had brought with her in her shopping basket.

It was like first day back at school, thought Sarah happily.

"So, what's it going to be, girls?" Aurora asked brightly. "Bestseller first as usual? Or shall we start with the auto-biography?"

"Oh, let's have Liz Smith's memoirs first!" said Miriam at once. "I've been dying to read this one. I loved *The Royle Family* on TV."

"So be it," said Aurora. " If you want more tea, Sarah, just ask. And do feel free to chat or bring up a non-book-related topic if you want to. It's not a library we're running. Now, let's chat about last week's book. Who'll start us off?"

Sarah smiled round the table at the three of them. The back door was only feet away from her if they turned out to be weird, but she hadn't heard of anything too dreadful happening at an Irish book club on the news recently. No, she felt these ladies were just lonely women of a certain age trying to hang on to some semblance of a social life now they were a little past the clubbing stage but still far too young for a knitting club. And they'd been more than nice to her so far. And Sarah liked them hugely already. Miriam began her critique, and the others listened politely.

And Sarah felt something close to contentment as she straightened up in her chair and poured herself another cup of tea.

13

This Charming Man

Aurora came bounding up the stairs to her luxury penthouse apartment on the third floor and let herself in with a spring in her step. The book-club meeting had gone very well today. Sarah Quinn was just the sort of person Aurora liked. Plucky, straightforward and respectful. She didn't waffle on too much about herself and she wasn't too secretive either: she was perfect book-club material. So even though Aurora had been slightly worried when Miriam mentioned she'd invited her new friend to their weekly meeting, she was feeling fine about it now. Aurora had a bit of a "thing" about book clubs, she knew that. But she was trying hard not to let it take over her life. Again.

The phone rang just as she placed her best court shoes neatly onto the rack in the hall closet and slipped her coat onto its allotted hanger.

This'd better not be David Cropper, she thought crossly as

she went to answer it. He'd been stepping up the desperation calls this month.

"Hello?"

"Aurora, darling? Don't hang up on me, please," a man's voice pleaded. "We need to talk."

"Oh for pity's sake, David! I told you yesterday, and the day before that, and I don't know how many times before that, I have nothing more to say to you. We are history."

"But I need to explain to you, tell you what happened. You never gave me a chance to explain myself, not properly. You just upped and left overnight."

"David, this is becoming tiresome. I left Belfast because of you. I sold my beautiful Victorian villa on the Malone Road because of you, and you don't know how hard it was for me to say goodbye to all my nice friends there. I gave up a good teaching job and I came here, to this remote little village, to start again."

"I know you did, my darling."

"Well, why do you think I went to all that trouble? Do you think I spent my first six months here working all hours to make the bookshop a success, just to let you come blundering into my life again and turn it all upside-down? I might have been foolish and silly and ridiculously naïve to believe you were ever in love with me, David Cropper. But I'm not a glutton for punishment. Now come on, act your age and leave me alone."

"You can't treat me this way, Aurora, you can't dismiss me like this. I don't believe you mean it when you say you don't love me any more!"

"I do mean it."

"You can't have forgotten what we shared! How we used to dress up in our book-club costumes and waltz around your conservatory cheek-to-cheek? You can't have forgotten how turned-on we used to feel, with all those lacy frills and ruffles so close to our skin?"

"Stop it, you're making me feel quite ill."

"Don't you miss our private poetry readings, my beloved? Don't you miss the book-club meetings, the power and excitement of it all?"

"No, I don't, David. I'll take the shame of our affair with me to my grave. My dignity was only the first casualty of our relationship. And as for the book club and that enormous bloody great conservatory I had built to accommodate it! To think that poor Henry's garden had to be bulldozed for it in the first place. You've some nerve calling me at all, you really have."

"How is your ex-husband these days, anyway? Is he still with that little cutey from the flower-shop?" David asked, slyly trying to attack the only man in Aurora's life that she claimed had ever truly cared for her.

"Yes, he is. He married that little cutey, as you put it, and they have a gorgeous baby daughter now, and they're blissfully happy, living in a lovely French farmhouse. You see, unlike your good self, my ex is a real man. He's not afraid of commitment and he's not too proud to be seen pushing a pram along the street, while you're still playing the field at your age. You know, you really are too much. Just how long can you go on chasing those skinny actresses and bowling out of wine bars at four o'clock in the morning?"

"It goes with the territory when you work in television,

117

Aurora. It's all just flim-flam and baloney. Producers are expected to flirt a little bit, to rip it up with the crew occasionally. It's good for team-building."

"Ha! Honestly, if it wasn't so pathetic, I'd quite enjoy this conversation. You need professional help, though sadly I doubt you'll ever have the wit to ask for it."

"But don't you miss me a little bit, Aurora? Don't you miss our evenings together in the conservatory, just the two of us, when we read Charlotte Brontë to each other? And I wore my frockcoat and you wore your petticoats and that criminally tight corset?"

Oh, the snake! Bringing up all that business again, she thought savagely.

"Yes, I admit I do miss you, a little bit, sometimes," she teased him. "You were so handsome in that coat."

"Really?" He sounded confused now.

"Yes, I'm not made of stone, you know. I'm a normal woman with normal feelings."

"I knew it! And I miss you too, darling. So much. And what's the point of both of us being lonely and bored, when all you have to do is come back to Belfast and love me again?"

Aurora could hardly believe what she was hearing. David Cropper couldn't be trusted to go to the corner shop for a pint of milk without pouncing on any attractive female he met along the way. He must be running out of options, and women, to be calling her at all these days.

"Oh, David," she cooed seductively down the line, "do you remember the first time we made love in our costumes, the day they finished filming the Brontë Bunch for that series on BBC2? Our little book club, famous at last! We were the talk of the city. Everyone who was anyone was clamouring for membership. They promoted me to vice-principal at the school because of it, because of the great work we did together to make classic literature more appealing to the masses. Good times, indeed."

"Yes, they were good times, weren't they?"

"And do you remember the day poor Henry accepted defeat and quietly moved out of the marital home? And he didn't even try to get half the house off me in court – he just walked away and made a new life with Rose?"

"Yes, of course I remember."

"Yes? And do you remember when you swore we'd be together forever?" she purred.

"Yes!"

Aurora took a deep breath. "And then you cheated on me with that twenty-year-old student from your drama class," she shouted down the line, "and she wrote to me and told me what the two of you were getting up to behind the curtains at the Grand Opera House!"

"Now listen, Aurora, I told you I could explain all of that."

"Go on, then." Aurora patted her hair in the hall mirror. She was looking rather good today, she fancied. The sea air and Miriam's home cooking were doing her the world of good. She'd gained seven pounds since moving to Redstone and her cheeks and chin had filled out a bit but it suited her. "I'm listening."

"I was having a mid-life crisis. I was feeling my age and I grabbed at any last chance I could get to prove myself attractive to a younger woman."

"Oh, please, David Cropper, what are you like? You're an

119

educated man, you can do better than that, surely? I'm bound to be worth a better excuse than a measly old mid-life crisis! You insult me, you know, bringing me such a dreary excuse. Oh David, you're really scraping the bottom of the barrel."

"Look, you don't know what it's like for a man, my darling. You don't understand how intrinsic our virility is to our sense of personal identity. I needed the boost to my confidence her attention gave me. I needed the creative surge that being with, em, that girl gave me."

"You've forgotten her name already?"

"I haven't forgotten her name."

"What is it, then?"

"Aurora, don't torture yourself with the details. Just give up that silly bookshop and come back to Belfast where you belong. I love you. I need you."

"And I need you like a hole in the head, you slimy little, two-faced, lying little toe-rag. Not to mention pervert! She was young enough to be your daughter. You never even said you were sorry. You must be out of your tiny mind to think I would allow you within spitting distance of me, ever again. And the book-club members killing themselves laughing at me – even my own students couldn't stop sniggering in the school. The scandal almost destroyed me. You dirty rat!"

"Aurora! Calm down, sweetheart."

"Calm down? You're the one who won't calm down, calling me day in and day out. Now don't put me to the inconvenience of having to change this telephone number again, I'm warning you. And don't call The Last Chapter any more either or I'll have you charged with harrassment. And if I can't have you charged with harrassment, I'll record you every time you call me, and I'll send the tapes to your bosses at the BBC in Belfast. And I'll go to the *Belfast Telegraph* while I'm at it. They might be stuck for a nugget of gossip."

"Oh!"

"You might not care about my reputation but you sure as hell care about your own. Now bugger off!"

Aurora heard him gasp with surprise. She never, but never, used bad language. Then she slammed down the phone with a triumphant flourish.

"Honestly, men are such twits," she told the mirror, shaking her head in amusement. "They still believe, after all this time, after thousands and thousands of years of living with us women, that they're the stronger sex. That man is an emotional cul-de-sac, like most of the rest of them. And hell will freeze over before I let him anywhere near my petticoats again. The very thought of him makes my skin crawl." Aurora made a mental note to dig out her Brontë Bunch costume and throw it in the bin. Along with the corset, the button-boots and the ostrich-feather hat. Honestly, she must have been going through a mid-life crisis of her own, letting a slimeball like David Cropper do all of those embarrassing things to her in the first place. Yuck!

"Oh well," she sighed. "Onwards and upwards!"

Then she switched on the central heating and went into the kitchen to make herself a nice cup of fresh coffee.

14

Love Resurrection

The last patches of snow had melted away. The Christmas festivities were winding down and making way for the end-of-year parties. The pub was having a special night of live music and stand-up comedy and the usual general-knowledge quiz and raffle. Sarah saw the poster in the shop when she went to buy some groceries and decided she might venture down to the pub for an hour or two before midnight, just to be sociable. (If she felt up to it when the time came.) In the meantime, she went to say hello to Mrs Casey and ask how she might order some more turf.

"Yes, dear, go ahead, there's the number," Mrs Casey said, passing Sarah the phone number which she kept scribbled on a small piece of paper in her purse. "Although I can't believe you've used all the turf in the cottage already?"

"The three baskets? Yes, I've gone through nearly all of it," Sarah confessed.

"But there's lots more in the wardrobe in the second

bedroom," said Mrs Casey. "Did you not find it? Miriam said I shouldn't leave it sitting out in the main room. She said it was taking the rustic theme a bit too far."

"No, sorry," said Sarah, laughing. "I never looked in there. Thank you and happy New Year!"

She went home to check in the wardrobe and, sure enough, there were three huge plastic sacks of the stuff, wedged tightly in behind the wardrobe doors.

"This house just keeps getting better and better," she laughed.

And then there was a knock at the door.

Sarah hurried up the steps to answer it, thinking it might be Miriam, Gemma or Aurora popping by to say hello, but she was surprised to find Ethan standing there. With a large Christmas tree in his hands.

"Oh, hello again," she said, trying not to appear too amused. "Are you taking your pet tree for a walk?"

"Ha, yeah! It's for you. Well, I thought that since there's still officially six days of Christmas left, you might like to have this? They were throwing it out at the garage. They didn't reckon they'd sell it at this late stage."

He set the tree up against the wall.

"Em, that's very nice of you, thanks, Ethan. I haven't any decorations, though."

"Not to worry, I got these at the checkout." He pulled a small packet of lights and one of baubles out of his pocket and handed them to her. "Not enough for a tree that size, I know."

But Sarah was delighted with the gesture. And also slightly embarrassed. Was he about to invite her out for a drink, she wondered.

"Would you like to come out later? To the pub, for the

New Year's Eve celebrations?" he asked brightly. "It's usually a great laugh. There's a quiz and two comedians and traditional music. And a raffle, though it's usually only a few bottles of booze and a hairdryer set or something. But it's fun – they go on as if it's the Lotto you're winning."

"Oh, thanks, Ethan, but I'm not sure what I'm doing yet."

Sarah felt torn between saying yes, and going along and enjoying herself, and saying no, and going to bed early and trying to sleep the night away. Gemma and Aurora were going to some posh hotel dinner-dance in Galway that they'd booked ages ago. And Miriam was spending the evening at home with Patrick, who hated all the "hyped-up nonsense" at this time of year. Sarah had already chatted to her parents and to Abigail (who'd been strangely quiet on the phone, obviously still not altogether forgiving her for running away) and now there was nothing left for her to do. But still, she didn't want to give Ethan the idea she was keen on him. Well, okay, she couldn't help fancying him but it was far, far too soon to even think about dating.

"It's okay if you have other plans," Ethan said, shrugging his shoulders. "Only I didn't see you in the pub all week, and I thought I'd just knock on the door and ask. No harm in asking, I said to myself, but anyway it doesn't matter." He shoved his hands deep into the pockets of his old reefer jacket and began to walk away.

Immediately, she felt sorry for him.

"Oh, all right, then! Thanks very much, I will," she said breathlessly.

"Aw, great. Will I call for you later? Say around nine?" he asked, a huge smile on his face.

Sarah noticed the way his eyes almost closed when he smiled. The corners of his mouth seemed to go all the way up to his eyebrows.

"Yes, nine would be good," she said, wondering how she was going to tell him tactfully that she really wasn't ready to see anyone romantically at the moment. And she wasn't looking for a holiday fling either.

Still, the pub was only a few doors away if they did have a falling-out or a misunderstanding. She hadn't flirted with him in any way. If anything, every time he'd seen her about the village she'd been a complete mess, like she'd been dragged through a hedge backwards. He could hardly accuse her of being a siren, she thought prudishly. (Must be Aurora's influence – she was so thoroughly prim and proper!)

"I'll see you at nine," he said. "Cheerio."

She saw that he had his car with him this time, an old Audi. It suited him, she thought, basically sensible but with a quirky kind of edge.

"Oh, Ethan, hang on," she said as he turned to go. "Is this a thing that people dress up for?"

"Dress up?"

"Yes, like, do the women wear dresses and heels? Or is it just smart-casual?"

Ethan began to laugh. "Dress up, in Redstone? Are you having a laugh? There's no dress-rule in Callaghan's. You just wear whatever you feel comfortable in. Jeans mostly, whatever. It doesn't matter."

"Okay, then. See you later."

"Are you okay with that tree?"

"Yeah, I'll manage. Thanks again. See you."

Sarah closed the door and dragged the Christmas tree

down the steps and over to the picture-window, where she had it propped up in one of the wicker baskets in no time, wedged in with some of the biggest pieces of turf. She turned it around and around, looking for the best angle. Some of the needles had fallen off but it wasn't too bad. They must have kept the tree in water, or maybe it'd been extra-cold this year. Then, satisfied, she draped the single string of lights across it and did her best to spread out the decorations. It wasn't too bad, she thought when it was finished. Nothing like the magnificent tree at Thistledown, though, dripping with so many heirloom baubles you could hardly see the branches any more. Oh well, she mustn't start thinking of those things now. She'd only get miserable again.

She plugged in the lights and switched them on. They were quite pretty really, little multicoloured miniature lanterns. Hopelessly out-of-fashion but somehow more Christmassy than those tasteful white opaque bulbs that her London friends went in for. Just then her mobile rang. That'll be Mum again, she thought, smiling. Worried about me, as usual. But it wasn't her mother. It was Millicent Campbell.

"Hello, Sarah? Is that you? I'm sorry for bothering you but I just wanted to have a quick chat. Is that okay?"

"Of course it is, how are you?" Sarah said, her pulse quickening with fear. Was Big Millie going to have a rant at her for leaving Mackenzie at the altar? Almost.

"I just wanted to say happy New Year, Sarah. And to say I'm sorry how things turned out. I genuinely believed Mackenzie was dealing with what happened to Jane and the two of you would be very happy together. I understand you modern girls want everything to be perfect but when you get to my age, you realize that perfection is extremely elusive."

127

"That's okay. I suppose I should have given him a chance to explain, but I did what I felt was right at the time. And when he didn't come after me, well, it proves I was right."

"Maybe it does, Sarah, and maybe it doesn't. You know, you don't really get to know a person until after you're married. The Campbell men take a long time to open up. I wish you'd gone ahead with the ceremony. Mackenzie's a good man despite his stubborn streak. You would have been a lovely married couple. You should have given him more time, my dear. However, I just wanted to say I'll miss you."

"Thank you, Millicent. I'll miss you too."

And she meant it.

"You could have come and spoken to me, you know. I wish you'd said something at the time."

"I'm sorry, Millicent. I suppose I didn't handle it very well. Even though I knew Abigail was right when she said Mackenzie was entitled to his feelings regarding Jane, it was still too much for me to cope with."

"I know, I understand. But men are such fools. He would've felt differently when the two of you were married. Is there any chance at all you might make it up? Or even get back together, without getting married, for a while?"

"Oh, Millicent, I don't think there is. I mean, I let Mackenzie down by running away and he let me down by giving up on us."

"But he's barely spoken a word since you left, Sarah. He's not eating properly. I'm worried about him."

"I'm sorry to hear that but I'm still trying to come to terms with this myself. It wasn't exactly how I planned to spend Christmas, you know. On my own."

"I know, I know. Well, what else is there to tell you? Em,

I've asked Abigail to come to Thistledown for New Year's Eve. Did she say anything to you about it?"

"No, she didn't," Sarah said, feeling slightly irritated with Abigail. "Mind you, I haven't been chatting to her much recently. This is their busiest time of year at the clinic."

"Yes, indeed. That's why I asked her to come for a few days, if she could possibly get away. She'll be here soon, as it happens. Sarah, will you stay in touch?"

"I don't think so, probably not, Millicent, it would be too painful for both of us. I'm really sorry."

There was an awkward pause.

"Well, will you look after yourself? Promise me now?"

Millicent was clearly doing her best to sound positive and friendly.

"I will. Thanks for thinking of me. Goodbye, Millicent."

"Yes – goodbye."

Sarah hung up, her heart about to burst through her chest with sadness. It was so hard to refuse Mackenzie's mother anything but she had already made up her mind. It'd been intimidating enough at times, the thought of marrying into the Campbell family. Now it would be ten times harder. Taking a few deep breaths, Sarah went to make yet another cup of tea and then light the fire. Two activities she seemed to have become addicted to in recent days. She had four hours before Ethan would call to accompany her to Callaghan's. Four hours in which to decide if she would go out with him and try to have a good night, or whether she would give in to the temptation to go home to Islington, crawl into her single bed and admit that life had beaten her. She knew which option she'd prefer. She just hoped she had the courage to go through with it.

Oh, what the heck, she thought suddenly.

Forget the "two glasses and no more" rule.

A good booze-up was just what she needed.

"Right," she said in a determined voice. "Where did I put my make-up? I refuse to sit here feeling sorry for myself for one more minute."

* * *

"Three, two, one! Happy New Year! Happy New Year, everybody!" shouted the lead singer, before continuing his homage to The Pogues. (Teeth and all.) The pub was packed to the doors and everyone was drunk, sweltering, exhausted and happy.

All except Sarah and Ethan.

She'd been all-too-aware that he was attracted to her and wasn't sure how to let him down gently. And Ethan had sensed her sadness and wondered what was the matter. He must have told her she looked gorgeous about a hundred times, but still she just shrugged her shoulders and went on listening to the band.

"Would you mind walking me back to the cottage now?" she shouted above the din. "I'm about to drop."

"Sure," he said, reaching for their coats. Moments later they'd squeezed their way to the door and slithered out into the inky blackness. The cold air hit them like a wave and Sarah's teeth began to chatter.

"Wow, that's cold," she muttered. "Thank goodness I left the fire lit."

Ethan smiled and turned up the collar of his coat. "It's not too far anyway, to yours. I had a great night, thanks for coming out. Wasn't your man with the permed hair hilarious? Telling all the old jokes – I think he was rubbish on purpose – did you think that?"

"Well, I'm not sure. They were all Irish jokes, sort of. I mean, Irish references."

"Yeah, that's what I mean. It was all old-hat stuff. Like, have you still got your Communion money hidden somewhere in a sock? And do you remember those Irish-dancing competitions that went on for days and the fiddler was asleep on the stage but still playing? And why did teachers in the 1980s wear such awful jumpers?"

"But the crowd was in stitches."

"I think they were laughing at his perm."

"Poor guy, he did his best."

"Yeah, he did, didn't he?"

A minute later, they were at the door.

"Well, now," he said. "I'm sure you'll want to get straight to bed?"

"What?"

"You said you were about to drop?"

"Oh, yes, so I did. Have you far to go to your own house? I mean, I presume you're not driving? We must have had, how many, seven or eight drinks each?"

"No, I'm walking tonight. It's not too far."

"How far, exactly?"

"Two miles."

"Oh, Ethan, why don't you come in and call a taxi?" she said, unlocking the front door.

"Dessie won't be running the taxi tonight," Ethan said, laughing. "He'll be comatose by now. Honestly, I'm fine."

"Please, come in and have a cuppa then? You'll freeze in this weather. Come on, I insist." She pulled him gently into the cottage.

"Okay, but I don't want to be in your way."

Sarah switched on the lights and they hung their coats up and went down to the sitting room. Luckily, the fire had stayed lit, just about, and the room was as warm as a room of that huge size could ever hope to be on a cold and frosty New Year's Eve. Sarah set back the fire screen, added some more turf and plugged in the Christmas tree lights. The room looked almost cosy, if they managed to overlook how empty it was. Sarah went to make tea and toast, chattering brightly about how good the music had been, trying to cover her nervousness. When she came back with the tea things, Ethan was perched on the edge of the sofa, gazing into the flames.

"What was his name?" he asked softly.

"Whose name?" she asked, handing him a mug.

"The guy who made you come here on a bus, on your own, just before Christmas?"

"Oh now, aren't you the clever one? That's a long story. It'd take all night to tell you," she said quietly.

"I've got all night, Sarah. Please tell me."

And so, against all her better judgement, she told him. She told him everything about Thistledown and how she'd been head-over-heels in love with Mackenzie. But then, how it'd all come crashing down. And how she could not forgive Mackenzie for loving Jane's memory more than he loved her. She understood, and she wanted to forgive him and accept him as he was. But she simply couldn't do it.

"That's a sad story," Ethan said simply, when she was finished. "I'm sorry your lovely wedding was ruined."

"So am I," she said. And then, before she knew what was happening, he had leaned across to her and kissed her gently on the lips.

"We never got to do that at midnight," he said.

"I'm not trying to be difficult but this is too soon for me," she said, tears coming to her eyes.

"I thought it would be. It was only a kiss for New Year's. Nothing more."

"I do like you."

"That's enough for now," he said, holding her hand tightly.

Sarah felt something in her heart wake up and begin to breathe again. She kissed him back. Maybe it was because she was lonely and it was New Year's Eve. Maybe it was because she'd drunk far too much and had no other way to release her frustration at Mackenzie's broken heart. Maybe it was because Ethan hadn't unbuttoned his coat yet, even though he was sitting right by the fire, and she found this strangely attractive and a weird sort of turn-on. But anyway she kissed him back again and found she rather enjoyed the sensation. Ethan's lips were very soft and he was so unsure of himself that she felt a kind of vulnerability in him that she'd never felt with Mackenzie. Ethan obviously wanted her, and it seemed he wanted her so much he was almost afraid to do or say anything wrong. His lips were trembling with nerves.

"Would you like to stay the night?" she asked him, shocking herself to the core. She'd never gone to bed with a man on the first date before. The second date, maybe, but never the first.

"Wow! I wouldn't mind sleeping on the sofa," he replied nervously. "I think that would be a better idea, don't you? I mean, you're not ready. You said earlier, it's too soon. I mean, the wedding and everything."

"Okay, then," she smiled, squirming with embarrassment. "But there's another bedroom through that door. I haven't made up the bed but there's sheets and blankets in the airing cupboard. You can sleep there, if you like? More comfortable than the sofa. Save you walking home in the dark, at any rate."

"Great," he said, as she got up from the sofa to go and fetch his bedding. "That'd be lovely, thanks."

"See you in the morning, then," she said when the bed was made up, mortified that he'd had the good sense to wait.

"Don't think I don't want to spend the night with you," he said awkwardly. "I'd like nothing more. It's just, we're both tired. Okay?"

"Okay," she said, switching off the tree lights.

Then both retired to their respective bedrooms.

Sarah fell asleep almost at once. The wine and the music (still ringing in her ears) covering up all thoughts of the exquisite Christmas decorations at Thistledown, of Mackenzie's comfortable four-poster bed and his lovely broad shoulders, of the endless bus journey here from Dublin. Of Ethan's dark, sparkling eyes and his wonderful, infectious smile.

Ethan, however, lay awake for most of the night, wondering what he should do next. Wondering if he was crazy to be falling for a woman who'd gone from Redstone before the spring. A beautiful woman who'd just had her heart broken and to whom he had nothing of any real value to offer. And would he bother telling her about the fairground accident and Patrick Gormley? Or would it be better to get all that out of the way first, before somebody else told her? His head was buzzing with questions and worries. So many things to consider, he hardly noticed how cold the room was. Shortly before nine o'clock the following morning, he got up and went to sit by the fire again, quietly building it up with more clods of black, powdery turf, and setting the kettle on to boil on the gas ring in the kitchen, so he could make both of them a cup of tea when Sarah woke up.

15

Last Night I Dreamt that Somebody Loved Me

It was almost lunchtime and Gemma was very pleased with her morning's work. Her little sage-painted terrace by the sea was spick and span throughout, all the vacuuming done, and the many books on her bookcases had been dusted and tidied. She'd blow-dried her short, punk-white hair into an artfully lopsided quiff. And she was wearing her favourite faded blue jeans and a soft cream sweater. Barefoot for the moment, though when she left the house she usually wore ankle-boots, she'd even found five minutes to paint her toenails pearly white. She always felt more attractive if her toenails were nicely done. Then again, since turning forty a few weeks earlier she had decided less-was-more on the make-up front. No heavy foundation or messy powder for her any more. Just a dot of expensive concealer under each eye and a touch of frosted gold lipstick.

She was tall and just curvy enough to be sexy without being

considered plump. Her large blue eyes were a little sad today, she thought, as she added a quick slick of mascara, then sprayed a light floral perfume on both wrists. Well, no wonder she was glum occasionally. Her love life had been a twenty-five-year saga of one failed "relationship" after another. The New Year's Eve dinner with Aurora had been great fun but hadn't yielded any interesting men. And she'd just had to turn down a couple of complimentary tickets to a lovely awards dinner in Dublin at the weekend because she couldn't find a date at such short notice.

The trouble was, she was hopelessly attracted to outgoing, flirtatious types who nearly always turned out to be rather dull behind closed doors or, even worse, who were somehow angry. Most of her lovers had turned out to be aggressive, self-obsessed or unpredictable. Or all three. Maybe they thought a strong woman would sort them out or support them or something, but in the end they only grew to resent her self-control and resilient nature. Well, she wanted a partner for life, not a project. Honestly, the men she met these days were getting worse, not better. Part of her blamed the media (her own line of work, it had to be said) for giving so much attention and column inches to badly behaved celebrities. These days, it was almost a badge of honour to have a personal life more tangled than a ball of old string. Well, she didn't want to live a life like that. Gemma wanted all the melodrama in her life confined to the pages of her novels.

She tidied her make-up away and checked her watch. Right on time, the phone began to ring. Normally she would be mildly apprehensive. But today, Gemma felt relaxed and ready for a good discussion with Mike, her newspaper-column editor. She padded across the cream wool carpet towards her glass desk, which was placed at an angle by the sitting-room window. Being a writer was a lonely old game, she mused, but it did have its few consolations. Like being able to work from home in a nice house like this with a stunning view in front of her. Not many people looked up from their computer keyboard to see the ocean gently rising and falling and the sea birds swooping and circling above it. She picked up the phone, determined to be friendly but firm.

"Hello. Mike?"

"Hiya, Gemma, how's things with you?"

"Sunny day here, looks lovely out. What's the weather like in Dublin?"

"Overcast," Mike said gruffly. "Not that I get to see the sky as much as you do. Up to my eyes here as usual. So what've you got for me this week?"

Clearly, he wasn't in the mood for small talk. She took a deep breath.

"*The End of Feminism*? How does that grab you?"

"Just a second, Gemma, I have to take another call."

Feeling suddenly hungry, Gemma wandered back to the kitchen with her cordless phone and opened the mini-freezer. She'd pop something in the microwave and then she'd have her lunch all ready to eat after this call. There was a chicken curry that only took five minutes. She set it into the microwave and switched it on.

Then Mike came back onto the line.

"Now, Gemma, we've been over all this before, more than once."

"I know we have."

And so, while her lunch twirled round and round on the microwave turntable, Gemma listened to Mike's standard lecture on the newspaper's relentless need for exciting and bold (okay, saucy) features. He concluded his spiel just as the time-up buzzer rang.

"Now, I get what you're saying but hear me out," she began. "We've got more important things to say! More than just features on boobs and boob-jobs and boob-job botch-ups and who's secretly gay in Hollywood. I mean, who cares? We've gone way beyond outing celebs. Look, Mike, it's embarrassing for me to have to write such pointless, useless drivel every week."

She had the phone balanced precariously on one shoulder as she tried to access her lunch. But the see-through cover refused to budge so she ended up stabbing it viciously with a sharp knife. A sudden blast of red-hot steam escaped and her hand convulsed with pain. She dropped the moulded container onto the counter in shock, where it bounced dramatically, split open and sent an arc of bright orange sauce right across her kitchen tiles. She knew the white grouting would be permanently stained.

"Stupid bloody thing!"

"Gemma, are you okay?"

"It's fucking agony!" she gasped, plunging her scalded fingers into a fat bag of ice-cubes from the freezer. "Sorry, Mike," she explained. "I burnt my hand."

"Careful, woman! Do you need to go to the hospital?"

"No, I'll live."

"Right, that's good to hear. Now, back to business. I'm sorry, but that title is a total *bust*. Geddit?"

"But, Mike, feminism is dead in the water! Most of us tried

our best, but we were let down by some of our sisters who got their tops off and made some easy money instead."

"Plenty of guys in this world also have a tough time of it. Look, why don't you write that nice little story I suggested last week? About the new metallic bikinis?"

"Oh, Mike, what am I going to do with you?"

"Here we go. Look, I'm a bit pushed for time today." Mike had a deadline looming over him and a stack of bills to pay. "Gemma, I need a hot title in the next five minutes. All joking aside. Because I need to fit in the Lonely Hearts section and the new diet-book feature and the cosmetic-surgery advert that we secured yesterday. And you'll have to keep the word-count to the stated amount this week, right? Because we really have to give priority to advertising. Okay?"

"Oh, Mike, why do I bother?"

"Because you need the money, Gemma love. Same as I do."

It was true, she realised. She did need the money. Literary novels just didn't sell very well these days, unless you were lucky enough to be selected for some glitzy promotion or a prime-time telly plug. And sometimes you lost a bundle on the discounts.

"You win, Mike," she said quietly. "I'll e-mail you something in the next ten minutes."

"Make that five minutes, thanks. Good girl, Gemma. And remember, if you're ever interviewed on *Ireland AM* about your books again in the future, make sure to slip in the name of our humble little paper, won't you? And next week could I please have something on *Big Brother*? Like would any of our readers turn lesbian in an all-girl house? See ya!"

"Wait, Mike!"

He hung up.

Gemma sighed, turned the phone off and went back to the sitting room, where she tapped out a slick little piece about chickens and cooking foil and beach-babes in silver bikinis, did a spell-check and pressed "send" without even bothering to read it back. What did it matter anyway, she thought crossly. Mike would do what he wanted with her submission and then ruin the whole thing with a smutty title. Even though Gemma's page was supposed to be aimed at women, they both knew that it was mostly male readers who looked at it. Hoping, no doubt, to discover some titillating new piece of information they could laugh about with their mates down the pub. Gemma was seriously beginning to think that men generally *hated* women. Because the more they lusted after, ogled and desired women (in every culture from the very liberal to the very strict) the more they seemed to despise and condemn them, too. Usually for possessing the very qualities (beauty and intelligence) that had attracted them in the first place.

"Ah, fuck it," she sighed, fixing her hair in the mirror. "Men want to look at bimbos, sleep with bimbos and marry skivvys. The end. Well, I'm neither so I guess that's me out of the race."

What now?

She was too annoyed to concentrate on her real work, her latest novel. She'd phone her daughter in New York again, that's what she'd do.

Twenty-one-year-old Victoria hadn't answered her house phone (or her mobile) for a few days now. Gemma called the beauty salon where Victoria worked (several times in recent days) but they'd always said she wasn't in that day. But there was no answer at home either, even late at night. It was very worrying. Maybe she'd met a new boyfriend and was spending time at his place. Surely she wouldn't have gone on holiday without letting her mother know? Would she? Gemma went back to the kitchen. By this time, what was left of her lunch had cooled into a congealed, heavy-looking lump so she threw it in the bin.

* * *

The following morning, when she strolled to the newsagents to buy a copy of the paper, Victoria still hadn't been in touch. Hurriedly, Gemma flicked through the solvent-scented pages until she found her column. Typical Mike! Half of the word-count had been slashed to make room for a picture of the new bikini. Silvery, shiny fabric (what there was of it) stretched to breaking point over the super-skinny model's jutting pelvic bones and obvious-implant bust. She was eighteen years old, the caption boasted, and from Cork. Eighteen years old! (Gemma was still sitting exams at that age.) She could practically see the model's Fallopian tubes, her costume was that skimpy. Gemma's cheeks began to turn pink with professional embarrassment.

But that wasn't all she had to put up with, unfortunately. There was also a picture of Gemma herself looking rather glum. Which she suddenly realized had been photo-shopped to make her seem a lot more despondent than she usually came out looking in author-portrait shots. But somehow, she also had a definite trout-pout. Her female readers (the few she had, probably) would surely think she was ranting on about the tyranny of the beauty industry, while secretly having all kinds of plastic surgery herself. She'd swing for that Mike the next time she saw him, she honestly would.

"But think of the money," she told herself sadly, later that afternoon.

And it did help.

But only a little bit. To cheer herself up, she raked her Zen-style pebble-garden perfect and then went for a long walk on the beach.

She joined Aurora and Miriam for coffee and biscuits in The Last Chapter in the afternoon. Aurora had recently introduced a tiny café area in her bookshop, painted a soothing dark green (inspired by the coffee-house on *Frasier*). Naturally, the two women were full of support for Gemma's world view and totally outraged at the way Mike had stitched her up with the dodgy trout-pout photo. And then they all broke into giggles and laughed about the whole thing for nearly an hour.

Wasn't she lucky she had such good friends, Gemma thought to herself on the way home. What would she do without them?

She rang Victoria again, twice, after supper. (Which was a microwaved shepherd's pie, tasteless and oily but edible enough with plenty of brown sauce on it.) Maddeningly, there was still no answer to the ringing telephone in Victoria's Manhattan apartment. Her mobile was still switched off, too. Maybe she had lost it? Gemma left yet another message at the salon and went to bed early but she did not sleep. This business of Victoria being out of reach was making her very nervous. She lay stiff as a board in her beautiful sleigh bed (the one and only extravagant thing she had ever bought for herself, to celebrate her first publishing deal), just staring at the ceiling.

Could addiction be inherited, she wondered. Victoria did seem to be missing an awful lot of days at work. And she had been rather too fond of the booze when she'd been a teenager, Gemma recalled with a lurch in her heart. Gemma hadn't been too hard on her at the time, and maybe in retrospect that had been a mistake. But as a single mother, Gemma'd had enough on her plate without her daughter hating her as well. She'd brought Victoria up all by herself. And most of it had been a struggle, to be both mother and father, nurturer and provider. Getting a place on that journalism course, then fitting classes and exams round her pregnancy and Victoria's baby years. Writing columns for three regional newspapers, child-minding for other mothers between jobs, proof-reading novels for a time and then writing six novels herself. None of them bestsellers but they'd garnered enough critical acclaim to get Gemma's name out there. And now she had this moderately lucrative gig on a national paper, albeit a tabloid. Even this little house she'd bought with no help from anyone, in the days before prices had gone completely off the scale, luckily enough. And she'd done the house up very gradually, too, as and when she'd had the money. But always putting Victoria's needs first.

Nobody could say she hadn't been a good mother. Nobody except her own parents, sadly. They'd stopped speaking to her back when she was eighteen and pregnant to a "head-the-ball" from Dublin. A flint-faced drummer in an up-and-coming rock band: she'd been obsessed with him. Except they never did make it into the charts. Only into the police cells a few times, for disturbing the peace. The band fell into obscurity in a few short months, mired in drink and drugs, and Victoria's father had lost interest in her before she was even born. (Last she'd heard, he'd gone to live in London.) He could be anywhere by now, Gemma thought. He could be cleaned up and respectable; he could be dead.

But Gemma had got over him pretty quickly anyway.

Nothing like a pregnancy to sort the men out from the boys. By the time the morning sickness had settled down, she'd known she never wanted to see him again. If it hadn't been for Gemma's grandmother taking her in for a while until she got her act together, heaven knows where she and Victoria would have ended up. She still hadn't forgiven her parents for the hysterical way they'd behaved. She'd tried to make allowances for the way they'd reacted, knowing they'd grown up in very strict times themselves, but really, they had acted like monsters. She couldn't believe the names they had called her, their lack of emotion even when Victoria was born beautiful and healthy. Gemma's own father was ill these days with a heart condition but still she couldn't bear to go and visit them.

None of the men Gemma had met in her twenties and thirties had wanted to "get involved" either. Because they didn't want to be "lumbered" with Victoria, they said. They didn't want to have to pay to raise another man's child. And now that Victoria had grown up and left home, they still didn't want to get involved with Gemma, or so it seemed. She was still on her own at forty. First she'd been too much trouble, a socially unacceptable embarrassment. (A burden on the State, as her father had put it, even though she'd never claimed benefits.) A young single mother with no nice granny willing to babysit for little Victoria. And now that she was free to date whoever she liked, she knew she was too opinionated and too set in her ways to compromise. She'd more or less given up hope of ever meeting a nice, normal man. Well, stuff the lot of them, Gemma decided.

Bloody men!

Who needed them anyway?

Untidy, lazy, dirty creatures.

Good riddance to bad rubbish.

Right! Now she'd focus on her one true love.

She'd call Victoria every hour, on the hour, all day tomorrow. And she'd write to her, a big long letter full of chatty news and funny anecdotes. They hadn't kept in touch nearly enough since Victoria went to work in America. And she'd demand to speak to somebody senior at the beauty salon, too. It was outrageous they hadn't been more co-operative.

And if she hadn't got in touch with her daughter by the weekend, she'd have no choice but to book a flight to New York and go over there herself and find out what the hell was going on. She couldn't go on not knowing, she vowed. Anything was better than this current shut-down in communication. Anything was better than lying awake at night, imagining all sorts. Yes, she would go to New York.

Flying phobia or no flying phobia.

16

Another Girl, Another Planet

Mackenzie finished his mug of tea, washed the mug and put it away on the dresser. The kitchen was spotless and he didn't want to leave anything sitting on the draining board and spoil it. His mother had been looking forward to putting her feet up and relaxing a little bit when Sarah took over as lady of the house. Not that she was ever going to turn into a pampered, glamorous granny or anything: she definitely wasn't. Some hopes now! And it would have been so nice for her to have another woman to share the house with, he thought sadly. And to share a laugh with, as well. It could be very lonely in Thistledown when the day-staff had gone home and he was out with his friends in the pub, he knew that. And he'd tried not to go out more than once a fortnight but still, he had to go out sometimes and talk to other people or he'd turn into a recluse.

Ever since Sarah and himself had become a couple, Millicent had been hoping for the sound of wedding bells. She'd tried hard not to ask all the time how the romance was going. But he knew she was praying he'd finally met the woman who would help him get over Jane. And for a while he'd thought Sarah would be his saviour, too. But then she'd run away in the middle of the night without even coming to talk to him. And he knew for sure that Sarah was not the one. Maybe he'd always known that. Maybe that was why he hadn't proposed sooner.

He saw Abigail and his mother coming back now from their walk with the dogs, and he waved out at them through the kitchen window. Abigail's cheeks were flushed with fresh air and exertion – clearly she wasn't used to so much exercise. The dogs were jumping up and down, delighted at having a new person to play with. Millicent saw him standing at the window and she waved in, smiling broadly. Minutes later, the three of them were sitting down to a late lunch of bread, cheese and home-baked apple pie.

"Does everything look okay?" asked Mackenzie, offering Abigail another cup of tea.

"Yes, the sheep are all happy enough," said his mother. "No injuries that I could see. And the youngest fir trees seem to have survived last night's gales." (They'd begun growing Christmas trees commercially a few years before.)

"Oh good, that'll save me a trip," nodded Mackenzie. "I'll get on with the new orders so. We've a batch going out to Canada today."

"Would you give Abigail a lift into the village later, if you have time? She wants to do some shopping. And I wanted to go to church to say a quiet prayer, so you could drop me off on the way?"

"Sure I will," Mackenzie said, getting up from the table.

"Only if it's no trouble," Abigail added. "Only I really didn't bring enough stuff with me. I mean, when you rang and invited me, Millicent, I was so surprised, I forgot to pack enough sweaters and socks."

"It's no trouble, none at all, it was good of you to come back and see us," Mackenzie said. "I didn't think any of Sarah's friends would still be speaking to me. I never thought I'd see you again, any of you," he added darkly.

Millicent appeared calm and composed as he said this but Mackenzie knew she was on tenterhooks with him, wondering when he was going to snap.

"Mackenzie, look, let me clear something up," said Abigail. "Now is as good a time as any. What happened with the wedding, it wasn't anyone's fault. I told Sarah that night, you couldn't help the way you felt about Jane, and that's still my view. You were trying to move on with your life and get married. But you found it harder to let go of the past than you'd expected. Guilt is a very powerful emotion, Mackenzie. And Sarah couldn't help the way she felt either. She's never had to share anything, not really. It would have been too much of a struggle for her to go into the marriage knowing that you felt this way. And knowing that everyone else *knew* you felt this way. So yes, it was a very sad thing to have happened, when we were all looking forward to a lovely Christmas wedding. But the main thing is, how are you feeling now? And how is Sarah feeling now? Everybody else will be fine – they don't know the full story anyway."

"I'm sure they worked it out."

"Maybe they did. But you don't owe it to the rest of the

world to live out some fairytale marriage, you know. And neither does Sarah. You're not some airbrushed celebrity couple, Mackenzie Campbell. You're both of you only human."

"I guess I can't argue with any of that. Thanks for putting me straight," he said, nodding, although he did sound a little bit peeved. As if she were mocking him for making a drama out of his cancelled wedding or something. As if he were enjoying the fallout of it all, when he definitely wasn't.

"You're welcome," she said.

They eyed each other across the table, neither one blinking or backing down.

Millicent said nothing but her cheeks were very pink.

Could it be that Abigail was *the one*, she prayed. Could Abigail be the one woman who was capable of taking her son in hand? Millicent held her breath. Everything could depend on what happened in the next few hours. Of course, nothing at all might happen. Abigail could simply go home to London and leave the pair of them behind with their broken hearts and their big, empty house. But still, she could feel something in the air. She could feel it!

Abigail suddenly broke the spell by pouring more tea. She patted Mackenzie's hand and smiled at him affectionately. "It doesn't matter what everybody else says or thinks about the wedding being called off. All that counts is the two of you, that you're both okay now. Even though the pair of you are mad eejits, in my humble opinion."

"Thanks, I think," he said and he stood up abruptly and strode off towards the workshops.

"Oh, Abigail, you're only brilliant," Millicent sighed, when her son was out of earshot.

"I am?"

"Yes! I've been trying to get through to him ever since it happened. Trying to make him feel better about himself. And now you've just said everything straight out, spelt it out for him. Do you always say what's on your mind?"

"That's what I get paid for! To tell you the truth, I'm amazed they haven't patched things up by now. I guess they really are the two most stubborn people who ever lived."

Millicent nodded and the conversation was closed.

Abigail went to freshen up and Millicent cleared away the dishes. But as she put the apple-pie away, she smiled a secret smile to herself.

Yes, she had indeed heard Sarah leaving the house that night. Millicent was a light sleeper and she had trained herself to wake up at the slightest hint of a noise in the manor house during the hours of darkness. A big historical house like this was a prime target for thieves. So yes, she had heard Sarah opening the front door and closing it softly behind her. And she'd seen her hurrying away down the drive with her bags banging against her legs in the moonlight. But she hadn't raised the alarm. She hadn't wakened Mackenzie or anyone. Because Millicent didn't believe in trying to go against fate. Of course later she had phoned Sarah and begged her to give Mackenzie another chance. And Sarah had refused, refused very emphatically. So Millicent's conscience was clear on that score.

But had she invited Abigail here because she felt in her heart that Abigail was a much better match for Mackenzie? Ever since Abigail had complimented Thistledown, Millicent admitted now, her wily brain had been working overtime.

So! Maybe she'd invited Abigail here for a reason. And maybe she hadn't. But Sarah definitely wasn't coming back. And her son wasn't happy on his own. And look, they were getting on quite well. And Mackenzie seemed to be cheering up, just a little bit. Not enough for anyone else to notice, but enough for Millicent to begin to have some hope again.

* * *

But later on, in the jeep, going on towards the village after they'd dropped Millicent off at church, Mackenzie seemed to have retreated into his dark mood. He didn't say much and, even then, it was mostly one-word answers to the questions Abigail had asked him.

Big Millie had been right earlier, Abigail thought sadly. Mackenzie was shutting everyone out again, just like he'd done when Jane died.

"Maybe you should have some counselling?" she suggested tentatively. "I think you could do with it. Grief counselling. You're stuck in your one bad moment, aren't you? Remember what I said about half a life being better than nothing?"

"Oh, no, please, don't start all that again," he sighed. "If counselling is such a great thing, why is half the country popping happy pills and having doomed love affairs and getting wasted drunk every night of the week? Obviously, all this analysis and self-awareness isn't doing much good."

"That's because life is more complicated than ever before, and most of us live a lot longer than Mother Nature intended. In the old days, war or illness probably killed most people off before they even knew they were depressed. And the ones who did survive were too busy looking for something to eat."

"Whatever."

She gazed out of the passenger window, determined not to lose her temper with him. She would not come back to Thistledown, she decided suddenly. Not any more. Even this visit had been a mistake. She liked Big Millie enormously and worried about how she would cope with her depressed son. But Mackenzie was like a black hole, pulling everybody else around him into his misery. And she had enough to deal with already – her career was making her emotionally and physically exhausted.

By this time, the silence in the jeep was becoming uncomfortable.

"I'm only saying, talking to someone might help," she muttered and then wished she hadn't. She thought she actually heard Mackenzie snort with derision.

"You think you have all the answers," he said, almost in a whisper.

"No, I don't," she half-shouted, making him jump. "I have to try, though. Somebody has to try. I had four suicides to deal with in Christmas week, if you must know. Four funerals to go to! That's why I got this time off, Mackenzie! You might have lost your girlfriend but we had to bury four of our patients! My job is bloody hard and nobody appreciates it. I counselled three of those people, you know. Two of them for a long time, months and months of counselling. But now, when something like this happens, people say we did nothing, they say we missed the signs. Well, I work my socks off in that clinic and I do my level best, every single day I'm in there. And you know what, Mackenzie Campbell? Sometimes it just isn't good enough. What do you want me to do about it? Give up and sulk for the rest of my life? Like you! I can't change the world on my own but at least I'm trying to make a difference."

"Jesus, I'm sorry I spoke. Women!"

"Women? What's that supposed to mean? Right, that's it! Stop this stupid jeep, the suspension is knackered anyway. I'll walk back to the house and pack my bags and you won't have to suffer another one of my pop-psychology lectures ever again. I'll leave tonight, don't worry."

Now he was worried.

"Please don't go, Abigail. Mum will be very upset if you leave early. She'll be very cross with me, too. She'll give me a right earful for upsetting you."

"Oh, Christ, why don't you stop sulking and ask Sarah to come back to Thistledown? Honestly, I give up on the two of you. That's it, I officially admit defeat. If I had a great big dope like you in love with me, moping around some enormous Scottish castle all day long, I'd have him marched up that aisle so fast his feet wouldn't touch the ground. If you were my fiancé, I wouldn't allow you carry on like this. You absolute, stonking, great idiot! Stop this fucking heap of scrap right now or I'll open the door and jump out of it, I'm not joking!"

Mackenzie slammed on the brakes, stopped the jeep in the shadow of a row of fir trees, reached across to Abigail and pulled her roughly into his arms. For one awful moment she thought he was going to hit her. Or push her out onto the road. But then she saw his gaze dropping down towards her shocked lips. And she knew he was going to kiss her instead. And she, numbed by the despair of having to attend four funerals in Christmas week, let him kiss her passionately on the lips. And then she began to cry with emotion and kiss him back, even more passionately. And the next thing they knew, they'd stumbled out of the jeep, into the darkness of the closely planted fir trees, and were kissing frantically on top of Mackenzie's winter coat. His surprisingly warm hands were slipping underneath her clothes, touching her breasts, circling her waist.

And she was trying to pull herself together enough to ask him to stop, but she couldn't. She wanted him badly. Abigail knew what she was doing was wrong, very wrong indeed, but suddenly she didn't care. She was so lonely and unhappy and weary. She was tired of funerals and tired of emergency meetings and tired of waiting for hospital clerks to get back to her with a spare bed and never having any time for herself. She was tired of all her friends using her as an emotional waste-paper basket. She was tired of missing Donal and waking up alone and going to bed alone. The world was in a mess, and she had no one. And Mackenzie had no one. And besides, he had amazingly smooth hands for a farmer. His lovely smooth hands now began to undo the buttons of her jeans and she didn't stop him. Then he was on top of her and it was too late to stop him. So she decided to stop worrying about everything for a few minutes and just enjoy his fabulously strong and muscular body.

For five minutes there was no sound in the air around them except for their laboured breathing and the occasional bird of prey fluttering in the uppermost branches of the Christmas-tree plantation. They rolled over instinctively then, Mackenzie being so much heavier and more powerful than she was, and Abigail straddled his iron-firm thighs and they came together like an explosion. Eyes open, holding hands, their faces tight with the urgency of it all.

When it was over, Mackenzie clung to her and would not let her go.

"I'm sorry," he said, pulling her down towards him and kissing her face all over. "I'm so sorry."

"Don't be," she soothed, stretching her back. Then pulling him up into a sitting position, stroking his back and shoulders, kissing his forehead. "I wanted you to do it."

"Did you really?" he gasped.

"Yes," she said. "I've always liked you. You knew that, surely? You're not exactly an unattractive man. Whenever we met in London, I did always think you were very nice."

"I didn't know you fancied me," he said quietly.

"Well, I did fancy you. From afar. But obviously I didn't tell you about it. Or Sarah. I'm not always in favour of honesty, you know. Some feelings you do have to keep to yourself."

"Abigail, what happens now?" Mackenzie said, looking at her intensely. At her dishevelled blonde hair, her hourglass figure, half-in and half-out of her clothes. He picked a leaf out of her stunning, gravity-defying cleavage and hugged her tightly.

"What happens now?" Abigail replied, gently getting off him and buttoning up her shirt. "Nothing happens now. I'm not some God-fearing, Victorian scullery-maid. I can take care of myself, you know. I *am* thirty years old." She stood up straight and adjusted her clothes, sighing with tiredness. "Forget it. Although I must say I feel a whole lot better now, don't you? That was very therapeutic."

"Forget what just happened? But what if something . . . What if you . . . Are you on the pill, Abigail?"

"Oh my God, you men really are hopeless, aren't you? You should have asked me that before we had sex, you dope."

"That's twice you've called me that."

"Don't worry, Mackenzie. I'm not pregnant, it wasn't my time of the month to be fertile. You're quite safe. And I won't tell anyone about this. It was just one of those things. It was lovely, I enjoyed it. But Sarah will never know, I promise you that." She walked back to the jeep.

Mackenzie leapt up, pulled on his clothes and followed her. Then he drew her into his arms. And kissed her again. Slowly, this time. Slowly and tenderly.

"You're lovely," he said in a husky voice.

"I know," she joked. "I'm absolutely gorgeous. Frankly, I don't know why I'm not on the cover of all the magazines. All those contracts must have got lost in the post."

"Don't go home tomorrow," he whispered. "Stay with me for a few days longer. Please. I need you to stay with me. I want you to stay. In my bed."

"Oh yeah, let's make a week of it! Shall we? Millicent will be delighted, I'm sure," Abigail sighed. "When she sees the two of us gallivanting round the house together in our pyjamas, she'll be just delighted. Besides, I might fall in love with you, and you might fall in love with me. And then where would we be? By the way, I'm joking. That's just my way of telling you I'm not a complete tart. No, really, I'll go home tonight."

"No, stay. Mum can go and visit the relatives for a few days. She was going to go anyway but then she said she would stay with me and keep me company. I'll suggest it at dinner tonight. And then you can decide if you want to give me a chance to make love to you properly."

"Are you mad?"

"Yes. A bit. It helps to be slightly mad when you live in an old house with gargoyles on it and you can't seem to hang onto your women."

"But why, Mackenzie? I told you already, this one time doesn't matter. But I'm not the type to have casual affairs. I wouldn't do that to you or to myself, or to Sarah. I don't know what happened back there but I want you to know I don't make a habit of it."

"Please stay, Abigail?"

"What if I really like you, though? And you really like me?" she said. "Just for the sake of argument, let's assume we began to feel something for one another. Where would we be then? We'd be out of the frying pan and into the fire."

"Not necessarily. The way I see it, we have nothing left to lose. And before you even think it, I am not doing this to make Sarah jealous. It's just, I'm so lonely I think I'm going to go out of my mind sometimes. I can talk to you, Abigail. I need someone that I can really talk to."

"I know exactly how you feel," she said quietly. "Hold me."

They stood in the gloom for a long time, hugging each other tightly, breathing in the scent of each other's bodies, listening to the wind blowing in the tree-tops, just enjoying the safe feeling of being together. Then they kissed again, tenderly, properly. And even though they were not in love with each other, they knew that they had become kindred spirits. And in that exact moment in time, they both knew that understanding was more important than chemistry. A bond had been forged between them. They were soul mates. Though it was kind of teenage-embarrassing to say it out loud so they didn't.

Eventually, Abigail's pulse slowed down again. So much so, her teeth began to chatter alarmingly. There were still patches of frost on the ground.

"I bet we've caught a cold, doing that," she said.

"Come on," Mackenzie smiled. "We'd better get back to the house. You slip upstairs and run yourself a hot bath – I see you've scratched your neck on some twigs or something. I'll drive Mum over to her cousin's house if she wants to go and then I'll fry us up some leftovers for supper and we'll just see what happens. You don't have to sleep in my bed tonight but I want you to, more than you'll ever know. I feel sort of peaceful when you're with me."

"Okay," said Abigail. "I like the sound of that fry-up. I'm starving."

She didn't ask him what they would say to Millicent, arriving back at Thistledown with no shopping bags. And she didn't ask him what they were going to do about Sarah.

But later that evening, as she lay tucked up in Mackenzie's beautiful four-poster bed, drinking hot, refreshing tea and waiting for him to come out of the shower, Abigail felt like she had never slept anywhere else.

17

Is This Love?

Abigail and Mackenzie had spent the day strolling round the estate, just enjoying the fresh (though still freezing) air and also enjoying being in each other's company. Now they were sitting on a rocky promontory near the house, looking out to sea. Mackenzie had brought a flask of hot chicken soup and they were both wearing warm scarves and gloves, as well as their heaviest winter coats. Abigail's cheeks were bright red from the searing gales and she feared she looked like a tomato wearing a blonde wig. Mackenzie poured the soup, shielding it as he did so by turning his back to the wind. Abigail watched the concentration on his face and her heart turned over. She did love him a little bit, she realized suddenly. More than a little bit. She did love being with him, talking to him. She loved his strength and his determination. She loved the way he took care of her. Most of all, she loved his sensible side. He wasn't a rolling stone or the type of man who would take chances. Maybe she was hankering after domestic bliss, after all?

"Thanks," she said, as she curled her hands around the piping-hot cup of soup.

"Smells delicious."

He smiled at her, then they both looked out to sea again.

They had made love about a dozen times since that first amazing experience beneath the trees. And each time had been just as heavenly as the one before. She had felt them growing closer and closer, anticipating each other's climax, knowing when to quicken up or slow right down. At night they fell asleep curled together, holding hands. Or companionably back to back, like book-ends. She could get used to this, she thought wistfully. She was trying hard not to think of the clinic and the massive workload that was waiting for her in London when this magical interlude, whatever it was, came to an end. She was also trying not to think of the repercussions of what had happened with Mackenzie.

"When are you going back to London?" he asked suddenly, as if reading her thoughts. "I mean, when were you thinking of going back?"

"Well, isn't Millicent coming home tonight from her little jaunt? I suppose I'd better make myself scarce. She'd know right away there was something going on between us, if she saw me still here. She's very perceptive – you know she is. And I'd hate to lie to her. I mean, didn't we say I was going home tonight, because they needed me at work?"

"Actually, I didn't say anything to Mum about it on the phone, one way or the other. And she didn't ask. If I didn't know her better, I'd think she was up to something. Usually, she's all questions about the farm and everything, if she's away visiting. But this time she was on and off the phone in five minutes."

"She's a wise old bird," was all Abigail could manage. Surely Millie wasn't on to them already?

"I'll miss you so much if you go," Mackenzie said, putting his arm around her.

"Mackenzie, listen, don't get me wrong. I don't want to leave you, or Thistledown for that matter. So much room here to walk about, after my little maisonette and the streets of London. These last four days with you have been so wonderful, a lovely experience for me, all round. Lovely and so unexpected. But we've got to face facts, I suppose. We've got to be grown-ups now."

"Here we go. I thought you said you weren't going to lecture me any more?"

"True. But maybe we should explore the possibilities? Maybe you were attracted to me – *let me finish please* – because you were afraid of being alone. And sometimes when I'm overwhelmed at work, I can think of nothing I'd like more than to live in a beautiful place like this. It's like standing at the edge of the world here, it's so gorgeous and peaceful. But this isn't going to cure you of your grief and it isn't going to cure me of mine. I think the world of you, Mackenzie, but we've got to accept we have responsibilities and move on. This isn't real."

She could hardly look him in the eye, she felt so guilty and sad.

"I knew you would say that. And I've got an answer for you: we could make it real."

"What?"

"You and me together, we're both intelligent people. We could make something happen if we wanted to. If we had the courage to."

"What are you talking about?"

"Think about this for a minute, okay? Most people believe in love at first sight, don't they?"

"I guess so."

"That second you lock eyes with someone special: and both of you will just know it, you'll feel it. Love! Why is that, Abigail? Probably because of some period drama on the telly! Some romantic notion planted in our national consciousness by Jane Austen. Or some other novelist who never really had a life anyway. Just years and years spent cooped up in their father's house, daydreaming their youth away."

"Where are you going with this, Mackenzie?"

"I'm just making a point. It doesn't have to be like that in this day and age. We're free now, free to make our mistakes and learn from them. Free to start over again."

"Mackenzie, don't say what I think you're going to say, please."

"Why not? I want us to give this a chance," he said, turning to face her. Touching her face and then holding both her hands tightly in his. She gazed up at him (he was considerably taller than she was, even when they were sitting down) and felt a lump of fear forming in her throat.

"Oh, Mackenzie, what have I done to you? I've made things ten times worse, haven't I? You said you would love Jane for the rest of your life. I don't expect you to give up her memory now, overnight. It's already cost you dearly. And me, well, I don't know what I'm playing at, to tell you the truth. Now we've trampled all over Sarah's dreams into the bargain."

"I'm glad it didn't happen, Abigail. The wedding, I mean. I honestly mean that, sincerely. It would have put too much pressure on Sarah if we'd gone through with it. I know she would have resented me always for what I said that night. I loved her, Abigail, but we didn't really connect as a couple. I could feel that from the beginning. She was too idealistic for me, too creative, too sensitive. I was always checking myself, watching what I said. You don't make me feel like that, Abigail. You're different. You're grounded and warm and I need you."

"Oh, Mackenzie, I can't think straight any more! Oh, this is great! I'm going to be a lot of use to them at work now, aren't I? I don't know what the hell I'm doing any more, what's right and what's wrong."

"Look, hear me out. You said you would never meet anyone who would make you feel special, the way Donal made you feel. And I can't forget Jane. Right? Well, doesn't that mean we have everything in common? We both know what it is to lose someone who meant the world to us. And maybe we can't say we *love* each other at the moment, but love can wait. It'll come, in time. We're friends, aren't we? The best of friends? I'd have withered away and died without you since Sarah went, despite the brave face I've tried to put on for everyone. At one point, I did wonder if I'd end up losing the plot altogether. You've saved me, Abigail."

"That's so lovely of you to say, Mackenzie, but still, I don't know if this is such a good idea."

"Please, Abigail, please take some extended leave at work and stay with me for a couple of months. I think we could be on the verge of something big here. What harm can it do? I think I'm falling for you."

"I can't deny I have feelings for you, too. But we're both tired out, Mackenzie. I've been through the wringer this Christmas and so have you. Maybe this new development would be too much for us? Too much pressure on both of us to rescue each other? Wouldn't it feel like we were starting off a relationship in a lifeboat? Could it be love, do you think? Or would we only be sharing a life-jacket?"

"No, absolutely not, this isn't about being helpless or desperate or anything. Aren't we having a lovely time together? The last four days have just slipped away, haven't they? I thought you said you enjoyed the nights we spent together, you like talking to me?"

"I did enjoy our time together, yes. I do enjoy your company."

"Well, then," he begged, looking into her eyes and pleading with her not to give up on him. "I like you an awful lot, Abigail, because you're strong and practical and direct, and you don't expect me to know what you're thinking all the time. And I accept that I can never be Donal, never be the man he was to you. We can relax together, knowing where we stand. Isn't that a far stronger position to be in than experiencing love at first sight and then waiting for it all to go wrong? We're compatible, Abigail. We're perfect together."

"I suppose so. But neither one of us has an awful lot of time to spare in the marriage stakes. I mean, don't you want a big family? Don't you need to get out there and find the mother of your children? Keep the Campbell dynasty going? I mean, you've got to be in love to bring children into the world. Whatever we tell ourselves now, at this point in time, a relationship's got to amount to something in the end. Otherwise, we're just housemates with added benefits."

"Abigal Halloran, I'm asking you to marry me. I thought you understood that's what I meant?"

"Oh wow, this is getting seriously weird."

She wondered if Mackenzie had gone mad with grief, and she was terrified she had pushed him over the edge, that this latest craziness was all her fault, for allowing their affair to happen at all.

"What's weird about it? You said I was an attractive man and I think you're gorgeous. You know losing Jane broke my heart, and I know you'll never get over Donal. We're great together in bed. You're worn out counselling those poor souls, you know you are. And I'm tired of being alone here in a house with ten bedrooms."

"And Sarah?"

"When I was with Sarah, I could never relax. She would have found me out eventually, you see. I lived in fear of calling her Jane accidentally. Ask Dougal, he'll tell you. He warned me about it several times."

"Oh, Mackenzie. We can't rationalize love into existence."

"We can. I think we should get married as soon as possible – if that's what you want, obviously. Grab this chance of happiness. Didn't you say that people could choose to be happy? That they could choose whether to be happy or sad? That it wasn't a case of allowing your emotions to dictate to you?"

"So we just get married? Get *married*. Just like that?"

"Yes."

"Wouldn't you be embarrassed? In front of all your friends

and family? The reverend? They'd say I took advantage of you, that you were lonely here, that you were on the rebound. Your mother would string me up."

"No, she would not. She likes you. It doesn't have to be another big wedding with all the trimmings. You said that was all OTT anyway. Sarah told me that you said you'd rather die than have six bridesmaids and a stuffy reception and sentimental speeches."

"Well, yes, I did say that. But that's only because I don't have the looks or the confidence to carry it off," Abigail said quietly.

"You're beautiful," Mackenzie said.

"No, I'm not," she sighed, shaking her head slowly.

"You are."

She wasn't beautiful. Not really. Not like Sarah, she thought guiltily.

Sarah had looked so gorgeous in her wedding dress, which Abigail suddenly remembered she still had hanging up in her London house.

"You are to me. And I never wanted a big wedding," he said quietly. "I'm quite shy, you know. I prefer my old jeans and a scruffy coat and boots."

"Well, what about having children together? Have you thought of that?"

"Yes. I think it'd be brilliant. I think we'd be the most understanding parents in the whole, wide world. If we had kids, they'd be so wanted. Aren't most of us the result of too much drink and a cheesy pop song anyway?" he said brightly, trying to make Abigail laugh.

"Mackenzie Campbell, how could you!"

"It's true."

"You know what? Everything you say makes perfect sense. Yes, I would love to get married and give up counselling and live in this gorgeous house with you. Of course I would. There's just one problem."

"Sarah?"

"Got it in one. I've stolen her dream, Mackenzie."

"You haven't. She wrote to me. She sent me a letter telling me there was no hope for us. It's too late for me and Sarah. Please, Abigail? Please, at least think about it. I'll ask only one thing of you: that you never leave me without telling me first. I've lost two women in my life. One died in a needless accident, and the other one disappeared in the middle of the night. I couldn't cope with it happening a third time. So, if we do get married, if that does happen, please don't do a runner on me. We can talk things through. I know you can't promise to love me forever and all that. But please, promise me we'll always be able to talk?"

"Okay. I promise I'll always be honest with you, Mackenzie."

"And I'll always be good to you, Abigail. I swear to God, I'll never, ever hurt you in any way. I'll spend the rest of my life trying to make you love me. And I'll love you as much as I can. I swear it."

"Okay, I believe you. I believe you actually mean this. But I don't want to go down in history as the wicked witch in this fairytale. So there's just one thing I have to do. All right?"

"Sure. What is it?"

Although he knew in his heart what she was going to say. There was only one person Abigail would really care about hurting or offending. (The rest of the world could say what it liked, as far as Abigail was concerned.)

"It's Sarah, I'm going to have to choose my moment and tell her about us. I'm going to have to ask for Sarah's blessing to marry you."

18

Interesting Drug

Aurora and Gemma were sitting at one of the dainty bistro tables in The Last Chapter, having coffee and a chat, with a huge confection of red roses, crackly cellophane and curly ribbons balancing precariously in a tall vase, between them, on the table. It'd been delivered to the shop the day before. The card attached read, *With lots of love from a fellow bookworm.*

"So, you were in another book club before this one?" Gemma said carefully. "You never mentioned that before."

The shop was quiet that morning; only one or two customers were browsing the shelves.

"And I never would have told you anything about it except that maniac David Cropper won't leave me alone," Aurora hissed quietly. "Sending a massive, great bouquet like this to the shop, the little weasel. I don't know what I'm going to do about him. He's a compulsive womanizer. I think he has some kind of personality disorder, to be absolutely frank."

173

"We did wonder who sent you red roses, I must confess. Miriam thought it was your ex-husband, trying to get back with you." Gemma was dying to know what had happened before in Belfast but Aurora wasn't the confessing type, unfortunately. It had taken her all this time just to divulge she'd been married before. Never mind that she'd had an affair with a sleazy television producer from the BBC.

"No, my ex-husband didn't send the roses, Gemma. He wouldn't waste his money on hothouse flowers. Not for me, anyway. I mean, he got married a good while ago, to a lovely girl. Her name is Rose, by a curious coincidence. I wouldn't be surprised if David sent me roses on purpose, to remind me of her. To rub it in. Well, maybe he isn't that clever. Whatever, it was just David being manipulative again, or trying to be. Thinking he can win me over with a dozen over-priced blooms and a bit of glossy cellophane. Doesn't that just go to show you how hopelessly outdated he really is? Honestly, he couldn't care less about me, he just loves the thrill of the chase."

"Well, don't ask me to explain how a man's mind works! I haven't the foggiest idea. You're a real mystery woman, though, Aurora Blackstaff. You and your roses and your obsessive admirer! What else haven't you told us? Go on, dish all about the book club. I'm going to die of curiosity if you don't."

"You should get out more," Aurora laughed, shaking her head. "The Brontë Bunch, we were called. I was a bit secretive about it, wasn't I? And no wonder I kept it to myself. It was possibly the most ridiculous period of my life, so far. Let me see, what's one of the worst things I can tell you about it? For starters, I sent out official cancellation notices in the post when I decided to move here from Belfast."

"You did what? Official notices, eh?" Gemma knew better than to push it. Aurora would tell her as much as she wanted to and no more. Still, she couldn't help prodding a little.

"Yes, I put on my best hat and coat and I went to the printers one bright Monday morning, and I designed the cards myself with a solemn, serious expression on my face. Lovely, laminated cards I sent out. One hundred and twenty of them altogether. In expensive, black envelopes. Oh dear, how they must have pitied me!" Aurora closed her eyes at the memory of it.

"Black envelopes? Well, that sounds very swish," Gemma said in her best plummy voice. "Sounds like a very exclusive sort of book club to me."

"Swish? Oh yes, they were very swish indeed. The Brontë Bunch was nothing but a vehicle for snobbery, Gemma sweetheart. All complete snobs, hand-picked by myself, and we often dressed in Victorian costumes and had tea and cucumber sandwiches in my double-height, period-style conservatory."

"Jesus! A hundred and twenty of you in a domestic conservatory? Must have been quite big."

"It was huge. Cost me a quarter of a million pounds."

"No!"

"We were on TV once. Only in Northern Ireland, mind you. Nowhere where it mattered. And even then, it was BBC2, at half past one in the morning."

"Still, that was brilliant!"

"No, it was quite dull, in the event." She sighed and sipped her coffee for a moment. "I held interviews before letting anyone join The Brontë Bunch, just to make sure they really loved the arts and weren't just lonely and bored. The poor people I turned down. Oh, Gemma! If only I could tell them now how sorry I am. How ashamed of myself I am."

"Black envelopes, though? And period costume!" Gemma laughed. "I'm sorry, but it is quite funny. I'm sure they loved getting those fancy envelopes in the post. I would. All very much in keeping with the theme, wouldn't you say?"

"Indeed. The death of a book club, and so on. I suppose it's hard to believe I was ever such an almighty prig but there you are. We were the talk of Belfast for a while. I daresay, so was the fact I was seeing a younger man. Well, a bit younger, not a toyboy, more's the pity. Gallivanting round the best restaurants with him and going to the theatre every weekend."

"Wow! You're making me jealous. I've never done anything as exciting as that. The details of my love life could fit on the back of a stamp."

"You're not missing much, don't worry."

Aurora decided she wouldn't bother telling Gemma about her secret fetish for too-tight corsets and frilly petticoats and having sex fully clothed up against a grand piano. She was grateful the menopause had descended, really she was. Otherwise she would be in serious danger of developing a sex-addiction problem. Oh, how she'd lusted after that graceful, artful snake . . .

"It didn't last," she said quietly. "And when my so-called affair with David broke up, I simply hadn't the heart to go on with the book club. Or my teaching career. My husband, Henry, was long gone, of course, with his new love Rose. And I couldn't even enjoy my lovely conservatory any more. It was all such a reminder of my vanity, my silly pride. And it cost me a blinking fortune to have built. Not to mention it instigated the break-up of my marriage in the first place because I had Henry's precious garden bulldozed to make room for it. So I sold my house for a fortune and I came here to recover."

"And where did Henry and Rose go?" Gemma asked before she could stop herself.

"Somewhere near here, initially. He was such a good man, Gemma. He kept in touch even though I'd treated him so badly. He used to send me postcards from time to time, telling me how peaceful it was in this part of the country. How slow the pace of life was, how good the landscape was for the soul. So I came here but I didn't pester him and his new love, no. I never went to visit them, not even once. They did invite me to dinner a few times but it would have been too awkward. We all knew it. Then they had baby Emily and moved to France to be close to Rose's friends and it was a kind of relief. Because by then, I'd fallen in love with Redstone and I wanted to make it my home and stay here forever."

"You didn't mind about the baby? Not even a little bit?"

"No, I wouldn't have been a good mother, Gemma. I'm far too neurotic and bossy. I would have had the poor child demented with my interfering and my advice and my worrying. I can't help it, you see. That's why I don't want our little book club to get any bigger. Because I might get carried away again. I'm trying to be less controlling but it's so hard. Such hard work."

"I understand. I'm going to bite my Victoria's head off the next time I see her for not calling me in recent days . . . Aurora . . ." Gemma paused and took a deep breath. "Aurora . . . can I ask you a massive, massive favour? I'm planning to go over to New York and see if I can track her down. But I'm dreading the flight, really dreading it. I don't like to go on about these things but I'm phobic about flying."

"Well, that's not so unusual. Do you really have to go to America?"

"Yes, I do. The manager at the salon where Victoria works finally spoke to me and told me they haven't heard from her in a week. They'd just assumed she'd moved on to another job. They hadn't even bothered themselves to go round to her apartment and check if she was all right. I had to phone the police in the end."

"The police?"

"I was at my wit's end, Aurora. They're looking for her as we speak but I have to go over there and file a missing-person thing, they said."

"The police are involved? For heaven's sake, Gemma Hayes! Why the hell didn't you say something sooner? Letting me babble on about my dimwit lover. You must be in pieces – you should have said something."

"I'm saying something now," Gemma said, her face flushing with anxiety and fear. "You, oh, you wouldn't like to go with me, would you? I'd pay for your ticket, naturally. Please, Aurora? It's just – I know I'm going to be useless on the plane. I've never been on a long flight before in my life. I'm scared stiff I might make a complete fool of myself. But unless I do something soon, unless I do something drastic to get in touch with Victoria, I'm going to fall apart anyway."

"I'd *love* to go with you, thanks very much for asking me," Aurora said.

"Oh, thank you, Aurora!" said Gemma in relief. "Thank you so much!"

"Not at all! I'm flattered you trust me enough to confide in me and want my company. What are friends for, after all? And it *is* New York, I mean to say! Not exactly slumming it for the pair of us. But I'm sure it's nothing, Gemma. Young people never think of calling home; time passes in a different way for them. They only look ahead to the future, never thinking of the old has-beens sitting at home beside a ticking clock. *Has-beens* meaning their parents and anybody over thirty, by the way."

"That's very wise advice and so marvellous of you to agree to chaperone me, Aurora. I absolutely hate travelling by myself. Silly of me, at my age, but I always think I'm going to have a heart attack when the plane door closes and they start that safety information rubbish. I wish they wouldn't bother. I wish they'd just whack the film on and let me get quietly pickled."

"You poor love!"

"I've only ever been to London three times on a plane, and even that left me in tatters for days before each flight and after it. I've never liked flying but it seems to be getting worse in my old age. I turned down a lovely book tour of Europe last year because of it, all expenses paid, saying my sales there weren't good enough to justify the expense. It could've been my big break."

"Oh, Gemma," Aurora soothed.

"And of course, Victoria says I can't love her all that much if I won't fly over and visit her in New York every few months. At least that's what she said to me the last time we spoke on the phone. Now I can't get in touch with her at all – my only child! What's wrong with me, Aurora?" Gemma whispered and the tears rolled down her cheeks.

"Hey, come on, you! Age does funny things to all of us, Gemma. We lose confidence as we get older, I know I have. It should be the exact opposite – you'd think you'd gain some bloody confidence. But, no. We begin to doubt ourselves and our beliefs. We realize how frail we are and how life can suddenly throw these big changes at us."

"Yes, it's true. I mean, I hate men usually. But sometimes, when I wake in the middle of the night and there's no one to talk to, no one to hug, I get terrified."

"You'll meet someone, pet," Aurora said automatically. She'd been telling her female friends they would meet a nice man soon for most of her adult life. They rarely did. It seemed that the perfect man existed only in the pages of classic novels. The kind of man who could scoop you up in his arms and walk for ten miles with you in the driving rain. The kind of man who would fight and struggle and sweat blood and go through any kind of hardship just to be with you for half an hour.

"Not for myself. I don't care about romance any more," said Gemma sadly. "I just wish I had someone to help me now, to look for Victoria."

"Well, you have me. And Miriam and Sarah."

Personally, Aurora was content on her own. It was very peaceful, living alone. There was never a chance that someone would come home from work one day and tell you they were leaving you for a young actress (as David Cropper had said to her), or that they'd gambled away the house (like her own father had told her mother). Or that your cooking was awful and what in the name of God had they married you for anyway? Which is what'd happened to one of her old colleagues at the Grammar School in Belfast. The poor woman had hit her husband over the head with a saucepan of mushy peas and knocked him out cold. (Aurora never did find out if the case had gone to court.)

"No, I'm finished with romance," said Gemma, trying to stop crying. "I'm hard to please, I know I am, and I'm not getting any younger. And I'm far too independent to start planning my life around another person or cleaning up after them. Plus, he'd have to sign a pre-nup because no way is any man getting my house when I shuffle off this mortal coil. That house is Victoria's legacy, whether she wants it or not."

"You're lucky to have such a gorgeous daughter to worry about, Gemma. I just hope she appreciates you."

"Thanks, Aurora. And thanks for going to America with me. Because nowadays with all these extra security measures they have in place, one of those gun-toting air marshals or whatever they're called might shoot me stone-dead if they saw me sweating and fidgeting and shifting around in my seat thinking I was a suicide-bomber or something."

"You'll be fine," said Aurora, thinking they might need to go to the doctor for some tablets before the eight-hour flight.

"At least you'll be there to tell them I'm just a silly woman with a flying phobia and a grown-up daughter who can't be bothered to phone home," said Gemma, wiping some fresh tears from her eyes with a paper napkin.

They both had visions of poor Gemma being arrested and cuffed to the arm of her seat, thirty thousand feet up in the sky.

"Oh, Gemma, you poor creature – this is almost as funny as me and my black envelopes for the Brontë Bunch. But it's a terrible phobia for you to have to live with. I mean, it wouldn't matter if it was only giving up foreign holidays, but you do have to go and find Victoria. I really feel for you, I do. And I'll tell Victoria, when I see her, not to switch her mobile off ever again or you'll cut her out of your will. It's only what she deserves. Come on, we'll go and walk on the beach for a while! I'll close the shop for half an hour when those two customers leave. What are we like, the two of us?"

"I know. We're both daft. And to think we had Miriam down as the one away with the fairies in our circle. It just goes to show you."

Ten minutes later, the two women put on their coats and locked up the shop, leaving the bouquet of red roses behind. They went down the sandy path to the beach, marvelling at how fortunate they were to live in such a lovely place and saying wouldn't it be just awful if all they had to look out on was a dismal train track or a tatty factory. It'd been raining and the sand was damp and darkened here and there. But a shaft of watery sunshine had broken through the clouds and was warming up the beach a little. Aurora slipped her arm through Gemma's and they went slowly down the strand together, breathing in the revitalising ozone.

"You know Mike?" Gemma began as she noticed some small boys giggling at their linked arms.

"Your editor, yes?"

"Well, he wanted me to write a piece about women turning lesbian out of desperation."

"What did you write about instead?" asked Aurora,

chuckling heartily and blowing a kiss to their mini-audience.

"I wrote that reality TV and junk culture in general was destroying the minds of an entire generation. Turning our young people into lazy, uneducated clones. I said, never mind turning lesbian, the kids today can barely read and write."

"Good for you! Listen, let's walk off some cellulite and then we'll buy two fish suppers and put it back on again."

"Agreed."

A short while later, as Gemma and Aurora were waiting for their fish and chips in the Golden Griddle, Gemma's phone rang out on her glass desk, and the answer-machine picked up a message. A nurse was calling from a private hospital in New York to say that Victoria Hayes was recovering, but still seriously ill, after an accidental heroin overdose. And could Gemma please get in touch with them? There was the small matter of payment, of several thousand pounds, for Victoria's medical treatment. But the main thing was, Gemma might like to consider visiting her sick daughter as the withdrawal process was taking quite a toll on her. The nurse left a contact number and stressed that Victoria was out of danger now. It had been touch-and-go for two days, though, she explained. Which was why she'd needed so much treatment. Victoria was presently very underweight and tired, as might be expected in the case of narcotics abuse. And she was also very depressed, but again this was not a great surprise. The hospital was sorry to be giving Gemma such bad news out of the blue like this, the nurse said, but the NYPD had asked them to call her.

19

Panic

O h, the state of joy Gemma was in when she got home and saw she had a message! The little indicator light winking merrily after ten days of blank inactivity. A message from America, she prayed, as she hurried across the floor with her parcel from the chippy still in her hand. An international phone number, yes! Glory be and praise the Lord! Victoria was phoning home at last. The little minx, had she any idea what Gemma had been going through? She'd give her such a telling-off, she really would.

"It's her," she called to Aurora. "It's Victoria!"

Aurora clapped her hands together with happiness and went to get two plates and a bottle of red sauce from the crockery cupboard in the kitchen. She grabbed two forks from the drawer and began to unwrap her own parcel. Oh, it smelled good. She closed the door to give Gemma privacy.

And then the nurse's recorded voice came spilling into the

sitting room, as Gemma stared down at her glass desk and then out of the window to the ocean beyond. There was a slow trickling of ice-cold water into Gemma's heart as she heard the news. Time seemed to have slowed right down: she looked at her watch but the hands were out of focus. She tried to call Aurora but the rest of the house was roaring with silence and the words would not come out. Gemma's heart seemed to have stopped beating altogether.

Aurora, in the kitchen, was unaware of what was happening, deftly slicing into her lovely, crispy cod fillet.

Victoria was in hospital; she was lying in a hospital bed. In a private hospital in New York, all alone, all by herself. Victoria could have died, she'd been very ill, an overdose. She'd had a lot of treatment. Visions of TV programmes came to Gemma then. Tubes, lines, vomit, beeping things, crashing doors, doctors shouting do this, do that. Heroin overdose, she'd been using heroin. Hard drugs, that was very bad. Out of danger now. Touch and go. Had the nurse actually said those words, touch and go?

Victoria could have died.

Then, the sudden rush of understanding and Gemma's legs buckled beneath her as if they were made of liquorice. Her lovely fish supper dropped to her feet. Gemma realized then that she had thrown it, in her anger and frustration at not being there to prevent this catastrophe. Her precious daughter could have died of a drugs overdose. Her little baby girl, with the silky blonde hair and the cat-like blue eyes, needed her mother. And here she was filling her face with fish and chips and feeling sorry for herself because she was a bit claustrophobic about flying. Feeling sorry for herself because she wasn't a globetrotter and a telly-babe and the darling of the party circuit. Aurora came rushing in from the kitchen and helped her to her feet.

"Gemma, what's happened?" she gasped, taking in the scattered chips.

But Gemma was struggling to remember how to speak English, it seemed.

"Jesus, Gemma, speak to me!" Aurora begged. "Take little breaths, now. Just little breaths, not big ones. Just tell me something, anything. Come on, make a start and I'll guess the rest."

Somehow, Gemma told her.

"Oh, love!"

The two women hugged and Gemma forced herself to breathe normally, with Aurora counting up to five like an idiot, over and over again, and rubbing Gemma's arms to comfort her. One, two, three, four, five and breathe in. One two, three, four, five and breathe out.

Gemma called the hospital back almost immediately, all the time trying to hold down galloping waves of nausea, as Aurora went silently to the kitchen and made them two mugs of sugary tea and then kept hold of Gemma's arm for moral support. Gemma told the nurse she would be at the hospital the following day (if it was humanly possible) and if she couldn't manage that, then at least within the next forty-eight hours. And all bills would be paid in full, of course. (She wouldn't think about that now, she decided. If she had to, she would sell the house.) And could she bring Victoria home again, please? That was the most important thing. Get her daughter home and tucked into bed before she wound up in prison, in an orange jumpsuit.

She was told, yes, she could take her daughter back to I-err-land. But she might have to stay in New York for a few days until Victoria was deemed fit to travel by the doctors. There were procedures to be followed in narcotics cases, the nurse said. Legal papers to be signed, possibly an interview with the police regarding naming her supplier, more medical tests to be carried out, and so on. It would have been easier to climb Mount Everest pulling a cartload of stones behind her, or so it seemed to Gemma, than it'd be to get her beloved child home from America. And she hated hospitals, too. Well, who didn't? Only people with Munchausen Syndrome were fond of that ubiquitous smell of disinfectant and the distant rumble of trolleys.

"I wish I had a magic carpet," Gemma sobbed when she'd hung up. She couldn't speak to Victoria at the moment, she'd been told. They'd given her a sedative to help her sleep through a bad patch. A bad patch. Gemma thought of Victoria's little pink patchwork quilt and the star-shaped cushions on her bed upstairs and her heart despaired. How had this happened?

"I wish I could fly to New York, right now on a magic carpet, and get there in less than a minute. I'd sail in through the window of her hospital room, scoop her up in my arms and be back here before this cup of tea goes cold."

"Here, drink this," commanded Aurora, worried sick herself and pouring a generous nip of brandy into both mugs. "Now, it'll be okay, didn't the nurse say she was over the worst of it?"

"Yes, she did, but you know what nurses are like? They're used to death: they see it all the time. Victoria could slip away tonight and they wouldn't care. Just so long as I paid the bill. God, I feel so fucking useless. Why did I let her go to New

York anyway? Why, Aurora? I should never have let her go."

"Sure, you couldn't have stopped her, she's an adult."

"I could have tried!"

"Are you going to tell her father?" Aurora asked suddenly. "Maybe he could help you with money and travel arrangements?"

They'd never discussed the father of Gemma's child before. But this was an emergency, after all. The rules of etiquette could be broken in an emergency.

"No way!" Gemma cried. "He'd only make it ten times worse. I don't want him involved. He was beyond useless when I was pregnant, in any case. Said he didn't want me any more, once my bump began to show. Aurora, I have to tell you something now, and I want you to promise you'll keep this to yourself. Victoria doesn't know this and she'll never hear it from my lips. Her father was an addict, too. Mostly drink but a bit of cannabis. For all I know, he died years ago. We never kept in touch. That's why I'm glad my own parents have had no contact with Victoria. They would have delighted in telling her that her daddy was no good. They're like that, vindictive."

"Oh, I see."

"Are you shocked?"

"Of course, I'm not shocked. I didn't come up the river in a bubble. Aren't I from Belfast? We had to evacuate the school plenty of times over the years because of bomb scares. When you've seen people being scraped off the streets, like I have, nothing shocks you any more. Come on, your supper is still warm, you should eat it."

"I couldn't eat a thing, pet. My stomach's doing somersaults. So much for single mothers being as good as anyone."

"Now, come on, we'll have none of that. Later, maybe, you can have a bowl of cereal. Porridge is good for shock, so I'm told. And get a cardigan on, will you? You're shivering like I don't know what. I'll turn the heating up. It'll be all right, Gemma, it will. We'll call the travel agent, check out flight times. I'll just give Miriam a shout, while I'm at it."

"Why Miriam?"

"Oh, just for the company. And Sarah too. They might be able to help, run errands, man the phone. They might have some useful advice for us. Didn't Sarah say her best friend in London was a psychologist?"

"I suppose."

"Right."

But the real reason was Aurora didn't want to be alone with poor Gemma, just in case she went into cardiac arrest. Gemma sat down on the sofa and went into a kind of trance, listening to the message again while Aurora busied herself with tidying up and making phone calls. Eventually, Gemma's blanket of numbness began to fall away and was replaced with a rumbling volcano of rage. Rage, like she'd never felt before in her entire life. Not even when Victoria's father had rejected her and called her a cling-on. Not even when her own parents had called her a stupid tramp. Not even when her best novel to date had been described by one (male) critic as a depressing, kitchen-sink tale of one woman's descent into self-pity and that he'd seen more erotic imagery on a pig-farm.

Bastard.

Gemma's loathing of the male of the species exploded into a molten ball of blinding-white rage and sulphuric vitriol, as Aurora hovered by the front window, eager for signs of the cavalry arriving. Gemma's language was bluer than Gordon Ramsay's on a boys' night out when she was riled up. The names she was calling men! The filthy rotten pinhead pimps, she roared. The evil and predatory nature of those demonic drug-dealers was beyond evil. The disgusting perverts who took advantage of the cravings of young drug-addicts ought to be jailed for life – no, hanged.

"Though there was no evidence of that in Victoria's case, thank God," Aurora pointed out.

According to the nurse, Victoria had only been into serious drugs for about six months and she'd been able to pay for them using her own wages from the salon. But she'd been missing a lot of days in the last month and her employment status had slipped into a foggy sort of arrangement, where she'd only be paid for the days she turned up. So she'd had to reduce her intake of heroin and then someone had given her a large dose and it'd been too much for her system. At least, that's what they thought had happened. Poor Gemma was beside herself with worry, anger and an awful, stomach-churning sensation that all of this was her fault.

"I can't believe it," she kept saying.

Aurora sent urgent texts to Sarah and Miriam, begging them to hurry up.

Meanwhile, Gemma's rant continued. The unhelpful attitudes of governments across the globe should be highlighted at every opportunity, she wept. The cruelty of the court systems which continually punished the victims and never the crimelords should be lamented from the rooftops. The dealers walked free every time, she hissed, and they flaunted their luxury villas and their pathetic shiny sportscars and their sleazy nightclubs in the faces of innocent tax-payers and concerned parents like herself. Not to mention the idiocy of the music industry which pampered celebrity addicts and protected them from the mundanities of this world so they didn't have to clean up their acts to be able to earn a crust, like normal people.

"Please don't torture yourself," Aurora pleaded.

And now poor, exhausted Victoria was lying in a hospital in New York, with no visitors to bring her flowers and hold her hand. In God only knew what condition, Jesus help her. And possibly facing a criminal charge, a criminal record. She'd lose her job and be deported and banned from America for life. Big loss there if they didn't even have the human decency to call round to her flat, and her not at work for a week. All this, and she was still only a child of twenty-one. It was beyond belief.

In fact, Gemma was so overwhelmingly angry, she rushed into the kitchen and grabbed the first thing she laid eyes on. She hurled her heavy aluminium food-mixer straight through the kitchen window. And two of her pine chairs after it. Just as Miriam and Sarah were coming in the front door. She then ripped her phone out of the sitting-room wall and smashed it to pieces before collapsing into Aurora's arms and crying and sobbing until she almost fainted.

"Thank God I came into the house to eat my chips, otherwise she might have been on her own when she found out," Aurora kept saying. "She might have spontaneously combusted and taken the entire terrace with her."

Gemma was hugged and placated and consoled and hugged again. And finally dunked in a hot bath, plied with herbal tablets to relax her, and much tea was drunk by all four women. At one point, Sarah got a call from Abigail on her mobile but she was too busy to speak to her.

"Sorry," she said, "I can't talk now, there's an emergency here. Call you later."

By teatime, Gemma *had* managed to get to speak to Victoria on the phone. Just for a minute, though, as she was still so weak and confused. Despite her current pitiful state of health, however, she'd been alert enough to want to cover up the scandal. She'd pleaded with Gemma to tell nobody. She said she would never come home to Ireland again if the whole country knew what had happened to her. It would be in all the papers because of Gemma's column, and everyone would be calling her a junkie and talking about her behind her back. So Gemma had promised not to tell anyone for the time being. Well, nobody else apart from Aurora, Miriam and Sarah.

Then there was the question of the medical bill. She had some money put by but not nearly enough. Was there time to get a bank loan, she wondered. Of course, she'd have to go to New York immediately now, Gemma knew that. There was no way she couldn't go. And despite the state she was in, she'd have to talk to the medical people and the police and try to convince Victoria to co-operate with them all. And maybe stay in the rehab wing with her until the worst of the withdrawal period was over, which wouldn't be cheap either. She'd have to sell her car, sell the house.

Gemma was in a blind panic over it all. She was throwing the herbal tablets down her throat by the handful, and the brandy too, and saying repeatedly that she couldn't handle it, she just couldn't cope. Aurora thought this was quite funny really but she didn't think she ought to point out the irony to

Gemma of relying on pills and alcohol to get through life's ups and downs. Miriam nipped back to her own house for a shepherd's pie which she brought round to Gemma's and heated up in the oven. They sat up all night, the four of them, making travel plans and comforting Gemma and phoning the hospital for updates. In the end, it was decided they would all go to New York, because Gemma couldn't go by herself and Aurora didn't want to be Gemma's only companion on such a difficult trip. All those trigger-happy security people and Gemma on the verge of hysteria. Sarah offered to accompany them since she'd been to New York several times and knew her way about. And Miriam insisted that she wasn't going to be left out, even though the other three didn't really see what she could contribute to the expedition. No way was she sitting here in Redstone on her thumb, she said. It was all they would ever talk about, for the rest of their lives, and she was going with them or else the friendship was finished right here and now!

Good old Aurora paid Vicky's hospital bill in the end, and the travel costs too, going behind Gemma's back the following morning with her credit card. And saying she had loads of money left over from her house-sale in Belfast and nothing important to spend it on, when Gemma had found out what she'd done. Aurora said she would fall out with Gemma if she didn't let her pay, at least for now, so the hospital wouldn't kick her out on the street. Gemma could always arrange some repayment scheme when she was able to, she gently pointed out. And so they were all booked, all four of them, onto the next flight. And they made a pact to bring only a small in-flight bag so there'd be minimal waiting around at the airport.

They'd go to see Victoria together, Aurora said, and assure her everything would be okay. And they'd be with her when she had the HIV and the other tests, and they'd bring her home again to Redstone the minute she was well enough to travel, so she could get her strength back. And no, they wouldn't tell a soul. None of them would breathe a word.

Gemma was so grateful she hugged them all so tightly they could hardly breathe and went to get her passport from her desk drawer, to check it wasn't out of date.

It wasn't out of date. It was crisp and clean and still new-smelling. She'd never used it, except to go to London. She'd only got it for ID purposes, really. The travel agent rang back to confirm flying times. They'd be on their way within twelve hours.

And then Gemma's fear of flying got the better of her again and she cried and cried until she actually blacked out for a few seconds. And then she drank a whole bottle of wine and fell asleep. The other women took it in turns to watch Gemma and go home to pack a bag.

Gemma was almost flatlining with exhaustion but she still had one more thing to do. She called Mike at the newspaper around six o'clock in the morning and told him he could stuff his tacky little newspaper up his backside. And snap a diamante thong over the top of it, and stick two big swinging tassels on his hairy fat moobs for good measure. Because Gemma Hayes was a serious news-journalist and she wasn't going to lower herself to write about boobs, bums and twinkles in Mike's tawdry rag of shame any more. And then she slammed down the phone on him before he could answer back. Which kind of left her on the breadline money-wise but no matter about that now. She had a child who needed her. Valium was procured from the chemist via a quick trip to the doctor's surgery at nine o'clock, and some more tears were shed in Gemma's kitchen. Which now boasted a boarded-up window. Then, they all sat down at the table for coffee and croissants before setting off for the airport in Aurora's roomy car.

Gemma was hyperventilating into a paper bag before the car had even left Redstone and all Aurora could think was, thank God, she had bought four plane tickets instead of two, because this was going to be one hell of an ordeal for all of them. If Gemma didn't calm down soon, they wouldn't let her on the bloody plane and then herself and Sarah would have to go on alone, leaving Gemma behind with Miriam to console her – and control her.

"That's it, girl, you get it all out of your system," she soothed, from the driver's seat. "Good girl! You'll be fine on the plane, I know you will. Won't she, Sarah? Won't she, Miriam?"

"She will, she'll be fine," they agreed, a little too enthusiastically.

But none of them believed it.

Then Gemma accidentally tore a big hole in the bag with her fingernail, her hands were shaking that much. Let's hope the Valium kicks in real soon, thought the other women, as Miriam patted Gemma's arm tenderly in the back seat and Sarah passed her back another paper bag from the stash she had with her in her handbag. With any luck, Gemma would have tired herself out before much longer and they would only have to support her through check-in and finally let her sleep most of the way across the Atlantic.

20

Making Plans for Nigel

"Now, you listen to me, Gemma Hayes," Aurora began in her best schoolteacher's voice. The serious, gravelly one she kept for very special occasions, like announcing the dates of university entrance exams or a visit from the Lord Mayor (or a bomb scare). "You've got to be braver now than you've ever been in your entire life before. Right?"

Gemma nodded weakly. She was severely hungover, sick to her teeth with worry, absolutely terrified of the journey ahead and emotionally exhausted. The second Valium pill of the day was kicking in and her sugar levels had bottomed out completely, or so it seemed. She'd just chucked up a cinnamon bagel and a cup of peppermint tea, and her hair was a windswept mess. The four women were having a last-minute meeting in the Ladies' loo at the airport. Miriam fetched a comb out of her big knitted handbag and began trying to do something with Gemma's "elfin" crop. Gemma stood mutely, gently rocking. Powerless to stop this nightmare that was taking over her life.

"They can be quite tough at the security end of things and so on, but it's all a big macho act, so don't let them upset you, please," Aurora added helpfully. "They all think they're in a Hollywood movie, that's all it is. Bruce Willis wannabes. Pathetic beyond words. As if we were going to bring down a jumbo jet, the four of us?"

Gemma only nodded again and closed her eyes. To be quite honest, she thought, she really wouldn't have cared. At least they'd be back on the ground a bit sooner.

"Actually, Aurora, can I say something at this point which might be helpful to Gemma?" asked Sarah, gingerly putting her hand up. As if she were back in junior form.

Aurora immediately began to blush. She just couldn't help being bossy, could she, she groaned inwardly.

"Permission granted," she said quietly.

"Thank you," Sarah smiled. "I just wanted to give Gemma some advice. It's a little tip that my friend Abigail passes on to her psychiatric patients. I mean, to the people she counsels at her clinic. It's just a little tip for anxious people, okay?"

They all nodded solemnly. This professional tip might be worth its weight in gold to all of them.

"Right, it's just something called visualization, and it's very easy to do. Now, Gemma, you should think of something nice and peaceful. Something that makes you feel relaxed and happy and positive. Can you think of anything, Gemma? When were you last feeling completely happy? Completely at peace?"

Gemma thought hard.

"When Victoria was born and I brought her home to my

granny's house and we were all there, the three of us, by the fire. And we were just looking at her little face," Gemma whispered. "And the room was lovely and warm, and my granny was smiling at me and saying well done!"

Nobody felt it was a good time to comment on the fact that the last time Gemma could remember being completely happy was twenty-one years ago.

"Okay, that's brilliant, that's lovely. Now, can you hold that picture in your mind, Gemma? Don't let it go. And while we're on our way to see Victoria, just keep thinking of that happy image. And if you do get distracted by the sights and sounds of travel, which is pretty much inevitable at times, just think of it all as a sort of tunnel. A tunnel with light at the end of it, okay? Just think of yourself whizzing through that tunnel, towards the light at the other end. Because that's all it is when you're worried about something. It's a transitory feeling. And it'll only last for a short while."

"Sarah, that's marvellous," sighed Miriam. "I feel all calm and floaty myself, now. Wow, that's really amazing. You should take up counselling yourself."

"Yes, excellent advice indeed," Aurora said in a clipped voice, slightly jealous of Sarah's professional wisdom and calming influence. She was the leader here, not Sarah. Oh well, Gemma did seem a little bit less stressed so maybe it had done the poor woman some good.

Then they heard their flight being called. Wordlessly, they filed out of the loo and towards the departure gate.

"Remember that tunnel and keep going towards the light," said Sarah, squeezing Gemma's arm gently. "And we're right here with you, holding your hand all the way, okay?"

199

"Okay."

Miriam and Aurora closed ranks and walked in front, trying to shield Gemma from the harsh, intimidating stare of the security men. Aurora began chatting about the weather to the four burly personnel on duty and deliberately boring them rigid, so their time spent under actual scrutiny was mercifully brief. Then they were through the gate and walking down the rattling connecting bridge to the jet. Minutes later, they were sitting on the plane, in a centre row.

Gemma closed her eyes again and thought of Victoria's impossibly soft baby cheeks nestled against her own, as the other passengers settled into their seats and busied themselves with fold-down tables and in-flight magazines and nervous glugging from small bottles of water. She still clung to that picture as the massive plane began to move down the runway, bumping and juddering, gathering speed, becoming more and more noisy with every second. The engines were going at full power and Gemma wanted to scream with fear and then, with a sudden drop in noise and vibration, the plane lifted off the ground and they were airborne. And it was too late to demand to be let off or make a break for the door.

"Jesus preserve us," she kept whispering, thinking of her grandmother's favourite refrain in times of trouble. She kept her eyes tightly shut the whole time they were climbing through the clouds. If I die now, she told herself, my earthly worries will be over. And I won't have to work or clean the house or struggle with the packaging on those stupid ready-meals any more.

Miriam was holding one of her hands and Aurora was holding the other one. Meanwhile, Sarah was keeping up her part of appearing relatively normal to the other passengers, studying a map of New York already, planning convenient subway routes and making a list of cheap hotels near the hospital.

Gemma decided to keep her eyes closed all the way to New York, imagining Victoria wrapped in her baby blanket. Small and perfect, and smelling of talc, and safe as houses. Eventually, as Aurora predicted, she fell into a deep sleep. They didn't wake her when the food was served (even though it was a lovely bit of beef and gravy) or for the coffee and fancy biscuit or even for the drinks, little plastic glasses with ice cubes rattling prettily and swizzle sticks. Aurora ordered a whisky and ginger ale, though, on Gemma's behalf and drank it in one. As well as her own vodka-tonic. The women took short naps occasionally but mostly they stayed awake to keep an eye on Gemma, silently thanking their lucky stars they weren't in her shoes. Even Miriam, who would have sold her soul to the devil for her own little bundle of joy, was grateful she didn't have a daughter who was addicted to heroin.

* * *

In the hospital, Victoria was shockingly pale, thin and lethargic looking. They could see her now, through the spotless glass partition, from the bright, white hallway. She was wearing a powder-blue hospital gown but they could see a small tattoo of a butterfly on her left shoulder, where the gown had slipped down a bit. Her blonde hair was cut short and had two pink streaks in it. Gemma touched her hand to the glass and tried not to cry again. She'd be dryer than the Sahara if she cried any more, she realized. She'd shrivel up on the floor like a raisin. Sarah went to fetch another couple of chairs so they could all wait in the corridor until the doctor came to brief Gemma on Victoria's progress. Miriam bought some cups of coffee at the vending machine and Aurora kept her arm round Gemma's shoulders constantly.

It wasn't too bad so far, Aurora thought happily. All in all, they had worked together very well. They were rather a tight little team when the chips were down. And this hospital looked the proper business, too. Yes, it was all ship-shape and oozing medical confidence. Then they saw the doctor coming towards them. A very tall black man, his skin was dark as could be against his crisp, white medical coat. He was shuffling through some notes and Aurora began to falter slightly. What if the news was bad, she fretted? The doctor, when he spoke to them, had very nice eyes. Sympathetic and surprisingly amused by them, it seemed. Maybe he thought they were a bit ridiculous, turning up like this in a little whispering huddle. Gemma, however, was beginning to rally.

"Hello, Doctor," she said, extending her hand graciously. "I'm Victoria's mother."

* * *

It was late in the evening and Gemma was speaking to the doctor again for a short while before he went off duty. From his accent he seemed to be African rather than American. Victoria was a little better, he said, which was great news. But she was still having nightmares and being sick quite a lot, and she was slightly dehydrated and, consequently, confused. Gemma nodded and did her best to look mature and sensible. There was no way they would let her take Victoria home if they thought she wasn't a capable mother.

"This has all come as a massive shock to me, Doctor I fe . . ." she said, sounding amazingly calm. Gemma could see his name badge but she couldn't pronounce his surname. She hoped he wasn't too offended when her voice trailed off, mid-attempt.

"There were no previous signs of addiction?" he asked politely.

"No, none whatsoever. It's just a recent thing, obviously. She must have fallen into bad company." Oh fuck it, what a parochial thing to say, she chided herself.

"What was that, Mrs Hayes? Fallen into what?"

She didn't bother to correct him, to tell him she was Miss Hayes. Surreptitiously, she covered her wedding finger so he couldn't see she wasn't wearing a ring. She didn't want them to treat Victoria any less kindly here just because her parents were not married. Funny how some silly notions persist in the mind, she thought sadly.

"She fell somewhere, you said?"

"No. I mean, she must have been influenced by someone in her social circle here. Don't worry, Doctor, I'll take good care of her when I take her home to Ireland. She'll get lots of rest and relaxation. I live right on the ocean, you know, in a lovely beachfront house," she added, trying to make Redstone sound like Miami. "I'm a novelist, as it happens. I work from home, so I can take good care of Victoria. There'll be no problems on that score."

"Indeed," said the doctor, who was working a double-shift and didn't get a lot of time to read novels these days. Still, Victoria's bill had been paid in full so that was a good sign, he noted. This woman must be solvent, at least, even if she did look a little "out there" with her feathery white hair and her low, lilting speech.

Then Gemma was finally allowed in to see her daughter, and she felt such a rush of love coursing through her veins, she almost staggered and fell under the weight of it.

"Darling, can you hear me?" she whispered. "Mummy's here. I'm here now."

Victoria opened her gorgeous, cat-like blue eyes and the hint of a smile played across her blue-tinged lips. Gemma kissed her daughter on both cheeks and on the forehead and on the fragile hand which lay above the hospital blanket.

"I'm sorry, Mum," Victoria said in a small dry voice. "So sorry."

"Hush, now, it's all right. I don't expect you to tell me what happened or anything. All that matters now is that you're alive and well."

"I look terrible."

"Yes, you do, you silly girl! But you'll get better soon enough."

"I want to go home now, Mum."

"And so you will, love. Home to Redstone with me, in a day or two."

"Will they arrest me when I'm better?"

"No. Not even a record, if you tell the police who sold you the drugs."

"Who said that?"

"The doctor. He told me."

"And I can go home with you if I tell them?"

"Yes, that's the deal, so I'm told."

"Promise?"

"Yes. Unless, of course, you don't know the name of the guy. They can't keep you here for not asking his name, sweetheart. If needs be, I'll get a solicitor, I mean a lawyer, involved, don't you worry, pet. I won't let them bully you, don't you worry about a thing. We're paying our way here – we're not freeloading off these guys. You just get your rest, my darling."

She held Victoria's hand and smoothed the pink-dyed hair out of her eyes.

"Love you, Mum," whispered Victoria and then she dozed off again.

"Love you."

Gemma's heart was pulsating with love for her beautiful daughter. At that precise moment in time, she could have killed dozens of drug dealers without a second's hesitation. Or any remorse whatsoever. Mown them all down with one of those shuddering machine-guns on a tripod they always have in war films, she seethed inwardly. When she thought of the excruciating labour pains she'd suffered, and the sleepless nights for six months afterwards, all the exams she had studied for, all the rubbish she'd had to write for Mike over the years. Just to make ends meet and support herself and Victoria. And it could've all been swept away with ten or twenty pounds' worth of dried poppy seeds or whatever the hell they made the wretched stuff out of. Oh, a thousand curses on the lot of them!

No, no, stop it, she told herself. Put the beast back in its cage and think of Sarah and her soothing tunnel of light. This was not the time to be ranting and raving about the world and everything that was wrong with it. She had to be strong now, she had to be the strongest woman of all time. So she could carry her beautiful baby home on a magic carpet (okay, on Aer Lingus Economy) and put her to bed in her own room, and love her and protect her forever more, Amen.

*　*　*

Gemma said she wanted to spend the night in the hospital. She couldn't be persuaded to leave, in fact. So Aurora volunteered to stay with her for another few hours to get her settled in. And Sarah and Miriam were dispatched to secure two hotel rooms after doing some shopping at the all-night grocery store for various bits and pieces. They all hugged again (it was rapidly turning into a televised talent show, there were so many hugs and kisses) and then Sarah and Miriam were out on the darkened street hailing a cab. The driver who pulled up was a young Chinese woman, very friendly and helpful, which Sarah took as a good omen overall. She asked the driver to drop them off at a street four blocks up, outside a fairly nice budget hotel she had stayed in once before with some of the staff from the cookery magazine. They had next to nothing to carry so that was good, too. Inside the hotel, in the all-beige foyer, Sarah got down to the business of booking two double rooms for the four of them, while Miriam spoke to a rather attractive barman about having some tea and biscuits sent up to their room. The barman's name was Nigel. It was written on a laminated badge attached to his chocolate-brown waistcoat. The name didn't suit him at all, Miriam told him. (For he was laughably good-looking. Flawless skin, a few freckles on his nose, a jawline like a razor.) She blew him a kiss as they went up the stairs.

"Miriam Gormley, what are you like?" Sarah laughed. "The jetlag must be getting to you."

"Don't think I don't appreciate we're here in New York on a mission of mercy," Miriam said to Sarah, as they unlocked their own room two minutes later. "But I must have my cup of tea and a biscuit before I go to bed or else I can't sleep."

"Fine by me," said Sarah, yawning. "I never turn down a cuppa, myself. Do you think I should call Abigail back? What time is it in London, now?"

"I haven't a clue. I don't even know if it's today or tomorrow there. Or yesterday."

"Oh, I'm too tired to work it out. I'll do it tomorrow," Sarah said wearily, pulling off her boots and socks. "I'm going to have a shower, okay? That hospital smell has permeated my clothes. I feel all germ-y."

"Work away, then. You go ahead and freshen up. And I'll listen out for the tea coming."

The knock sounded about ten minutes later. Miriam answered the door at once and was pleased to see Nigel standing there with a little silver tray in his hands. He was a male model between gigs, obviously, she decided. With that shoebox jaw and that lovely dark hair styled into curly strands, like a surfer. He must have been about twenty-five.

"Hi there."

"Marvellous," she sighed. And she wasn't talking about the tea and biscuits.

She thought of Patrick in his old fishing clothes, for a moment. Patrick was fifty now. Sometimes days would go by without the two of them speaking a word to one another. Days when he sat in that study of his, alone with his lighthouses. Never mind discussing sperm counts and sperm donors. Never mind going to that place in Dublin for tests, with the luxurious pale carpet in the waiting room. And he had nothing else to do with his time, did he? Just that boring old page in the fishing magazine that she was so ashamed of she told her friends they lived off inherited money.

"Thank you, Nigel," she said graciously, accepting the tray carefully and giving Nigel a five-dollar tip.

"Thanks," he said simply, before nodding to her politely.

"Having our little cup of tea already, what are we like? And we just got here from Ireland," she laughed, flicking her plum-coloured curls out of her eyes.

"Welcome to New York, then. I guess you Irish like your tea a lot," he smiled and then he was off again, pacing down the corridor in a very nice pair of tight-fitting black trousers. Or pants, as the Americans would say. Tight, black pants.

"Yes, we like our tea. And that's not all we like," Miriam sighed hopelessly.

She closed the door with her foot and looked at herself in the mirror, still holding the tray in her hands. "Sometimes, we'd like to get our teeth into a nice set of rock-solid hips like yours, Nigel, but we have to make do with a Digestive biscuit." She sat down on the bed to drink her cuppa. The room wasn't too bad, she thought, looking round. A colourful, modern print of some tulips in a black bowl. Clean sheets on the beds, soft lighting at the touch of a switch, even the buttons on the telephone were spotlessly clean. The hotels in America were very well-kept, she decided idly, even if the streets outside were not always. She wondered if Patrick was missing her yet. He'd been outraged when she told him she was going to New York to give Gemma a hand.

"Serves him right," she said now to the tulips on the wall.

"He never talks to me anyway. Serves him right to be on his own for a few days. Silly old sod."

In spite of herself, she couldn't help wondering what Nigel looked like naked. And then, suddenly, the strangest thing that had ever happened to her: Miriam had a sort of vision. Almost a religious visitation, or so it seemed. For in her mind she was imagining Sarah's transitory tunnel, with a bright and blinding light burning at the other end. A baby! She could have a baby in a different way, without having to expose herself and Patrick to the people at that clinic in Dublin. Like two lab rats in a glass box, they'd be. Two lab rats sniffling for a nibble beneath the sawdust. But, if she were to have a little liaison here in the Big Apple . . . If she were to have a New York Minute with a handsome young man like Nigel, for example . . . If she were to somehow seduce a gorgeous young man like that, then maybe she would be going home with more than just a miniature of the Statue of Liberty as a souvenir. Whoosh! The answer to all her prayers, in his tight, black pants: Nigel!

* * *

Five days later, and the situation had more or less stabilized. Gemma kept up her vigil at Victoria's bedside, sleeping at night in an armchair by the bed. The staff let her stay on after visiting hours because Victoria seemed to be much more relaxed when her mother was there. Gemma had a quick shower in the adjoining bathroom each morning, changed into a fresh set of clothes brought from the hotel by Aurora, ate small mouthfuls of food from the hospital canteen and held Victoria's hand constantly. Sarah and Aurora were her faithful assistants, doing anything they could to help. Packing up Victoria's clothes at her flat, washing them at the launderette and settling up her unpaid rent with the landlord. Bringing things for both of them to and from the hospital, buying new pyjamas for Victoria, keeping the hospital room tidy and supplied with fresh flowers, scented tissues, refreshing cans of lemonade and glossy magazines. Most of their gifts went untouched, naturally, but it all served to make Victoria feel much less of a freak and more like a normal patient. Gemma almost forgot she had the return flight to get through.

Victoria was becoming much more lucid by now and was even beginning to relax a little bit. She told the police she had bought her heroin from a street dealer wearing dark glasses. Average height, average build, tanned skin, could have been anyone. She couldn't even say what nationality. Of course, they didn't believe her. But they would be back, they said. Before she was allowed to leave the country, they would be back for another little chat. Gemma shooed them out of the room then. The cheek of them, she fumed. Threatening poor Victoria like that! Hinting that she'd never be allowed home.

"If my daughter has any information to offer, Officers, rest assured I will pass it on to the appropriate authorities. Thank you for your help."

* * *

Miriam was the only one not totally committed to the project of Getting Gemma & Victoria Home. She seemed to spend most of her days wandering about the city, and when they asked her what she was doing, she told them she was just looking at the shops. Just browsing, she told them. They didn't quiz her too much about her comings and goings. They'd known it was going to be like this anyway. Miriam was a daydreamer, a leaf on the stream of life. She didn't do an awful lot at home either, it had to be said. Just pottering around the lavender house, playing with her trinkets and then visiting the elderly on Wednesdays in the local nursing home. Doing a bit of light shopping, maybe, for them. She went to Mass a lot, too.

"To tell you the absolute truth," Aurora whispered to Gemma late one evening as they sat side by side in the hospital room, painting Victoria's toenails, "I think she only came here to get away from Patrick. Now, I know that's an awful thing to say but have you noticed she rarely mentions his name? I don't think she's even called home once."

"Do you think they'll split up?" Gemma asked, curious in spite of herself.

"Who knows, but I don't think they're very happy together. They don't seem very lovey-dovey, do they?"

"True. Other people's marriages are often a mystery, though. But it's weird because Miriam is the only one of us who's got a husband at the moment," Gemma said, shaking her head. "I never had one to begin with, and you're divorced, and Sarah left her man practically at the altar. We're not doing too well, are we? Maybe it really is the end of marriage in the western world, like they say here in this magazine." She indicated the inch-thick publication sitting on the side-table. "It says, there won't be anyone getting married in a couple of centuries."

"You don't want to believe all that alarmist twaddle. Sure, there'll be nobody left if global warming steps up. Married or not married. Who cares, anyway?"

"I care. I want Victoria, and her children, and their children, to live in a nicer world than the current one. Without war and racism and poverty and oppression."

"Yeah, right on, sister. Listen, you do know Sarah's been seeing a fair bit of Ethan Reilly, don't you?" Aurora asked as casually as she could. Slightly ashamed of her gossipy nature, of course, but also wondering furiously if there was anything going on between them.

"Is she? I thought they were only being friendly. He's about her age."

"No, I think there's definitely something going on. She's taking it slowly, it seems. For obvious reasons, I suppose. Her wedding being called off and all that business. But he seems very keen on her. I've seen them walking round the village together. Haven't you?"

"I must have been too busy lately. Or distracted perhaps. I don't know about him, though – if he isn't a bit shady. He was mixed up in a suspicious fire at the fairground ten years ago."

"Was he?" Aurora was agog. "You mean, the fire was set deliberately? I knew there was a fire but nothing about a deliberate fire."

"Nothing was ever proved. But he was working there in his younger days, as a general handyman, and then one of the rides broke down and a young girl was hurt. Broke her back, she couldn't walk for two years. There was an investigation, of course. A big court case looming, to sort out the compensation. Half a million or something, they said she would get. And this was back in the days when half a million was still considered a lot of money, don't forget. Then, before the ride could be properly inspected, the whole lot burned down. The fair was nothing but a pile of scrap and that was the end of it."

"So they never found out what happened?" Aurora asked thoughtfully.

"No. The family of the injured girl settled out of court and Patrick sold the land to a developer."

"Patrick, you said? Patrick who?"

"Miriam's Patrick," Gemma said quietly. "They were going to build private homes on the site but it's just been lying empty ever since. I think the new owners are looking into building a hotel and spa instead. Anyway, there's only weeds growing there nowadays. Oh God, I shouldn't have told you. Look, don't mention this in front of Miriam, will you not? She's very sensitive about it all. And it was after that whole ordeal with the court case that Patrick started going a bit odd and began spending so much time by himself. You know the way he is, he'd rather die than talk to anyone. Well, he wasn't always like that. He used to be a good laugh, as it happens. He was forty when it all happened; Ethan was just twenty-odd. Promise me you won't say a word, now? Miriam would kill me if she knew I'd told you all this. But after what you've done for me and Victoria, well, I know how you love your little bit of gossip!"

"I do not!" protested Aurora, her face a picture of wounded indignation.

"Yes, you do, you love it," Gemma laughed, feeling happier than she had in ages. She sat up in her armchair, put the lid back on the bottle of nail polish, stretched her arms and yawned widely. Keeping this vigil was very tiring. "Go on with you, you're dying to know everything about everyone in the village. You know what I think? You should start up another book club when we get back to Redstone. I mean open up the current one to other people, besides ourselves. It would be lovely for the people to have something to go to, some kind of community spirit in the village again. There's been nothing much for years, really."

"I'll think about it," said Aurora, already wondering how many bookworms she could squeeze into The Last Chapter at any one time. "It might be good for business." One thing was for sure, though. If she did extend the book club, and it was a very big "if", but if she did, she definitely wasn't going to invite people to gather at her home any more. No, she was finished with conservatories. And she wasn't going to make anyone wear a costume either.

* * *

Back at the hotel, Miriam and Nigel were perched on the side of the bed in Nigel's tiny room on the seventh floor. He'd been living there for about six months now, since moving to New York from Montana in the hopes of getting into an acting class. Or a theatre company. However, most of that time, he'd spent clearing tables and reading the newspapers. He was on the verge of giving it all up, in fact, and going back to night classes: get a trade under his belt. He told Miriam about his plans now. She was a very good-looking woman, he thought. He'd never slept with anyone of Miriam's age before. But she had beautiful, silky white skin. Few Americans were as pale as Miriam was: her skin was almost transparent. And soft as soap. She'd told him she didn't want anything serious, just a holiday romance. Not even a romance, she said. Just a fling, a New York Minute. And he liked her a lot. She wore funny clothes with little flowers stitched onto everything, and she said hilarious things. She was like a fairy godmother. A modern one, not an old-fashioned one with a crown on her head and a magic wand. The way she dressed, she was very theatrical herself. Like Helena Bonham Carter, but with more colour. Yes, he liked her. Leaning across to Miriam now, he kissed her on the nose. She laughed out loud.

"You're so good looking," she said. "You should forget about acting and be a model instead. I'm sorry for laughing but that's how you make me feel. I just think it's hilariously funny when I meet a man as handsome as you are, in real life. Usually, I only see men like you in the movies."

"That's the plan," he said, touching her plum-coloured ringlets tenderly. They lay down on the bed together and she laughed again.

"Sorry," she giggled. "I can't help it."

"Laughing is good," he replied. And then he kissed her on the lips.

21

Come on Home

When the plane touched down on Irish soil again, with just the tiniest bump and skid, Gemma felt such a surge of relief flooding through her body, she almost cried out with pleasure. It was a wonderful feeling to be back on terra firma, much more pleasurable than the best sex she'd ever had. Which, admittedly, hadn't been much to write home about, even then. But she imagined that nothing could ever feel as good as this, as euphoric as this.

Yes, Victoria was still in pretty rough shape. Yes, she owed Aurora several thousand pounds, but no matter about all of that now. They'd left the hospital and they were away from the tubes and the sick bowls, after ten long days of watching the minutes crawling by on a stainless steel clock. They'd satisfied the police that Victoria knew nothing that could help them to make any important arrests. They'd paid the hospital for the remainder of Victoria's treatment. And Gemma had been so preoccupied with making sure Victoria was comfortable on the plane home that she'd barely thought about how high up they were. How confined they all were in that claustrophobic metal cylinder in the sky. They were home and dry. They were home.

People were clapping. Well, some of them were clapping and saying thanks to the cabin crew and what a smooth flight. How embarrassing! Then the lights flickered on and everyone started rousing themselves, getting up out of their comfortable, linen-headrest-covered seats and yawning and stretching and blinking. Gemma fussed over Victoria until the poor girl begged for mercy. No, she didn't need a coat, thank you. Yes, she was able to walk without Gemma's arm linked through hers. No, she didn't need anyone to carry her handbag. Yes, she had taken her medication earlier, thank you. No, she hadn't a mobile phone to switch on again, she'd lost her mobile weeks ago. Soon they were all out in the car-park, trying to remember where they'd parked the car. It was raining heavily. The sky was a blanket of grey. A red-breasted robin was picking crumbs out of a dropped sandwich at the edge of the pavement.

"Welcome home, darling," Gemma said tenderly to her only child. "I've missed you so much."

"Come on, Mum, let's go," Victoria replied, smiling warmly at her mother.

"It's so, so good to be back in the rain, isn't it?" Gemma sighed. "What date is it, anyone?"

"It's somewhere near the middle of February, my darlings, that's all I know for certain," Aurora yawned.

"It's Valentine's Day," said Miriam, smiling from ear to ear.

"Unless I'm very much mistaken, it's Valentine's Day." And her eyes looked very bright and starry.

* * *

Sarah was walking on the beach, thinking she'd missed Rose Cottage more than she ever thought she could. And every week she spent here in Redstone was costing her 250 Euro and now she'd wasted almost eleven days of rent money by going to New York. Oh well. It was worth it to see the transformation in Gemma's entire personality. And it was a small consolation to herself, too, because she hadn't thought about Mackenzie as much as she'd feared she would. After all, she should have gone to New York with Mackenzie on their dream honeymoon.

Sarah's mobile rang, making her jump.

It was Abigail.

She answered at once.

"Hi there," she said simply.

"Hello, Miss Quinn. What have you been up to these last few days, exactly? You've been switched off most of the time recently," Abigail said accusingly. "I've been calling and calling."

"Sorry, I kept forgetting to switch my phone on. I've been to New York," Sarah told her proudly.

"What? On a cookery-shoot?"

"No, I'm between jobs at the moment, aren't I? No, I went over to do a friend a favour. It's all hush-hush, sorry I can't tell you more about it. But I was able to pass on some of your famous advice about visualization."

"But New York? I thought you said you were skint?"

"I am. Someone else paid for my ticket."

219

"Very mysterious. Listen, Sarah, I've got something important to tell you. I've met someone."

"Oh, wait! Abigail, hang on, can it wait a little while? I've just seen this person that I've got to talk to. I'll call you back later, okay?"

"Oh, right, okay then."

"Cheerio."

Sarah clicked her phone off and hurried towards Ethan who was walking up the beach towards her. As they drew closer, Ethan broke into a run and when they met up, right at the water's edge, he lifted her into the air and swung her around and around, before kissing her passionately on the lips. And this time, she responded naturally and happily. Not because she was lonely or frightened but because she liked him a lot. And because it was Valentine's Day.

"I've missed you so much," he said, gazing deep into her sparkling green eyes, smiling hugely and holding both her hands tightly.

"And I've missed you," she laughed breathlessly. "I thought you were going to drop me in the water there! Hey, better not do that again, I'm heavier than I look."

"You're a sight for sore eyes, that's what you are. How did it go?" he asked.

"Not too bad. She's home now and on the mend. Though I think she'll need a lot of attention and minding, if you know what I mean?"

"Right, yeah, definitely. That's great she's home anyway. Don't worry, I haven't told anyone the details. I just said the four of you were away on a shopping trip if anybody asked. And Aurora's shop is okay and so is Gemma's house. I've been checking them."

"You've been a busy boy!"

"I have – Sarah, listen, I've been thinking of a way you could make some money, and I've picked out some lovely views for you to photograph."

"How do you mean?"

"You could take pictures for the tourist people. I saw an article in the paper, asking for submissions."

Sarah didn't expect the local paper would be able to deliver her from penury but Ethan was so enthusiastic about the competition, she couldn't bear to burst his bubble. She had no money in the bank, besides, so she'd have to do something soon.

"I was going to ask them for a job in the sweet shop, actually," she told him as they went on up the beach, hand in hand. "I might as well start selling ice-cream, instead of only eating it."

* * *

Aurora and Gemma watched them going past, as they opened the windows and aired Gemma's house after the trip to New York.

"You see, I told you!" Aurora said triumphantly. "I told you they were getting closer. Now, you can't deny that was one serious kiss."

"Well, I just hope she knows what she's doing," said Gemma. "I'm very fond of Sarah. I don't think I could have got on that plane without her."

"Are you cured then, of your flying phobia?" Aurora asked, plumping up the pillows on Victoria's bed. And then she set them down again and stood back, sensing this was something Gemma would rather do for her daughter.

Gemma smiled at her, understanding the gesture.

"No, indeed I'm not cured. I'm never getting on another plane, ever again! That's all I kept saying to myself on the way home. Never again, I will never do this again!" And then she laughed heartily and smoothed down the pillows and the bedspread.

Aurora thought her friend looked years younger. They went downstairs together to let the glazier in to fix the kitchen window. Aurora said she'd slip away soon and go back to her apartment and have a long soak in the bath. Gemma thanked her for about the tenth time for the loan and, when she'd gone, began preparing a delicious lamb casserole for supper, using ingredients she'd bought at the supermarket on the way home from the airport. Victoria had about twenty pounds to put back on before the rosy bloom would return to her once-beautiful complexion. And Gemma didn't want her daughter to have to live on microwave dinners. No, she was almost going to enjoy the time-consuming process of peeling and chopping root vegetables and browning chunks of flour-coated meat on the pan. Because every minute of her time in the kitchen would be put to good use. She might even buy a slow cooker and then she could fill it up with nice things in the morning, forget about it and have a home-cooked dinner every night. It would almost feel like going out to eat.

Victoria was curled up on the sofa in the sitting room, watching television with a soft throw over her shoulders. It was just like old times. Gemma was in seventh heaven as she put the kettle on for tea. They were like two birds in their little nest, she thought happily. Who knew when Victoria would fly away again? Until that day came, Gemma was going to enjoy every minute they had together.

22

Sonic Boom Boy

Miriam and Patrick had not spoken to each for three days now. Patrick's long-ago-handsome face was even more drawn and despondent with worry than it usually was. He'd left a small posy of pink and white flowers and a Valentine's card for his wife on the kitchen table. But Miriam barely noticed it, and when she did notice, she didn't bother to open it. She didn't want cards and flowers any more; she was fed up with gentle hugs and polite conversations about the lavender house. She wanted a baby and, at the very least, she wanted a man who was loving and spontaneous and who listened to her when she was speaking. She thought of her New York lover and the way they'd made love slowly and intensely in that tiny hotel room. She'd almost had an orgasm when he was only kissing her neck. And then she'd had three actual orgasms within two hours. And then they'd had a shower together and he'd shampooed her hair. And caressed her all over with body lotion. It had been the most exciting afternoon of Miriam's entire life to date. Truth be told, she'd have enjoyed another few afternoons with Nigel but she didn't want to push her luck. As far as he was concerned, it was a one-off thing and she didn't want him to suspect anything. She didn't want him to realize that she was using him as an unofficial sperm donor. So sadly, it had been only that one magical time. But she had lain down all evening afterwards, in her own room, with her feet up on a pillow, praying for a baby.

He was the perfect male specimen. That muscled stomach, those perfect sculpted legs and lean, hard shoulders. His kisses were perfect, barely touching her lips, making them melt with desire! Where had he learned such techniques, she wondered. Or was that simply how some men were, naturally? If they'd had a normal upbringing without too much tragedy in it, was this how they turned out? With enough generosity of spirit to give a lonely woman like herself an afternoon of blissful, daydreamy sex?

Was there something wrong with Patrick, she thought. Some fundamental reason why he was so cut off from her? She'd tried talking to him over the years. But he wasn't much of a talker. And now the years were slipping away and the sands of time were cascading down and she was running out of patience.

She'd given Nigel some money when she was leaving the hotel. Two thousand dollars in cash, inside a blank card. Just a little love heart on the front of it. Made of red glitter. The money was not a payment for what they'd shared during that wonderful afternoon, she'd said to him when the other women were not looking. No, indeed. It was to help support him for a few more weeks in New York, so he could go to another round of auditions and maybe find his big break in acting before he went home to Montana. Besides, she'd been prepared to pay thousands for the IVF treatment. This way had been so much more enjoyable.

She went darting round the house now, from room to room, straightening up the things Patrick had disturbed and making everything neat again. While Patrick hid in his study and then went fishing for the rest of the day.

When she heard the back door closing, Miriam came downstairs and finally opened his card. Just a plain old Valentine's card with *Love, Patrick* written on it. Nothing else. She threw it in the wastepaper basket and made herself some tea and a huge BLT sandwich with potato-chips on the side. Like in New York. There were seven days to go until her next period was due.

23

The More You Ignore Me, The Closer I Get

Somehow, Victoria knew who it would be when the telephone began to ring. She'd been home in Redstone for a week and she was getting restless, waiting for him to get in touch. Maybe it was intuition but she could sense his presence in the room with her already. She didn't pick up, she only stood by the sofa, her back poker-straight, and waited until the hateful ringing stopped. Ten minutes after that, there was a loud knock at the front door. She ignored that, too. Perhaps it was only the postman with a script for her mother to proofread, she fretted. Or maybe some new books that she'd ordered online? Victoria's heart was beating like a drum, wondering, waiting.

And then she heard the back door opening and quiet footsteps in the kitchen. Her mother must have forgotten to lock the door when she went out. Stupidly, Victoria's next thought was that it was Gemma's grandmother come back to haunt them. Or at least, to see how they were getting on. And in a way, that would've been quite nice. She'd much rather have seen a ghost at that moment than Buddy. But then her body temperature suddenly dropped and she knew who it was, without even turning round.

"Thought you could run away from me, did you?" he said, his voice barely above a whisper.

She froze.

"Not going to say hello? Not going to kiss me?" he asked.

Now, she turned around and there he was, white-faced as usual, his slender neck covered in that familiar tattooed graffiti. Which she'd initially found highly attractive and dangerous, but which now reminded her of ink-stains in the bottom of an old school-bag. Dirty, he looked dirty and crumpled. He was wearing a battered trilby and a white vest. A double-breasted navy coat over a posh felt blazer and thin, red braces. Heroin chic. Skinny jeans and a stripey school tie and red sneakers. Buddy (real name Stuart Holly) was a lot of things but he wasn't unaware of fashion trends. She had to give him that. And besides, who else but a heroin user could get away with skinny jeans?

"How did you find me here?" she whispered. "I never told you I was coming home."

"I followed you to the airport when you left hospital," he said. "I had to know where you were going. Sorry I couldn't visit you, by the way, but I guessed the cops would be sniffing around. You shouldn't have left New York without saying goodbye."

"Buddy, listen, I can explain," she said, feeling rather faint. There was a steely look in his eyes that had not been there before.

"I think I know what happened, Vicky sweetheart. You

decided you wanted to run home to Mummy, and so you just bailed out on me without saying goodbye."

"No, I was at death's door in that hospital. I had to come home – they would have deported me anyway. The police were in to interview me and everything. Twice, as it happens. Looking for information."

"Did you give them my name?"

"What do you think? Of course I didn't."

"Good girl." He sat down on the sofa and put his feet up on the coffee table. "Nice pad you got here."

"It's not mine, it's my mother's."

"Be yours one day, though."

"Look, she'll be home in a minute, Buddy. She only went out for some chips and a pint of milk. You'd better go."

"Excuse me, Vicky baby, but I'm not going nowhere. I just flew nine fucking hours to get here and then I had to sit on a fucking coach until my ass went numb. The least you can do is invite me to supper."

"You're going to have to leave and that's final. Mum said she would call the police if any of my old friends from New York ever got in touch with me again. She's not joking, Buddy. She's got a mean temper on her when she gets started." Victoria walked across the room to push Buddy's dirty sneakers off her mother's immaculate coffee table but, as she bent down over him, he slapped her hard across the face. Stunned, Victoria fell against the edge of the table and hurt her shoulder. She couldn't believe it. Yes, Buddy had been an unbelievably possessive and jealous and suspicious boyfriend. They'd argued all the time, him accusing her of looking at other boys. But he'd never hit her before. Not even when he'd been high.

229

"I'm sorry, baby," he said in a soothing voice, as if nothing at all had happened, "but you can't just order me to leave. You can't just order me out like that when I came all this way to see you. I'm your boyfriend, you know? Not some guy you picked up off the street for the night. Now, you start paying me some respect and we'll get along much better. Okay?"

"I'll decide who comes into this house," said a breathless voice from the kitchen and they both looked up to see Gemma standing there with her shopping bag still in her hand. "Get out of my home immediately. I don't like the look of you," she said to Buddy. And then spotting the red welt on Victoria's face, she drew herself up to her full height with sheer horror.

"Did he just hit you?" she asked in a quiet voice.

Victoria didn't answer but her blushes said it all.

"Did he?"

"Mum, please don't make a scene!"

"I'll make a fucking scene, all right!"

Gemma dropped her shopping and reached for a knife from the chopping block in the kitchen. In one swift move, she was standing between her daughter and this new threat in their lives. This new man who reminded her so much of her own youthful indiscretion. Victoria had clearly inherited her mother's taste in men. She liked the bad boys, too. Unfortunately for this bad boy, though, Gemma Hayes had wised up.

"I'm telling you, now," she spat at him. "Nothing would give me greater pleasure than to gut you down the middle like a fish. You get your scrawny backside out of my home and never come near this house again or I swear I won't be responsible. You touch my daughter again, you even look at my daughter and I won't be responsible for my actions."

Slowly, Buddy got up, winking at Victoria as he went into the hall.

"You can see yourself out," Gemma told him.

"I'll be back," he said softly from the front door, blowing Victoria a kiss. "Happy belated Valentine's Day."

When he had gone, Gemma locked all the doors and windows and closed the curtains.

"Is he the one who got you into drugs?" she asked Victoria, plainly in no mood to be fobbed off with vague answers.

"Yes."

At least she had the good grace to look ashamed about it, Gemma thought, still shaking from the encounter.

"And why did you let him do something so damaging to you? I have to know why, Victoria."

"I loved him."

"Jesus Christ. Is that all you can say? Whatever happened to the Feminist movement? That's just the saddest thing I ever heard, Victoria. You actually loved that piece of trash? He's never done a day's work in his life, has he? By the looks of him."

"I know, I'm sorry."

"Do you still love him? Am I wasting my time here? I can't believe you would ever have listened to that little idiot."

"I suppose I still love him a little bit. But I hate him, too. I hate him much more than I love him. He left me on the floor at that party and went out for something to eat. I could have died. Or been assaulted. I never want to see him again."

"Thank God! Promise me you're telling the truth."

"I promise, Mum. I'm finished with drugs. And him, and boys like him. Look at the state of me – I'm not cut out for that kind of life anyway. I was only doing it for a few months and I almost lost everything. You've got to be really tough to live very long when you're an addict. I'm too soft to go for days without eating or washing. I'm telling you the truth. Mum, put that knife down, you're scaring me."

"Oh, sorry, I forgot I had it in my hand. Right, interrogation's over. I believe you. We'll say no more about it. But if he shows up again, I'm calling the guards. Right?"

"Okay."

"And always check that the doors are locked from now on."

"Okay."

Somehow, they both knew they hadn't seen the last of Buddy.

"But, Mum, you were so brave," Victoria sighed, falling into Gemma's arms for a big, long hug.

"Thank you, my darling," Gemma said, kissing the top of her daughter's head with a loud smack. "I might be a jellyfish at thirty thousand feet. But on dry land, I'm telling you, I'm an absolute shark."

24

The First Picture of You

Sarah looked through the lens and panned her camera along the horizon. She took a few snaps, just to get some idea of scale.

"The thing is, Ethan, I've seen panoramic views like this before," Sarah said, trying to be tactful as they stood, panting heavily, on the top of the mountain. Sarah was gazing down at the village below them and at the pale grey beach and the dark green ocean beyond. "I mean, it's stunningly beautiful but I think I need something different. Something with more narrative."

"Narrative?"

"Yes, I mean, something that tells a story."

"How can one picture tell a story?" he asked, genuinely interested. "It's only a photograph of one moment in time. How can one picture tell a complete story?"

"That's the whole point of photography," she laughed,

finding his confusion endearing. "That's what we snappers try to find, every day of our lives. This view is gorgeous but it's also timeless and sort of closed off, emotionally."

"You mean boring?" he smiled.

"Not at all – it's not immediate enough, that's all. Not personal enough, I suppose. I need more detail."

"I see."

"Still, bloody good exercise, traipsing all the way up here," she said, tucking the camera into her rucksack and taking a sip of water from the bottle. She offered it to Ethan. He took some and they smiled at each other.

They began to walk back down the mountain, slipping here and there on the damp, pebble-strewn path. The air was crystal clear, though, and Sarah breathed it in and felt it blowing the London smog right out of her lungs.

"This is such a beautiful place to live," she said sadly. "I don't want to go home yet."

"Then don't," he said simply.

"We'll see."

"Did you ever ask about that job in the shop?"

"Yes, they said they would be looking for someone in May, but not until then," she sighed. "They were very nice about it, though. Said they would get in touch if a job came up."

"Well, you're too talented for that kind of work anyway."

"Beggars can't be choosers, et cetera. Hey, wait a minute, Ethan, what's that over there?" She pointed to a small field at the bottom of the mountain and a pile of colourful rubbish or something nestled behind a clump of ancient, dark trees. "Is that a junkyard? Seems to be full of old cars. Old tractors, is it? Yellow and red things, it looks like."

"That's nothing," Ethan said huskily. "Just some old scrap metal."

"But look how brightly painted some of the bits are. That could be quite interesting, viewed up close. Shall we go and have a look?"

She turned back to look at him and saw his face was clouded with unease.

"What's the matter, Ethan?" she said. "Have I said something that's annoyed you?"

"Look, that stuff down there," he said, "it's from the fairground. The old fairground at Redstone. It's been lying there for ten years because that's where they dumped it when the fair closed down."

"But what's the matter? I can tell you're quite upset. I'm not blind, you know."

"It's just, I used to work there. I don't like to think about the past. It makes me feel old."

"You worked at the fair? How sexy! Well, come on, tell me all about it. I mean, Aurora did mention something once about a fair here at the village but then we didn't get around to talking about it, for some reason."

It began to drizzle as Sarah hurried down the lower half of the mountain and towards the pile of brightly coloured metal debris. Ethan remained very quiet on the topic of the old fairground. Sarah asked him again for more detail.

"Was it a big fair? Why did it go out of business? What did you do there?"

"There's nothing much to say about it, really. It was a medium-size fair, about twenty attractions, bit of a shambles, not very pretty in broad daylight. I was the dodgems operator and general repairman. Tidyer-upper, at the end of the day. And then it burned down."

"What happened?"

"Nobody knows for sure."

Sarah stumbled down the final part of the narrow pathway and then struck out to cross three overgrown fields, Ethan trailing in her wake. Eventually, she came to a five-bar gate which she had to lean against to catch her breath.

"I'm definitely not getting any younger, myself," she joked. "I'm so going to get fit this summer, wherever I end up. I can't believe I'm not strong enough to climb a very small mountain and then walk for half an hour on flat ground."

"Well, I hope you're pleased with the results, now you're here. Look, it's only scrap. Rubbish."

But Sarah could see a lot more than scrap. She could see a group of carousel horses, beautifully painted and life-like, with big black eyes that seemed alive with emotion. She could see fluid, golden manes and tails on the sleek, black horses. And gold-coloured barley-twist poles sticking up from their backs. They were badly charred in places but there was still enough of their beauty left for the camera to capture. And there was a lovely painted sign, too, announcing *Welcome to Redstone* in curly red and yellow letters, in a bold, circus-style design.

"Now that," she declared happily, "is what I call a narrative photo-opportunity." She climbed over the gate, mindful of the valuable camera in her rucksack, and began looking at the various pieces through the lens, bending down to get better angles, standing on top of other bits of junk to get a different view.

"Careful," Ethan warned, as she nearly fell off the base of a small trailer at one point.

"You know what?" said Sarah. "I've just had a brainwave here. Yeah, I'm definitely getting an idea. Aren't these carousel horses just the most exquisite thing?" She craned to see past the wreckage of a popcorn stall. "Look at the craftsmanship: they look almost alive."

"If you say so," Ethan muttered. He turned away and walked on for a few steps, his head full of dark thoughts. He should tell her now, he knew that. This would be the perfect time to tell her, and then he could stop fretting and maybe get some sleep at night. But how to find the words to tell her he had once been directly involved in a serious case of arson?

"Hey, Ethan," she said now, and he looked up from his reverie to see Sarah push the button on top of her camera. "The first picture of you!"

"Ah, don't," he groaned. "I'm not photogenic."

"We'll see about that," she laughed, coming towards him while checking back over the shots she had taken. "This thing is digital so you can see yourself right now."

"No, thanks."

"There you are, that's lovely," she said. "You look great with the hills in the background: that's a great picture. Now let's see the carousel horses . . . Oh, yeah, baby! That's terrific . . . see the way it's been foreshortened, with the pole going out of focus like that?" She showed him.

"Yeah, that's nice. But you can still see the scorch marks on the side of the face there," he pointed out.

"That's my narrative, that's what that is," she said, extremely pleased with her morning's work. "Looks even better in black and white. But then again, I need the colour to show up the charred bits. Hey, Ethan, do you know what? I'm going to take shots of everything here, and of that old derelict ballroom down the road, and there's a wooden deckchair chained to the railings outside Gemma's house that's been there for ages apparently. I'm going to put some pictures together for a project on the seaside, on the theme of the decline of the traditional seaside holiday. You know, like someone eating fish and chips in the rain, a solitary seagull standing on the turnstile to the pier, empty beaches at the height of summer?"

"Sarah, listen, there's been something on my mind for a few weeks now. I'd really like to get it off my chest, if you don't mind."

"Fire away," she said, wiping some spots of drizzle off her camera lens. Her hands were cold and she had trouble putting the cover back on. She looked up at him expectantly. "What is it?"

"It's something that happened ten years ago. And it's why I didn't go to bed with you that night. New Year's Eve, remember?"

"Yes, I remember."

"Even though, God help me, I was so tempted to. Even though the timing was all wrong anyway because of what you'd just been through with your man. But still, it was very hard to say no."

"Ethan, it's okay, you can tell me. Just say it and then we can hammer out the details later. I won't bite your head off, you know. I'm not like that."

"Well, okay, here goes . . . I'm badly scarred, you see. On my back and side. I was caught up in the fire. When the fairground was on fire, I got caught up in it, and I got quite

238

badly burned. I didn't want you to see me without my clothes, to see my scars."

"Oh, you sweetheart! I'm sure I wouldn't have been all that shocked," she said, touching his face tenderly.

"You would've been."

"No."

"But anyway, there's more. I don't know why I'm telling you this, Sarah. The chances are, it never would've come up. But it's been on my mind all the time. I think maybe it's because . . . I love you."

"Oh, Ethan, that's so amazing and so lovely of you to say, but we're still getting to know each other."

"I know, and it's pathetic but still it's how I feel. It was love at first sight for me, Sarah, when you came into the bar that night and then dropped all your things on the way out again. So I have to tell you what happened at the fair, just in case it ever comes up and you lose your trust in me. I don't want to keep secrets from you, Sarah. It's been such a long time, ten years, keeping all this to myself."

"Come on, back to the cottage," she said then, putting her index finger to his perfect bee-stung lips. "Come home and we'll sit by the fire and get warmed up and you can tell me everything."

As they walked back towards Rose Cottage, Abigail called Sarah again on her mobile but somehow Sarah knew now was not the right time to have a cosy chat about some new guy Abigail had met in London. She let the phone ring out, and they walked on together, wordlessly. Ethan reached for her hand and they went the rest of the way in silence.

An hour later, the little teepee of turf had crackled into

life, the curtains were drawn for privacy and the tea was made.

"Okay," Sarah said gently as they sat down awkwardly together on the sofa. "I'm ready now, so tell me all of it, from start to finish."

"Right. It was Valentine's Day, ten years ago. We'd had a good day at the fair: business was brisk enough despite the bit of rain in the afternoon. I was working on the dodgems as usual that day – some of the cars kept getting stuck against the barrier. Then Patrick Gormley told me not to bother clearing up the litter at the end of the night. Just go on home, he said."

"Miriam's husband?" Sarah asked, totally surprised.

"Yes, he owned the fair, didn't she tell you? Didn't Gemma Hayes mention it to you?"

"No, I didn't know that."

"Okay, well, I can see why they didn't bring it up. So anyway, Paddy, I called him Paddy though nobody else did, he owned the fair. It was a family business, set up in the 1950s by his grandad. And he'd only had it a couple of years when I started working there. I was good with engines and stuff, and there wasn't a lot of other work going at the time. Obviously, the fair was closed down in the winter months, but Paddy used to open it for a few days around Valentine's Day, for the passing trade on the way to the ballroom. And then it would be shut again until the beginning of May."

"I'm with you so far."

"Okay. So I went home that night, about eight o'clock, when the last of the stragglers had drifted on to the ballroom. The place was covered with chip papers and cigarette butts, but Paddy was the boss, so I left it. I just assumed he wanted to get away himself because he told me he was going to propose to Miriam that night at the dance."

"Right."

"But then, as I was having a pint in Callaghan's at about half past eight, I got a bad feeling about the court case."

"What court case?"

"A young girl was seriously injured falling off the carousel the previous summer. The girl's family were suing Paddy for a fortune, and he was worried sick about it. He couldn't sleep at night, he said, and he couldn't eat; he was losing weight over it all. Thought he'd lose everything, actually, if the amount of compensation he had to pay was anything like what the young girl's lawyers were suggesting. And he wanted to get married, too, you see. And Miriam was quite a catch for him, her being so much younger than him and all. So there I was in Callaghan's and I got this feeling . . . a premonition maybe . . . or just a suspicion."

"So what did you do?"

"I went back to the fairground, just to check if everything was all right. But by the time I got there, it was already well alight. And I knew then that Paddy had done it for the insurance money and to hide any evidence of negligence. I mean, some of the rides were past their best, though we did keep all the safety checks up-to-date. We definitely didn't cut corners on the upkeep. The thing is, I heard Paddy shouting and swearing, somewhere in the middle of it all. I tracked him down to the dodgems eventually. He'd got his foot caught in the barrier at the edge of the dodgem track and he couldn't get it out. I think the barrier was bent out of shape a little bit at that side: it didn't always fit snugly to the surface, as I remember."

"Oh my God! And you went in to him?"

"Yes, I ran into the dodgems marquee, playing the hero, as you do. And I tried to pull him out but he was stuck fast. So I kicked off a bit of the fencing and I levered the barrier off his ankle with it and I pulled him out just as the roof came down. Part of the roof-supports caught me on the back and shoulders. It was hot and there was burning canvas attached to it. I put it out right away, surely, rolling on the wet grass, but the damage was done. Paddy was speechless with the shock of it. He was shaking like a leaf, poor guy."

"Poor guy, nothing. You could have been killed, both of you. It was a crazy thing to have done."

"Aye, well, he didn't mean for anyone to get hurt. There was nobody there at the time and the site was a good way away from the village. He'd pushed some of the litter up against a portable heater and, really, it didn't take long to go up. The whole place was covered, like I said, in chip papers and axle grease and popcorn butter."

"Didn't anyone else see the fire and call the fire brigade?"

"No, it was sited in a hollow between two small hills. Anyway, the nearest fire station is ten miles away. And most of the structures at the fairground were made of canvas and wood and chipboard. It was all destroyed in about ten minutes."

"But why did he start the fire in the dodgems if it was the carousel he wanted to get rid of, mainly?"

"Well, he didn't want to make it look *that* obvious, did he? I mean, he was crazy, right enough, but he wasn't thick. He was going to start the fire in the dodgems and then drop a bit of burning canvas onto the carousel a minute or so later. He didn't have to do anything else though, in the event, because it all went up like a tinderbox."

"But you said it was raining?"

"It was raining earlier, but the insides of the various marquees were bone dry."

"I see. What happened then?"

"He begged me to keep my mouth shut, naturally. I said, I wasn't going to grass up my friend, what did he take me for? But I told him somebody would put two and two together and work it out, but he was nearly hysterical at that point. He said it didn't matter what anyone suspected, they couldn't prove a thing. There's always talk after a fire, he said. That's the first thing people think of, that it was arson, for the insurance money. But as long as we both kept our mouths shut, nothing could ever be proved."

"That would've been true, Ethan, except you were both right there when it happened," Sarah said thoughtfully.

"That's the next bit of my little story. Well, Paddy pulled himself together eventually and went off home to get ready for the dance. He said he'd wave in to a few people in the shop, to make it look like he was on his way home already when the fire happened. He didn't look any messier than usual so that was okay. I was injured, of course, so I couldn't get away so easily. I had to hang around for twenty minutes or so until the fire brigade turned up, and say I'd got injured trying to put the fire out. It would've taken me that long to walk to the village for help."

"Didn't Patrick have a car?"

"Not that night, it was in the garage for a service."

"Okay. So you said you'd just come on the fire, and it'd started accidentally?"

"Yeah. I said I'd come back looking for my wallet and just found it all ablaze."

"Wow. Did they believe you?"

"Not really. But they had to let me go to hospital, didn't they? And afterwards, Paddy and me both stuck to our stories and the case looked like it would go on for years. Then Paddy got the insurance money, and the family of the young girl settled for about half of what they could have got in court. I still feel terrible about that, actually. Poor kid was in hospital for eight months with her back broken in two places."

"And did she get better?"

"Eventually. But she had to walk with a stick."

"Oh dear . . ."

Ethan rubbed his eyes and sighed.

"That was an awful ordeal for you," Sarah said, holding his hand. "And your back?"

"It was fucking sore for a long time!"

"I'm sure it was."

"Yeah, I was in and out of hospital a few times – it took ages to heal up."

"Did you not get any compensation money yourself?"

"No."

"Why not?"

"Paddy hadn't insured me."

"But he gave you nothing? He could have given you some of his own insurance money?"

"He said he needed all of it to buy a new house for Miriam. The lavender house, she had her heart set on it, he said."

"But you were badly hurt, for heaven's sake. You saved his life!"

"Whatever. I wasn't going to leave him there to burn to death, was I?"

244

"Now, this is ridiculous, Ethan. You saved his life and he gave you nothing? I don't believe it. He could have slipped you a bit of cash, surely?"

"He said he would do that, yes, if he was ever in a position to, somewhere down the line."

"And did he?"

"No. We haven't really spoken since it happened. Look, it doesn't matter, Sarah. My parents left me their house when they went to live in England later that year. My father got a live-in gig as a college caretaker in Sheffield. And I got a job at the garage a few months after that. I wouldn't have taken the money off Paddy anyway – it was just going too far, what he did. And I would have been guilty by association. He knew I didn't want the money."

"But that was unforgivable of him! You risked your life to save him and he didn't give you a penny. They've got plenty of money – Gemma said they had plenty of money. Old money from the Gormleys of Galway. That's why the two of them don't have to work."

"They haven't got a bean, Sarah. I know that for a fact. Paddy Gormley makes a living writing a column for some fishing magazine in England."

"But Miriam makes out they have money."

"Miriam is away with the fairies, Sarah. Or haven't you noticed? I mean, she's a lovely woman but she's not really dealing with a full deck."

"She is not away with the fairies! Don't say that about Miriam! She wants to have a baby using IVF but Patrick won't have anything to do with it."

"I suppose he has his reasons. He's pretty old-school, is

Patrick. He might not want to go through the medical tests. That would be my guess. Also, like I said, they're not exactly minted."

"Oh, Jesus! Miriam just spent a wodge of cash going to New York with us. She bought her own ticket and paid for her own hotel room. She said Patrick didn't want her to go so she just whacked it all on a credit card and went anyway. And she was flirting with one of the barmen."

Ethan shrugged his shoulders helplessly. "That's not our problem. But Patrick's crazy about that woman, Sarah. Just plain crazy about her. I sincerely hope she isn't going to leave him over this IVF business, because quite frankly I don't think he'd be able to live without her. And that's another reason I didn't push him for any dough. He's not rational when it comes to Miriam. He'd do anything for her. Well, almost anything. He bought her that house, anyway."

"Show me your scars."

"What?"

"Show me them, please."

"Can't we wait until it gets dark, at least?"

"No. I want to see them now."

"Okay. Brace yourself."

He unbuttoned his coat and shirt and stood up. Dropping both garments off his shoulders, Sarah finally saw the seven diagonal, red welts across his back, as if he'd been whipped by a bunch of red hot rods. Which, in a way, he had. And a patch of melted, shiny skin all down his right side. The skin that had not been burned was soft and white.

"Does it still hurt to be touched?" she asked gently.

"No, not for a long time, now."

"Come on, let's go to bed!"

"You what? Hey, this is all moving a bit fast! Give me a minute to get my head round this, will you? I didn't think you'd fancy me at all when you saw the state of me!"

"Relax! I meant to sleep, that's all. We're both tired. It'd be nice to go to sleep together, wouldn't you say?"

"Yes, I'd like that, thank you."

But later, after they'd showered and had supper and were climbing into bed together, and Sarah was cuddling in to Ethan's lean, sexy bare chest and shoulders, there was a knock at the front door. They could hear muffled voices and a car door shutting.

"Ignore it," she whispered. "Probably someone's got the wrong house."

"What time is it?"

"Nine o'clock. It's too late to be visiting, really. I'm not expecting anybody."

Another knock, louder this time.

"Oh, bugger it," Sarah sighed, getting up and pulling a sweater on over her pyjamas. "I might as well answer it – it might be Mrs Casey."

She hurried up to the front of Rose Cottage and wrenched open the door.

And there, shivering on the doorstep, were her parents, Agatha and Richard Quinn, in the flesh. And three massive suitcases beside them. And a taxi on the road, still dislodging a further two suitcases. And a set of golf clubs.

"We came to visit you, darling," said her mother. "And we brought you some of your clothes and stuff. Surprise!"

"Oh my God . . ."

And coming across the road towards her were Gemma and Victoria, both looking rather upset.

"Can we stay here tonight, Sarah, please?" Gemma asked at once. "Oh, hi, hope I'm not interrupting anything?"

Sarah was flabbergasted. She battled on with the introductions despite feeling like shutting the door and going back to bed.

"Gemma, meet my mum and dad, Agatha and Richard Quinn. Mum and Dad, meet Gemma Hayes, the famous novelist, and her lovely daughter, Victoria."

Lots of hellos and handshakes followed. Sarah watched it all unfolding, leaning on the door jamb for support.

"Just chat away there amongst yourselves," she said, smiling determinedly. "And come on in when you're ready."

"Oh, Sarah, we're in a spot of bother, you see," Gemma explained quietly, trying not to let Mr and Mrs Quinn hear too much of what she said. "We're being stalked at my house. Just nuisance calls but we don't want to take any chances."

"Gemma! Who is it, do you know?" Sarah whispered.

"Victoria's ex. He won't take the hint, the brute. I've called the guards and they told us to go somewhere else for the night. And they're going to keep an eye on the house for me. I didn't want to bother Aurora after all she's done for us recently. You wouldn't mind, would you?"

"Not a bit. Come on in, the lot of you," said Sarah, standing back and opening the little Hansel-and-Gretel door wide. And wondering how she was going to tell her parents she didn't really need all this extra stuff they'd brought over from London because she had literally only days left until her rent ran out. And now she had four guests and only one extra bedroom with a double bed in it. Gemma and Victoria would have to sleep on the two sofas, obviously. Or she could give them her own bed. But Ethan was in it at the moment. And that was her main problem: how would she possibly explain to everyone what she was doing with Ethan Reilly lying topless in her bed, when she was supposed to be resting up in Redstone, nursing a broken heart?

"Well, that was some slog but we're here now," said Agatha Quinn, bustling into the cottage hauling the first two suitcases. "You forget how long it takes to get here when you haven't travelled in a while. Give us a kiss, sweetheart, and then give us the guided tour. I'm just dying to see everything! What have you done with the place?"

"Well, Mum, not much. I've done nothing except buy a nice little Buddha for the sitting room, to bring me good luck," Sarah said brightly, knowing her mother would be worried about her Christian daughter having *false gods* in her home.

"You bought a what?" Mrs Quinn said, her forehead already wrinkled with confusion and concern.

25

Happy House

Needless to say, it was quite a night at Rose Cottage. First of all, Mrs Quinn had to be quietly taken into the kitchen and warned by Sarah not to ask Gemma for more information about their mysterious stalking incident. Then, she was so bothered by the sight of Sarah's Buddha statue that it had to be taken off the bookcase and stored in a corner behind the wicker baskets. And then moved right outside to the yard because she said she wouldn't be able to get to sleep under the same roof as it.

"What if I died in the night?" she kept asking.

"Don't tempt fate," Sarah whispered to Gemma and they both collapsed into giggles.

Sarah then had to make an excuse to go into the bedroom and warn Ethan that her parents had turned up unexpectedly. And that her mother was asking for a "look-see at the sleeping arrangements".

Ethan, now out of bed and dressed, was still feeling very emotional after unburdening his conscience and his scars to Sarah earlier in the evening, so that was the last thing he wanted to have to cope with.

"I'm kind of tired, actually," he began.

"You can climb out the window and go home if you like," Sarah said, holding the door shut behind her in case her mother barged in. "I'll give you a call when they've gone home again." They she blew him a kiss and went back into the fray.

When she had gone, Ethan looked longingly at the bedroom window. All he had to do was nip out and walk home along the beach. That would have been the easiest option by a long chalk but then he worried Sarah might think him a will-o'-the-wisp. And he didn't want to get into her bad books, like that Mackenzie. Sarah obviously had very high standards when it came to her menfolk. Then he had an idea.

He flung open the bedroom door.

"Hello, everyone," he said merrily, holding up a hard chair and advancing into the sitting room with it.

Mrs Quinn jumped two feet into the air with surprise.

"Oh my word! You didn't say you had a visitor, darling," she trilled accusingly.

"Didn't I? Must have forgot with all the excitement. Ethan just came round to fix the radiator . . ."

"Here you are, Sarah," Ethan said loudly, setting the chair down by the kitchen door. "You can't have too many chairs when you get surprise guests, I always say," he added sheepishly.

"Thanks, Ethan, you're terrific," Sarah said, pleasantly surprised to see him sticking around but so glad he was putting on a little act. Yes, it was ridiculous to be tip-toeing round

Mrs Quinn like this. But some things were just too much trouble to explain to her mother, she thought wearily. Like the fact she could spend the night with Ethan and not have sex with him. But that if she *did* have sex with him, it was their business and nobody else's. And also that it *didn't* mean they were going to buy the ring and announce their engagement forthwith.

"This is one of my new friends, Ethan Reilly," she added, trying to sound ever so casual. As if it was no big deal to have a gorgeous man popping into the house to fix radiators at nine o'clock at night, with no socks on under his shoes and his shirt hanging out of his jeans at the back. And when Sarah herself was wearing pyjamas and a pair of slippers.

Gemma's eyes were popping out with amusement. Good for you, Sarah, she thought, trying very hard not to laugh. Good for you for luring such a looker into your lair. Ethan Reilly might have had the name of keeping himself to himself in the village but Gemma was always willing to give the underdog the benefit of the doubt. She was one of life's underdogs herself, after all.

"Have you met Sarah's parents at all?" Gemma asked him cheekily, nodding her head towards the well-dressed yet twitchy couple, Mrs Quinn resplendent in a grey wool twin-set and trenchcoat and her husband sporting a neat beige raincoat and cloth cap. Obviously, Ethan hadn't met them before but she had to find some way to get the conversation up on its feet, she decided.

"No, indeed, the pleasure is all mine," Ethan said warmly, coming forward at once and shaking hands with the two of them. "How are you, Mrs Quinn, Mr Quinn? Lovely to meet you both at last. Well, I'll just head on, then, shall I? Goodnight, all. I think you'll have no more trouble with that old relic, Sarah. Should be working the best from now on." And he nodded towards the bedroom.

"Don't go, Ethan. Please stay a little while!" Sarah almost begged him, not wanting to be left alone with her parents *and* Gemma and Victoria. She could have managed quite well on her own with either pair, but having them all in the house together was definitely going to be awkward. A severe case of two worlds colliding. Her parents were religious, conservative and they liked to know if other people were, too. No matter what faith they actually belonged to. And her parents didn't know about Victoria's ongoing detox programme either. And she didn't want them to find out. Especially since Gemma might accidentally describe her sheer relief that Victoria hadn't died of a heroin overdose at that three-day party in the Bronx.

Oh dear, Sarah thought, her stomach suddenly feeling rather unsteady. This was going to be tricky. Her parents were sweethearts, and she loved them with all her heart. But still, it was very embarrassing when Mrs Quinn started up her Columbo routine. She simply had a compulsion to get to know certain details about people. Right on cue, the questions began.

"You're a local boy, then, Ethan? Would you have gone to the boys' school here? Saint Michael's?"

Ethan nodded in the affirmative. Of course, he'd gone to Saint Michael's. Where else would he have gone? "Yes, Saint Michael's it was," he smiled. "Fourteen years of happy memories. Luckily, they'd done away with the cane by the time I got the length of them. But yes, we had some great times there. I was part of the hurling team, also. We won the County Cup in my last year."

Mrs Quinn nodded at him, pleased to be with someone so forthcoming. This was a good start.

"And would Father Healy have been teaching there around your time?"

"Yes, that's right," Ethan smiled.

"He used to say a lovely Mass."

"Yes, he did."

"And tell me, Ethan, does Father Healy still hold the men's prayer week every year?"

"Oh, yes indeed, he still does all that, Mrs Quinn. I never miss it, myself. In the front row every night, I am. Seven o'clock sharp. Top stuff."

"Really? How does it go, again? I forget the running order," she said to him.

Sarah held her breath but Ethan was one step ahead of her. He didn't go to the prayer week any more but the running order hadn't changed in four decades. And anyway, he heard odd details from one of the guys in the garage who was rather religious.

"Well, there's the Mass first, obviously. And then we get the sermon on the evils of modern life. It was – pornography last year. Pardon me for saying. But oh, Father Healy should have been in show business, he's such a comedian. *There's girls from every nation*, he shouted from the pulpit, *cavorting in their underwear, in every newsagent in Ireland!*"

"I wish!" laughed Mr Quinn, in spite of himself.

"Richard, please," scolded his wife.

"Sorry, Agatha."

255

"Go on, Ethan," she prompted.

"Where was I? Oh, yeah. We all say the Rosary when the sermon's over, walking in a line up and down the aisles, and then we light a candle for our good intentions. And then we sing "Star of the Sea". It's just lovely, very nicely done in harmonies, you know." Ethan did his best to look pious. "It's a great experience altogether."

And all delivered from his lips without a hint of mockery. The man was a genius, thought Gemma admiringly.

Mrs Quinn didn't know quite what to do with herself. She was speechless at such a high level of devotion.

Clever old Ethan, Sarah thought, as he winked at her behind Mrs Quinn's back. He'd put her mother firmly in her place without actually being rude about it. And really, she deserved it. Agatha Quinn could never understand that people were *allowed* to be secular nowadays, even though she was a gentle little soul in most other respects.

An awkward silence then filled the room. Everyone stood in a kind of untidy circle, looking at one another, hoping someone else would break the ice or be the first one to sit down. Then Victoria yawned and swayed slightly on her feet. She did look tired, Sarah thought guiltily.

"I'm starving," Gemma said bravely, sensing the mood was becoming strained. "What say I get Victoria tucked up in bed and then we'll fix some supper for ourselves? Oh, sorry, Sarah, you won't have a room going now your parents are staying here. I'll just call Aurora and ask her if she can take us in. Sorry about all this carry-on."

"No need to call Aurora at this time of night," Sarah said, coming out of her reverie and reaching out a hand to stop

Gemma dialling Aurora's number on her mobile. "I'd love you to stay," she added firmly.

"We don't want to be in your way. I'm so sorry," Victoria said in a small voice. She was very embarrassed by her obsessive ex-boyfriend's behaviour being made public like this. She wished she'd never met Buddy in the first place. Thank goodness she'd left America before he could talk her into getting his name tattooed on her arm. She'd have been reminded of the useless layabout forever, if she had.

"You take Victoria into the spare room: it's just through there," Sarah said, pointing the way for Gemma. "Switch on the electric heater, Victoria, there's a good girl. The switch is behind the bedside table on the left. You'll have to share the bed, the pair of you, is that okay?"

"Thank you so much, Sarah," Gemma smiled. She nodded her gratitude to Sarah and then to Ethan as well. She was very grateful to have a strong young man about the place tonight. Two men, actually, just in case things got out of hand. And then she was cross with herself for thinking in such a girly, fluttery way. She ushered Victoria towards the bedroom door.

"And, Mum and Dad, you can have my room," Sarah continued. "You can put your cases in there now, actually. Get them out of the way. I'll kip on the sofa. Now, Ethan, I'd be grateful if you could build up the fire a little? And I'll see what I can find in the way of supper. I haven't much in the cupboard. Some tins of chicken soup and a fresh loaf might be the height of it. And a pack of custard slices. Oh, and some nice fresh peaches. Is that all right for everybody?"

"Sounds great, love," her father said, beginning to relax. He could see Sarah had found herself a new boyfriend here in

Redstone. Richard Quinn was a bit hen-pecked but he wasn't stupid. He knew chemistry when he saw it. And at least this fella here was a lot younger than Mackenzie Campbell, which was a good thing. But by the looks of him, he didn't have an awful lot of money. Those scruffy old clothes on him. Oh well, he thought charitably, maybe they were only his working clothes. Sarah was a sensible girl, and that was good enough for him.

And so, they settled onto the sofas, huddled round the fire for something to look at, more than anything, having a sort of picnic. All except Victoria, who was soon sleeping soundly in the second tiny bedroom, with Gemma keeping a watchful eye on the doors and windows for any signs of an intruder. Sarah knew Ethan would have to leave when they all went to bed for the night and she was missing him already. He was so good at papering over awkward moments. She smiled at him now and mouthed "thank you" to him. And he smiled back at her and winked again.

"Ethan, you wouldn't mind staying here tonight, would you?" Gemma asked then. "On the other couch? Just in case we have a visitor?"

"Sure," he said, "if you think it'll help."

"Thanks a million," Gemma said gratefully. "I'll turn in, then. Goodnight."

Mrs Quinn pursed her lips until she could have fitted them through the eye of a needle. But she said nothing.

"Goodnight," Sarah said to Gemma.

And then the four of them were left alone. But Ethan kept up a harmless line of chat, tracing back through the various families in the area and what they were doing nowadays. It wasn't too bad, really. It wasn't too bad at all. Sarah was almost enjoying herself as the night drew to a close. She and Ethan washed the dishes as her parents eventually went to bed and shared a triumphant hug in the kitchen.

But outside on the beach, someone was waiting.

26

Life in a Northern Town

Abigail sat at the desk in Mackenzie's bedroom – well, in their bedroom now – and looked across at the telephone. It sat there, shiny and silent, patiently waiting for her to walk across the carpet and pick it up. Really, she ought to say everything she had to say to Sarah in person. But by now, far too much time had elapsed and the news was too big, and she had chickened out. There was no way she could formulate the words, let alone say them out loud: she knew that for a fact. She had been on the verge of calling lots of times in recent days. But it was too hard. And so, going against all of her professional training, she decided to avoid the potentially fraught confrontation altogether. Sighing heavily, Abigail pulled the writing pad towards her and reached for a pen. She didn't want to leave a written record of her treachery either, but this was definitely the lesser of two evils, she decided.

Dear Sarah,

I hope this letter finds you well.

I also hope you don't mind me writing all this down on paper when the two of us are supposed to be best friends. Of course, we still are best friends. But I've tried calling you a few times over the last few weeks and you're either madly busy with your new life there in Redstone or else you're not available at all. So, I've decided it might be better for you this way. And it'd be a lot easier for me, if I'm honest. Which is strange, since I was always such a big one for not avoiding the issue.

Well, here goes.

I mentioned a while ago that I was seeing someone. Well, it isn't some man I've met in London. And it's not just a casual thing. Sarah, I'm so sorry to tell you the news this way, but I have to be completely truthful with you. I'm going out with Mackenzie now. Mackenzie Campbell. Your Mackenzie. I'm sure you're as shocked to be reading this as I am to be writing it. But some of the girls in our set have their suspicions about the situation and I'd rather you heard the details from me and not them. Sarah, please try to understand. If it's any consolation, this isn't a rebound thing or some stupid plan by him to win you back by making you jealous. It's real, Sarah. It's a real relationship.

I can't tell you how guilty I felt when we first realized we had feelings for each other. Not feelings of purely romantic love, naturally, but a bond of friendship and companionship. We'd both lost loved ones and I suppose we were both ready to settle down and live a quiet life. It was simply a case of the timing being right and a little bit of serendipity, I suppose. I spent a few days here at Thistledown over the New Year's holiday (Millie invited me) and some kind of understanding just grew up between us. And we decided to give things a chance and see what transpired. Anyway, the thing is, I'm still here in Thistledown, nine weeks later. I've resigned from my job at the clinic and I've put my London house on the market.

Mackenzie has asked me to stay on, you see, and help him to manage the estate. We're going to use the money from my house sale to renovate that old row of derelict cottages on the edge of the village, and we're going to let them out to artists and writers. And maybe call it something whimsical, like Quill Lane. Hopefully, some of the houses can be let for the whole year and not just for the summer months, which would be the makings of a nice little community, if it works out. We might even start up an online art gallery. Or maybe run courses in forest management, or shooting at targets, or archery. I'm very excited about the plans we've made. And I don't miss my old job one little bit. I've been to Mackenzie's church with him every week and I've met most of the villagers at Glenallon. What I'm trying to tell you is, he's asked me to marry him.

Now, Sarah, I know you're going to hate my guts for all of this. But I promise you, I never had any intentions of going out with Mackenzie, even when I knew for certain that the two of you were definitely never going to reunite. I did my best to get you back together, if you recall, and I still feel I failed you there, as a counsellor and as a friend. But I never, in my wildest dreams, envisaged myself and Mackenzie getting together. It's important to me that you understand that, Sarah. Whatever happens, between Mackenzie and myself, it's important to me that you give us your blessing at this point.

Because I can't seem to come to terms with the fact that if Mackenzie and I do get married, then the friendship I had with you might well come to an end. I am dreading that possibility. We've shared so much together over the years. But now that Mackenzie and I have been this close, all these weeks, I have truly fallen in love with him. And he says he loves me, too, as much as he can love any other woman after Jane. And I'm willing to live with that. Because a part of me will always belong to Donal.

Mackenzie has set a provisional date for our wedding, the 30th of June this year, and whilst I don't expect you to attend, it would mean the world to me if you could send us your best wishes. Millicent has been surprisingly relaxed about everything. I think she is just pleased that Mackenzie is not going to be by himself for the foreseeable future, like she's been for all these years.

Please, Sarah, please don't hate me for this. Remember when we sat on the swings in the park and just talked and talked about our future lives and what they were going to be like? Well, that's how I feel right now. Like I'm sitting on the swings again, waiting for something to happen. I sincerely hope you are having a lovely time there in Redstone with all your new friends. And I also hope that you can spare a minute now to get in touch with an old friend. It would mean the world to me.

Love always,
Your friend,
Abigail.

P.S. I have given your wedding dress back to your parents. Sorry to mention it here but I know you must have been worried about it.

Better not sign it "your *best* friend", she decided wisely. Well, it was done now, so before she bottled out of posting it (as she had from phoning), Abigail folded the sheets carefully into a matching envelope and wrote out the address.

To: Sarah Quinn, Rose Cottage, Redstone, Ireland.

The letter looked quite beautiful when it was finished. Nice and elegant in its cream, watermarked envelope. Addressed with Abigail's perfect, italicized handwriting. She fixed on the stamps very neatly, too. This was such an important letter, she wanted to do everything perfectly and correctly. She didn't write her own address on the back, however. That would have been showing off.

After breakfast, she borrowed the jeep to drive into Glenallon, taking with her Millie's old shopping basket and a small list of things to buy at the grocery shop.

"Be careful driving," Mackenzie said to her as she went out the front door.

"I will," she assured him, knowing he would be using these self-same words to her for the rest of their time on earth together. "I'll be very careful, don't worry."

Mackenzie watched her as she went down the drive, knowing she was going to post her letter to Ireland and hoping that Sarah would not be too disappointed in them both. The dogs were barking to be let out into the fields but he wanted to see Abigail setting off. And when she went out through the gates and onto the road, he raised his hand high above his head and waved to her.

27

There is a Light That Never Goes Out

It was the fourth day of cramped living conditions at Rose Cottage. Gemma and Victoria were doing their best to keep a low profile by staying in the kitchen or in their bedroom. They should have gone home again by now but it was so nice having company with this threat hanging over them. Sometimes they even managed to forget about Buddy, they were having such a nice time getting the lunch ready or chatting by the fire. But Mrs Quinn would keep glancing out the window to see was there any sign of the bogeyman on the horizon. And in so doing, she managed to keep both Gemma and Victoria in a state of high anxiety. Sarah was forever telling her mother to relax. Mrs Quinn would make a gold-standard stalker herself, Sarah thought, shaking her head. The woman had the strength and determination of ten men.

"I wouldn't mind if I could just shoot the fucking little shit and get off without being charged," Gemma whispered to

Sarah, as she made sandwiches for Victoria in the kitchen at noon. "But if they hauled me into prison, who'd look out for her? I'm all she has in the world, poor love. I don't know how it happened, but it's just me and Victoria now. There's nobody else to rely on. I wish I had a big family round me. I wish I knew what to do."

"It's okay," Sarah told her. "The police will catch him if he's still hanging around somewhere. I mean, where is he staying at night? Not in a hotel or a guest house, that's for sure, because they'd have found him by now. He can't be living rough or sleeping in a car or whatever for much longer. No, he'll go home to America soon and that'll be the end of it. If he isn't gone already. These bullies don't stick around when they know they're outnumbered. They're nothing but a bunch of cowards, at the end of the day. All bullies are snivelling little cowards, beneath their posturing."

"Thanks, Sarah. I'm so grateful to you for letting us stay."

"You're very welcome. Besides, right now, I'm delighted you *are* staying here with me. You're a great buffer between me and my parents. They can't quiz me with yourself and Victoria around. And as a distraction for my mother, you take some beating! If she wasn't trying to find out what's going on with Buddy, she'd be giving me the third degree on my plans for Ethan. Honestly, I'd be getting twenty questions every morning before breakfast."

"Is Ethan coming back again today?" Gemma asked, putting the sandwiches on a plate and pouring a glass of milk to go with them. "I mean, I know he had to go work but will he come back later?"

"Yes. He said he would ask for a half-day and bring my

father for a round of golf at this fantastic course about twenty miles away. And Mum's going too, for the ride."

"That's nice of him. I didn't know Ethan played golf."

"He doesn't."

"Oh, he's a keeper, Sarah! What a lovely thing to do for your parents. I'll just take this through to Victoria, then I'll tidy up the kitchen, okay? It's great to see her eating well again. I think we're really getting back to normal."

"Fine by me, no hurry. Oh, listen, is that the post?"

Sarah went hurrying up the little steps to see what the postman had brought. Not that she was expecting anything exciting but it always gave her a little thrill of pleasure to see an envelope addressed to Rose Cottage. Even if it was only from her bank. There were two letters lying on the mat. One was from, yes, the bank. She tore it open immediately. Her second request for a (smaller) overdraft had also been turned down. The tight-fisted buggers, she thought, dismayed. What would she do now for money? The only things she had of any value were her camera and the gold bracelet Mackenzie had given her as a wedding present. Should she sell them, she wondered, as she studied the other envelope. She recognised Abigail's distinctive handwriting at once.

"Wow, this is a lovely surprise," she said happily.

But before she could get a chance to open it she heard the sound of a plate dropping to the sitting-room floor and Gemma's voice calling to her, softly but urgently.

Somehow she knew at once what was going on.

"Sarah, come quick!" Gemma called for a second time, and Sarah, letters in hand, darted down the steps and into the sitting room. Gemma was standing by the curtains, peeking out of the picture-window. Sarah's parents were hovering behind her.

"We believe our stalker has returned," her mother said in an ominous voice.

"Look," Gemma gasped, "look there, that's him. That's Buddy. Oh God!"

Sarah looked.

Buddy and Victoria were sitting on the backyard wall, heads together, talking earnestly.

"She went out to get some air, Sarah. The little bastard must have been waiting close by. I don't know what to do. I don't know how he found us here. Should we call the police and hope they arrive before he leaves again? Or should I go out there and thump him?"

"You call the police. I'll go out. You'd better not go near him in case you do anything stupid. Mum and Dad, you stay right there and don't make a fuss," Sarah commanded.

"As if I would make a fuss," her mother began.

But then her husband put his arm round her and guided her over to the sofa.

"Hush now," he said tenderly. "This isn't our business. Sarah, love, you should stay indoors too, and let the guards handle this. If you're going out there, though, I'm going with you."

"I think he's going to slap her! Oh, it's too late!" cried Mrs Quinn.

They all heard Buddy shouting, calling Victoria names. And she was sobbing on the low wall, all cowed and subservient, and Buddy had slapped her again.

"That's it," Gemma growled. "I've had enough of this!"

She ran outside, flinging the back door wide open, and raced across to Buddy, grabbed him by the lapels and pushed him away from Victoria. Then she was slapping him and thumping him and kicking him on the shins. Mr Quinn scrambled to get one of his golf clubs from the bedroom and Mrs Quinn went up the street to see if there was any sign of Ethan.

Sarah watched, frozen, as Buddy rallied himself enough to start fighting back. Obviously a few days hanging around in the damp Irish weather had weakened him. But now he made his bony hand into a hard fist and punched Gemma square in the eye. Victoria began to scream. Gemma was lying in the yard, obviously too stunned to get up. Victoria was bending over her and it looked like Buddy was going to punch her as well. He really seemed to have lost it. His face was contorted into white-hot rage.

"You can't finish with me!" he roared. "I won't let you! We love each other!"

"You love my wages, you mean? You lazy sponge! Leave me alone!" Victoria shouted through her tears. "Can't you see nobody wants you here! I don't want you here! I'm tired of taking drugs and I hate you! Go *away*!"

Sarah finally snapped out of her shock-inspired trance. She dropped her mail, bounded out the back door like a fox and, in a flash of inspiration, grabbed her Buddha statue from behind the dustbin and clobbered Buddy with it. Right across the back of his head, hat and all. He staggered for a few seconds and then fell limply onto the sand on the other side of the wall.

"Oh my God, Mummy, are you all right?" Victoria wept, helping her mother up off the concrete yard. "Are you blinded?

271

Your eye, your poor eye, oh, it looks so sore! I can't believe he did that to you, Mum. I swear I never thought he'd turn nasty like this. He was never like this in New York. Just possessive, but not violent. Oh, Mum, is your eye okay?"

"I'll live. But what about that good-for-nothing prick over there?" Gemma gasped. "Is he dead?"

"Oh God, he's not moving! Oh my God, this is turning into a complete disaster! Sarah, I think you've *killed* him," Victoria mumbled, glancing over the wall again at Buddy, utterly beside herself with misery and guilt. She couldn't believe she had inflicted all of this damage on her own mother and her mother's friends.

"I didn't mean to kill him," Sarah choked, her mouth drying up. "I only meant to stop him hurting Gemma. Oh, what have I done? I'm a murderer . . ."

But then the moment of panic was gone when Buddy groaned and opened his eyes and then groaned louder and closed them again.

"Don't move a muscle, boyo," said Mr Quinn, hurrying across the yard and standing beside Buddy with a golf club gripped in his hand. "Sarah, don't worry, we were all witnesses to what happened. It was self-defence."

"This village . . . has gone downhill a fair bit . . . since we moved to London," Mrs Quinn panted, coming back with Ethan. Both of them were out of breath from running. Mrs Quinn had practically dragged Ethan down the little set of steps, in through the main room and out to the yard.

"Cancel the golf, Ethan," said Mr Quinn in a weary voice, wiping some beads of perspiration from his brow as Ethan tried to take it all in.

Gemma's left eye was swelling up rapidly and Victoria's face was red and sore-looking.

"We've just made a citizen's arrest here," added Mr Quinn, pointing towards Buddy with his golf club. "This young man assaulted both Victoria and her mother. We all saw what happened. It was his fault. He was completely out of control."

"I did hit him before he hit me," Gemma admitted quietly.

"Only after he slapped your daughter," interjected Agatha Quinn. "He nearly took the face off her, so he did. I saw it happening." (Because she'd been glued to the window, not wanting to miss a thing, obviously.)

"That's correct," said Mr Quinn. "What sort of a man would hit a woman anyway?"

"And her mother as well," said Mrs Quinn.

"No kind of a man, at all. A proper waster."

"Then Sarah walloped him with that idol thing," Mrs Quinn added. "And put a stop to his gallop."

Sarah nodded, too shocked to speak.

"Wow, right, have you called a doctor yet? He doesn't look too hot," Ethan said quickly. "Everyone, get back in the house, and Richard, could you call a doctor? I'll stay out here and keep an eye on this guy. We'd better not move him."

They all trooped inside to wait. Mrs Quinn went into the kitchen to make tea.

"I'm so sorry, Mum. Now you'll really get into trouble," Victoria sobbed, dabbing at Gemma's eye with a clean facecloth dipped in cold water. "And Sarah will, too. She'll be done for assault."

"Nobody will get into any trouble," Mr Quinn said, suddenly sounding very authoritative. "I'll have a word with the guards.

I'm sure all of this can be sorted out very quickly indeed. An aul' skirmish is all it was."

"I need a drink," Sarah said, heading to the fridge for a glass of wine. "I'd offer you all one but there's only a drop left. And I'm having it in case they arrest me."

They all nodded in agreement. Nobody wanted to deny Sarah her spoonful of wine after what she'd just been through.

"I'm so sorry, all of you," Victoria repeated. "I promise I'll never do anything stupid for the rest of my life."

"I don't care, darling. I don't care about anything else as long as you're all right. That guy needs some serious help, and I don't mean just physically." Gemma hugged her precious daughter to her as if she would never let go. Victoria was going to be fine, she knew that now. Her dalliance with the dark side was finally over. Her own genes had won out over those of Victoria's father, and she wouldn't have to tell her daughter the tawdry truth of her lineage. As far as Victoria was concerned, her father had been a lovely man Gemma had dated briefly before he emigrated to New Zealand and he'd died a long time ago in a climbing accident. If Victoria ever suggested visiting his grave, Gemma was going to tell her he'd been cremated and that she didn't think he had any family. Luckily, so far, Victoria hadn't wanted to start discovering her family tree.

Outside, a trickle of blood ran down the side of Buddy's face. This country was something else, he thought bitterly. Even the women were deranged here. He'd been told by some friends back home that the Northerners in Ireland were all nuts but that the Southerners were lovely, friendly people. He longed for the safety of his own neighbourhood in the Bronx.

A huge, pulsating pain was thundering through his skull and every beat of his heart made his head feel like it was splitting open. He wouldn't press charges, he decided. He didn't want his own personal circumstances being under the spotlight. And he'd used a stolen credit card to pay for this trip. As soon as he could walk unaided, he'd be out of this awful place and on his way home to America. Buddy lay his head down on the sand again and closed his eyes.

28

This Perfect Day

Sarah's parents had gone home. Their trip to Redstone had done them the power of good, they said. It had made them appreciate their little floral-patterned palace in Islington. For once and for all, they had given up on their vague dreams of coming home to Ireland, to grow old by the water's edge. No, they wouldn't be hankering to return to the peace and tranquillity of the Irish seaside any more. Anyway, a few trips to Callaghan's had reminded them how few of their contemporaries were still around to talk to. The majority of their friends were Londoners, now. English people. And what was wrong with that?

Sarah went with them on the bus as far as Galway, and while she was there, she reluctantly sold her gold bracelet to a second-hand jeweller's for a fairly good price. Enough to cover the rent and basic expenses for another month, at any rate. Her father had offered her money but she didn't want to dig into his little nest egg. Richard Quinn had worked hard as an electrician for forty years to save that money, and she wasn't about to go spending it, sitting with her feet up in Rose Cottage. She would get a job soon, somewhere, she vowed. Maybe in the chippy!

Next, she went into an Internet café and downloaded her digital camera pictures of the carousel horses and the other nostalgic shots of the old ballroom and the chained-up deckchairs, and she e-mailed them to a publisher friend in London. A publisher who specialized in coffee-table books and illustrated diaries. It was a long shot, of course. Such a long shot it was hardly worth trying at all. But still, she knew it was a good idea. A lovely, glossy desk-diary with lots of blank pages to write notes in, but also lots of full-page photographs of the Irish seaside of yesteryear and suggestions where people might stay nowadays on short breaks in the Emerald Isle. And very timely, too, in these days of paranoia about global warming and too many people criss-crossing the globe in too many planes. She added a brief outline of the plan for her book idea in a short e-mail, attached her contact details and explained that she didn't have a home computer at the moment. Then she sent it all off with a click of a mouse. Magic!

Finally, she went to another second-hand place and sold her camera. She was offered a good price and she agreed to it immediately, before she got all sentimental and changed her mind. To celebrate her windfall, she bought some nice food and wine in the deli in the town centre. Coming home on the bus afterwards, her purse containing the cash she'd swapped her two fat cheques for in the bank, she decided that she would give herself until the start of the summer to enjoy her sojourn in Redstone. And to spend some more time with

Ethan. And after that she would go home to Islington and start looking for work. Any kind of work, even on the check-out in her local supermarket if nothing else turned up.

When she let herself into Rose Cottage again, the restored quietness of it was like a balm to her senses. The guards had been and gone – she wasn't going to be arrested or charged with assault. Thank God. Buddy had been treated in the nearest hospital, delivered to the airport and was now back home in New York again. They were pretty sure he had been cured of his "love" for Victoria Hayes.

Gemma and Victoria were the best of friends once more, laughing over and comparing their "Buddy-bruises". Gemma had scraped a few local columns together and things were looking up. Aurora had told her not to worry about the money she'd lent her, that it could wait until she was on her feet again and what was the world coming to if women couldn't stick together in a crisis?

And Ethan had also proved himself a dependable person in times of trouble. And he hadn't been put off by meeting Sarah's mother. Or by the fact that she was so poor, she was reduced to flogging her possessions in second-hand shops. All in all, life was not too bad.

And then she remembered Abigail's letter. There it was, sitting patiently on the bookcase, where her mother or someone must have set it the day of Buddy's dramatic acquaintance with her lovely statuette from The Silver Birdcage in Dublin. Sarah made herself some tea, marvelling at how addicted she'd become to the feel of a warm cup in her hands. And then she lit the fire, enjoying the barely there powdery texture of the firelighters between her fingers. And finally she sat down in the rocking-chair to read her letter from Abigail, thinking it would be full of hilarious news about the girls, especially Eliza's various antics.

Recognition was slow in coming at first. Even when she read the name, Mackenzie, she couldn't take it in. Abigail and Mackenzie were getting married. Sarah couldn't believe it. They were getting married in June? Abigail had fallen in love with Mackenzie? She had given up her important career in London?

This was so wrong, it was all so *wrong*. This was only happening because they were both lonely and hurt and bereaved and tired of being the strong ones. And yet, when Sarah thought about it, it was obvious the two of them were made for each other. Her eyes were filled with tears by the end of the letter. Dear, sweet Abigail, considerate to the end. Yes, she would give them her blessing. And yes, it would break her heart to do it. Because she would never be able to be friends with Abigail now. It would be too difficult to pretend that Mackenzie had not once been engaged to Sarah. It would be too awkward to pretend that she hadn't slept with Mackenzie for five years and that she knew his body intimately and that she had left him before their own wedding.

"I will write to her tomorrow, or the next day," Sarah told the dancing flames in the grate, glowing orange and purple around the central pyramid of peaty, black turf. There was a small cracking sound as one of the clods of turf split in half with the heat. She watched a shower of bright sparks floating up the chimney and couldn't help having a little cry. It was selfish of her to expect other people to stay in one place, she knew that. Mackenzie and Abigail were free agents. They had done nothing wrong. But still, it was very hard for Sarah to accept they were a couple now. She had lost her best friend, her emotional safety net. She was on her own now in the world, it seemed.

"Yes," she whispered, "I will make this as easy for Abigail as I can. She deserves to be happy, and so does he. But God, I'm going to miss both of them so much." And then she cried again.

Sarah decided then that she didn't want to be reminded of this moment forever more, the moment when she knew she'd lost her best friend. So, when she had read the letter again, she folded the sheets back into their crisp, heavy envelope and she set it reverently on top of the fire. She sighed as she watched Abigail's letter burning down to ashes, and then she also burned the sale-receipt for Mackenzie's gold bracelet and the one for her camera. She would never be able to buy them back, she reasoned, so why bother to keep the receipts?

Sarah made more tea, her hands holding the cup tightly, and said a short prayer that everything would go well for Mackenzie for this, his third attempt to trust and believe in the power of love. After a while, she nipped up the street to pay Mrs Casey her overdue rent money and to buy some things in the shop to complete her dinner plans. Candles, yet another box of matches, napkins, ice-cream.

When Ethan called round later that evening to ask if she wanted to go for a drink in Callaghan's, Sarah pulled him into the cottage, closed the door, put her arms round his neck and kissed him for a long time.

"What was that for?" he asked, laughing, afterwards.

"Are you complaining?" she teased him.

"I am not indeed. I'm delighted."

"It was for being so nice to my parents, that's all."

"Why wouldn't I be nice to them?" he asked, sounding genuinely puzzled.

"Oh, well, not every man would bother going to such trouble for a girlfriend he'd just met. And they're both such dotes when you get to know them. They've got hearts of gold, really."

"No bother to me. I like them," he smiled.

"So do I."

"Well, are we going for this drink or what?" he asked. "Thought we might get some pub grub? I'm starving."

"Actually, if you don't mind, I bought some decent food and a bottle of red wine in Galway this morning. I thought I might attempt to cook for us this evening? Just a steak, nothing gourmet or anything. But I don't really feel like going out to the pub. Do you mind?"

"Surely we can stay in, that'd be much better."

"Plus, I don't want the guards to think I'm out revelling so soon after committing an act of violence, now do I?"

"Good point."

They looked at each other for a moment.

"It's funny to be saying this at our age but … I really like you, Ethan."

"Thank you for the vote of confidence, Miss Quinn. And what I said before still stands," he said softly. "But I know it's early days so I won't say it again for a while."

"Okay. Well, hang up your coat and come on through to the fire. Oh, listen to me, I'm sounding very Irish these days. You'd think it was the 1940s or something and everybody was catching pneumonia!"

She went into the kitchen to fetch the steaks and the salad ingredients out of the fridge.

"Can I do anything to help?" Ethan asked brightly, following her and looking in at the tiny kitchenette.

"No, I don't think we'd both fit in here at the same time," she laughed, "but you could take that little table there and set it beside the big window in the sitting room. I bought some tea-lights as well, so you could light a few of them and maybe set the table?"

"Sure thing," he said. "I'm right on it."

An hour later, they were both sitting comfortably at the tiny table, the steaks eaten, along with a green salad and potato cakes. Sarah had made them by adding chopped salad onions to the mashed potatoes and then forming the fluffy mixture into little flat circles which she fried in butter, the way her mother always did it. The bottle of wine was almost gone and the tea-lights were going out, one-by-one, on the table. Ethan lit some more and made a joke about Rose Cottage looking like a shrine.

"We will have a shrine, when I get my Buddha back from the police station," she laughed.

They could hear the waves crashing onto the beach, less than forty feet away at high tide. None of Sarah's new friends would be calling round to see her tonight. She'd told them she was having dinner with Ethan and they understood what that meant: some serious talking was going to be done.

"I got a letter from Abigail a few days ago," Sarah said. "But what with all the drama that was going on with Buddy, and then my parents staying here, well, I wanted to save it for when I was on my own. Anyway, Abigail said, in the letter,

283

that she's going to marry Mackenzie."

"What? Your Mackenzie?"

"Yes," Sarah smiled. "That's what she called him, too. But he's not my Mackenzie, is he? None of us belongs to anybody, not really."

"Bit sudden, though? What's it been? Not even three months?"

"Yes. They got together at New Year's."

"Are you okay with this?"

"I suppose I'll have to be. The funny thing is, I can't deny they're well suited."

"I don't know what to say. He's a fast mover."

"Yes, he is. But then, he is forty-nine years of age. I suppose he can't afford to mope about for another ten years."

"Really? Forty-nine? Wow, I just assumed he was your age," Ethan said, slightly overwhelmed by this fact, and also by the knowledge that Mackenzie had a country estate in Scotland and that he lived in a listed building with gargoyles on it.

"It wasn't something I gave much thought to when we were together," Sarah said, getting up from the table.

"That was a lovely meal, thank you," Ethan said quickly, getting up as well and lifting their plates. "I'll wash up."

"Leave it," she told him. "Let's just sit and talk for a while."

"Okay."

But when they were sitting close together on the sofa, listening to the wind outside begin to pick up and whistle round the corners of the cottage, they began to kiss again. Very gently and tenderly, each unsure of the other's mood.

Both wishing Sarah hadn't brought up the subject of Mackenzie, for now it seemed as if they were somehow the leftovers in this love story. Well, Sarah still felt a little bit like that. Like she was the immature one, the one who couldn't handle adult emotions.

Ethan didn't *really* feel that he was second best. But the shadow of Sarah's cancelled wedding was definitely hanging over them still. Maybe it always would, he thought sadly. Maybe this new development would make Sarah realize what she had lost, and then she would begin yearning to go back to her life in Scotland. Women were very complicated creatures. He hated even thinking such a prejudiced thing about them but it was true. But until he knew for sure that Sarah was over Mackenzie for good, he couldn't ask her to make any kind of commitment to himself.

"Will you stay with me tonight?" Sarah asked meaningfully, cutting across his thoughts.

"What?"

"You know, *stay with me*, tonight?"

He nodded.

Maybe she wasn't still yearning for Mackenzie after all. At least, he hoped she wasn't . . .

"Come on," she said then, taking him by the hand. "It's cold in here. When the wind blows like that, you just can't heat this room. I did wonder why Mrs Casey hadn't sold this house for a fortune years ago but now I'm beginning to understand. I think perhaps the locals know a cold house when they see one."

Together they went into the bedroom. Sarah had made it much cosier, Ethan noted at once. She'd hung heavier curtains at the window and there was a puffy aubergine-coloured satin throw across the foot of the bed. There was a small lamp with a purple beaded shade on the bedside table. And hanging on the previously bare wall was a small love-heart made of twigs. And there was a small rag-rug on the floor.

"Have you been shopping?" he asked, sitting down gently on the bed, trying not to dislodge the extra few cushions Sarah had placed on it.

"No, just some things my parents brought over from London for me, from my old room. I can take them with me when I leave."

"But you're not going yet?"

"No, I'm staying until the start of the summer at least. After that, well, who knows?"

She switched off the overhead light and left only the smaller lamp on. It threw its mottled violet shadows across the white-painted walls, turning the tiny bedroom into a magical space. The shiny aubergine throw caught the light and sparkled dimly. The fresh white pillowcases were criss-crossed with pleats where she'd ironed them. It all looked very inviting. Sarah sat beside Ethan and kissed him again, tracing the contours of his face with her hands. He had a beautiful face, she thought again. It was almost a pity they were going to sleep together tonight. She didn't want her illusions about him to be shattered. Ethan was very sexy in everyday life: he had graceful hands and sensuous, pouting lips. She'd hate it if he was selfish in bed. Still, it was an experience that she didn't want to put off any longer. It was time to move on. She wasn't Mackenzie's girl any more.

"Shall we get into bed?" she asked him. "It'd be a lot warmer."

"Are you sure we should be doing this yet?"

"Yes, I am."

"Is it because of Mackenzie?" Ethan asked quietly.

"What, because he proposed to Abigail?"

"Yes. I don't mind waiting a bit longer, if it is."

"No. It's not about them. I'm ready now, that's all."

"Okay."

They took off their clothes and slipped under the covers. Sarah could see Ethan's damaged back and his burned side quite clearly, even by the dim light from her beaded lamp, but the scars on his body did not upset her. They were a part of his life and she admired him for saving Patrick Gormley. Even if the poor man hadn't appreciated Ethan's wondrous gesture enough to give him some money for his efforts.

It began to rain heavily, the drops making a pleasant drumming sound on the roof above them. Ethan began to caress Sarah's body beneath the sheets.

"You have beautiful skin," he said. "It's so smooth, like marble . . ."

She initially felt incredibly shy but after a while she began to relax and let him lead the way. He did seem to be every bit as considerate in bed as he was out of it. She slipped one arm around his neck and kissed him again. Soon, she was longing for him to make love to her. Tenderly, gently, as friends, as best friends. She wanted a best friend now because she had just lost the two people she'd once looked up to most, in all the world. She wanted to fill the void left by Mackenzie's huge strength and Abigail's wisdom. And to take away the loneliness she feared would envelop her if she withdrew into herself and wallowed in the end of her relationship with Mackenzie. But she did love Ethan's company and she also fancied him, much more than she had admitted, even to herself. Those perfect lips of his were so beautiful, she couldn't help letting her gaze linger on them when he was talking sometimes.

Now Ethan turned over onto his back and pulled her gently on top of him, pushing one of her knees across his chest.

"Oh, Ethan, let me put the light out first," she whispered.

"Why?"

"I don't want you to see me."

"Why not?"

"I just don't."

"I want to see you."

"Not yet."

She leaned across and switched the lamp off, but there was still some moonlight coming in through a chink in the new curtains. He gently pushed her upwards so that he had a better view.

"You're gorgeous," he told her, admiring her small, high breasts catching what was left of the light. "You shouldn't mind me seeing your body. Your waist, look, it's so small . . ."

She leaned down and kissed him again. A long kiss, this time, long and lingering, and the mood altered suddenly from one of shyness and politeness to something more urgent and immediate. She kissed his neck hungrily. He touched her gently between her legs. Just the lightest of touches but he could tell she was ready. He eased her body back slightly and she guided him inside her and then they were locked together at last. And it was very calming and wonderful and not nearly as embarrassing as she had feared it might be. He had his hands circled firmly round her waist and he was gazing up at her, and they were both smiling.

Then Sarah closed her eyes for a few moments, suddenly shy again as Ethan began to move inside her, pressing gently on her back, asking her if it was okay.

"Yes," she told him. "It's lovely."

Gradually, she gained enough confidence to take over, rocking ever so slightly backwards and forwards, getting into a steady rhythm until she could feel a familiar tingling sensation building up inside her. And then she felt a long, electrifying shudder of pleasure, and Ethan felt one too and they both began to laugh.

"Sorry that didn't last very long," he said, pulling an apologetic face. "It was just too good. It'll be better, next time . . ."

"It was lovely," she said. "Thank you."

She lay down beside him and he kissed her again and she rested her head on his chest and they just lay together under the aubergine-coloured throw, listening to the rain drumming on the roof and the waves hissing and splashing on the beach and wondering which one of them would speak first.

"I love you," he whispered to her, his hands twirling her hair into dark, glossy spirals.

"I love you, too," she answered, on the verge of sleep.

"Sarah, do you mean that? Do you, really?"

"Yes, I do."

"How do you know? I thought it was too soon for you?"

"It feels right," she said. "It just feels right. You're very easy to be with. I can be myself with you. I like that. It's a good feeling."

He kissed her again and they fell asleep.

29

I've Changed My Plea to Guilty

At breakfast, Miriam was in a foul mood. She was banging plates and cups down on the table and spilling the milk and not bothering to clean it up. Patrick looked at the milk stain spreading slowly across the pink checked tablecloth and he was afraid to speak. This open display of bad temper was a new milestone in their relationship. Normally Miriam was so house-proud, he couldn't move anything by half an inch or she'd notice and put it back again.

"You might as well know," she said then, sitting down heavily and glaring at him over the toast-rack. "I slept with a man in New York."

"What did you say?" Patrick's voice was barely a croak.

"I went to bed with a man. A younger man. Just once, mind, just the one time. But it was *wonderful*."

Miriam looked at Patrick as if she hated him. Loathed him. And at that moment, she did hate him. She wished she'd never married him, never even met him.

Patrick's heart was racing with stress, but then again, this was nothing new. He felt the familiar hot flush of panic creeping up the back of his neck, making him feel dizzy and light-headed.

"Well, well, is that right? I wondered why you went to so much bother for Gemma Hayes' daughter. So you fancied a little bit on the side, as it were? Fair play to you. But what are you telling me about it for?"

"I wanted to get pregnant. I did it to get pregnant."

"Oh my God! You mean you didn't use protection? He could have been anyone."

"He wasn't anyone, he was nice. And we did discuss that side of things, if you must know."

"Jesus, have you gone mad altogether?"

"Well, you needn't worry yourself, Patrick dearest. It didn't work. I got my period this morning."

"I see. That explains a lot. The milk –"

"Spilt milk! Is that all you can say?"

"What do you *want* me to say? I'm sorry your American gigolo didn't give you a child? How much money did you spend over there, anyway?"

"A few thousand."

"We can't afford it."

"I know we can't."

"Then why did you go?" he said, his voice getting louder.

"Because I don't care," she said flatly.

"About what?"

"For a start, after this morning, I don't care about having a child any more. It's obviously not going to happen for me. But apart from that, I don't care about the *money* we haven't got. I don't care about you and your blessed *agoraphobia*. I don't care about this fucking house and all the stupid trinkets and crap I've wasted so much of my life collecting. I just don't *care* any more. About anything."

Patrick stared at her.

"I don't believe you," he said in a hoarse whisper. "You love this house."

"Not any more."

"I bought you this house as a wedding present."

"I'm sorry, Patrick. I've changed. I'm bored with the *lavender house* now."

"Are you?"

"Yes. I am. Bored rigid."

Silence.

"In a way, that's a good thing," he told her, then.

"What do you mean? How is it good?"

"We're bankrupt."

"What?"

"I got the letter when you were away. I couldn't keep up the repayments on all the credit cards, Miriam. So last year, I used the house to borrow a massive consolidation loan."

"I didn't sign for any loan."

"I forged your signature on the form. Anyway, it's academic at this stage. Because the consolidation loan has got too much for me as well. They're going to repossess in a couple of months."

"Are you telling me the truth, Patrick?"

"Yes. I am. I owe the loan company forty thousand Euro. There's no use even asking the bank to help us. Neither one of us has a decent job. Anyway, there's no more time to negotiate.

They want their money by the end of next month or we're finished."

Miriam sighed softly.

The room was reeling, or so it seemed. Trinkets and bright colours were whirling round and round her head. She felt as if she might faint.

"I'm sorry I let you down," Patrick was saying. "In more ways than one . . ."

There was no sound in the room for a few minutes except for the ticking of the clock on the wall. Miriam poured herself a fresh cup of tea and drank it, averting her gaze from her husband's shocked, colourless face. There was no point in living in denial any more, she told herself. Patrick hadn't worked in years because he was unable to face people or talk to them in everyday situations. The fishing column was the only work he had and it brought them a mere £150 a week. He didn't like being indoors for long unless it was in his own house. He didn't like being on planes, in trains or on buses. He didn't drive any more either. He didn't like being confined anywhere, in fact, where other people might witness his distress. He never went to the cinema or to the supermarket. He didn't go to weddings, funerals or parties. Or to the hairdresser or to the doctor or to the clinic in Dublin that might have arranged IVF for them. And Miriam didn't go out to work because he didn't like her to be too far away from him during the day. Just in case he got one of his dizzy spells and needed her to talk him out of it. Well, things were not getting any better. He'd said they would get better in time. He'd promised her they would get better, and they hadn't.

"He probably had a vasectomy, that guy I met in New

294

York," Miriam said suddenly, as if to herself. "He probably sleeps with a lot of women. He probably had to get himself sterilized to avoid fathering *dozens* of kids to support. I'm such a stupid bitch, I never thought to ask him if he'd had a vasectomy. Only if he was healthy."

"Would you still have slept with him, if you'd known there was no chance of a child? Did you want to be with another man?"

"What do you care, Patrick? Haven't you got enough worries on your plate already?"

"It would help me to think you only did it to have a baby."

"Would you mind if I was pregnant this morning?"

"I don't know. I really don't know."

"Oh fuck, Patrick. We're in such a fucking mess, aren't we? I don't know what the hell we're going to do."

"Don't leave me, Miriam," he said quietly, his eyes suddenly filling with frightened tears. "I was going to tell you anyway, this morning, about the money. It was only a matter of time before they began calling on the phone. But it needn't be the end of everything. The end of us. We'll sell the house and pay off the debts and buy something smaller. I'll go to the clinic in Dublin. I promise I'll go. And anywhere else you want me to. I'll do it, Miriam, I'll go to the doctor, whatever it takes."

"Will you?" she gasped, her face a study of amazement. "After all this time? Ten years? You always said you would recover by yourself. In time, you said."

"Well, sure, I haven't got better. If anything, I'm getting worse. I made an appointment to speak to the estate agent about getting a valuation but when he turned up with his tape measure and his camera, I couldn't answer the door. I just stood in the hallway, at the side of the bookcase, until he went away. We can't go on like this, Miriam."

"I know we can't."

"And if we did split up, the house would have to be sold anyway. You couldn't run it by yourself, and my wages can't support one house, never mind two. We might as well sell it ourselves and get the best price we can. Otherwise the loan company might be tempted to offload it quickly, at a discount. Plus, they'd hold the purse-strings for months and we'd be destitute in the interim."

"But what about me and that other man in New York? I thought you'd throw me out on the street when I told you."

"Why would I do that? Miriam, I love you."

"But I cheated on you."

"Yes, you did. But I don't blame you. I'm not an easy man to live with."

"Oh, Patrick! I'm so sorry."

"Well, the last ten years haven't been happy years, have they? I haven't been much of a husband."

"But *why*, Patrick? What happened to you? You were so different before we got married. You were such fun, always. You were so much fun to be around, everybody said so."

"I did a bad thing, Miriam. I might as well tell you, since we're in confession mode today. I set fire to the fairground."

"What?"

"You heard me. I set fire to it."

"Why?"

"For the insurance money, for God's sake! It was very well insured."

"But you could have gone to prison. Oh, Patrick, you

complete fucking idiot! Is that why Ethan Reilly got burned that night? Was he trying to stop you? I always thought he was mad for getting so close to the fire when there was nobody else at risk! How could you have done something so mindless, so absolutely stupid?"

"I took a huge chance all right. But my fingerprints were everywhere anyway so there was no way they could prove I did it on purpose. I pushed some chip papers into the grill of the gas heater in the dodgems marquee."

"Patrick! It could have blown up!"

"The cylinder was nearly empty. I checked first."

"But still, you could have been killed."

"Maybe it would have been better if I *had* been killed."

"Don't say that!"

"Why not? It's true, isn't it? I've been living in a nightmare ever since it happened. My fucking nerves, in tatters. Can't even go to the dentist or anywhere without thinking I'm going to have a heart attack. I should have ended it all years ago."

"No!"

"You don't love me any more. You just said you didn't care about anything."

"I was disappointed about not being pregnant."

"Maybe if I was to walk into the sea today and never come out of it . . . You could go back to America and meet a real man and sleep with him over and over, until you knew you were pregnant for sure. Never mind America, you'd have no problem finding another man anywhere. You're a gorgeous woman. You could get married again, no bother to you whatsoever."

"Patrick, don't be like that. You just said you would do

whatever I wanted – you said you would go to the doctor and try to get better."

"Yes, I did say that. Because I hate being like this, Miriam. I hate it, can't you see?"

"Oh, Patrick!" She was sobbing now. "I'm sorry, really sorry. I do love you. I do."

"Do you?"

"Yes! Of course I do. Even though you're such a fool sometimes."

"I know I am. Sometimes I wish Ethan Reilly had never come back that night."

"What do you mean? Because he paid the price for your madness?"

"Of course, there's that! I never wanted anybody to get hurt, in any way. Never mind scarred for life, like he was. But there's more to the story, my darling. Ethan came back to check on things, you see – yes, he did. I think he knew how much the court case was getting to me. A big payout would have ruined us. He told the court he came back to look for his wallet. Anyway, what folks don't know is, when Ethan came back he saved my life. I was still there, Miriam."

"Jesus, Mary and Joseph! This just keeps getting worse and worse! What the hell are you talking about? You were still there? Why the hell were you still there? Patrick Gormley, this had better be good. Or I might just have to pack my bags and go, after all!"

"I had no choice, sweetheart. I was still there because I was trapped in the marquee – my foot was stuck in the dodgems track. We should have got it fixed the day we noticed it, I know that, but the dodgems were our main attraction and I couldn't afford to close them down for a week. To have that piece repaired would have cost me a small fortune in lost revenue. And then, when the fire took hold, I was hurrying to get out, and I jumped over the fence, and I got stuck in that one particular place. Can you believe it? That I would have got my foot caught in the one, single area that was damaged? Poetic justice, I suppose."

"Oh my God!"

"I'd have died if Ethan hadn't come back. There've been times, though, when I wish he hadn't saved me."

"Please, stop saying that! For heaven's sake, Ethan Reilly risked his life to save yours, and you're not even grateful! You didn't even pay him very well when he was working there, now I come to think of it. Pocket money was all you gave him really. And you certainly didn't give him any money after the event. You should have told me. You shouldn't have bought me this house if we couldn't really afford it. Poor Ethan, and there's the whole village thinking he's a bit simple. Ten years, they've thought his behaviour that night was very odd. Running into fires for no good reason and getting himself severely burned. Jesus flipping Christ! I don't know what to think now. Fucking hell! What kind of a man are you, Patrick?"

"I'm a nutcase, Miriam! Isn't that what you think? What Gemma and Aurora think? What *everyone* in this village thinks? Patrick Gormley is a fucking space cadet! Lurking in corners, afraid of his own shadow!"

He stood up and with a roar that nearly scared the life out of Miriam, he up-ended the kitchen table, scattering plates, cups, teapot and milk jug, toast and cutlery in all directions.

"Calm down," she cried. "Stop it! What good will wrecking the house do you?"

"I might as well not be living at all, as living this half-life!" he cried. "Terrified of what'll happen next. I can't stand it, Miriam. I just can't stand it any more!"

"I'll help you, Patrick. Jesus Christ, don't be raging like this. You're scaring me to death. I was used to you the way you were before, but this is scaring the hell out of me. Please be calm and quiet again! I don't want to lose you, Patrick. I don't want to lose you. Please! I love you. *I love you.*" She was crying hysterically now, her heart thumping like a drum.

"What did you say?" he asked, his whole body shaking with ten years of pent-up frustration.

"I love you, Patrick," she whispered.

"Despite everything? The crazy way I am? The debts we've run up because of it?"

"Yes, I love you. Don't leave me alone in this world."

"What about your young lover?"

"He won't remember my name by now," she said in a small voice.

"And he won't turn up here, on our doorstep, declaring his feelings for you?"

"Don't be ridiculous. There's more chance of you starting up an Elvis tribute act," she scoffed, and then they both smiled at each other and stumbled across the remains of their scattered breakfast to hug one another.

"Oh, Patrick, I've been such a fool. Shopping for butter knives and storage baskets when I should have been helping you. When I should have been coaxing you into trying some exposure therapy, like the self-help books suggested."

"Me too. I've been such a fool. What'll we do now?"

"Right, let's think! I'll tidy up this lot, and we'll call the estate agent again. We'll say we forgot about the other appointment altogether. You can go and sit on the pier while he's here and I'll arrange the sale. He might even have a list of potential buyers ready. Then, we'll pack up all of this bloody tat and we'll move somewhere else, just temporarily, and I'll sort out the loan company. And then we'll find a smaller place to buy. And when the dust has settled, in about eight weeks or so, you'll have to get some professional help, and that's final."

"Okay," he said. "Okay to everything."

"And no more secrets. Ever again?"

She wanted it confirmed.

"Agreed. But there's just one thing I want to know."

"What?"

"Why did you wait for ten years to have an affair?"

"It was a one-night stand, not an affair," she said sadly. "Not even a one-night stand, either. A one-afternoon interlude."

"Well, why did you wait so long?"

"It was Sarah," she told him simply. "She told Gemma to think of her flying phobia as a tunnel to float through, not as a brick wall to push against. And that's what I did. To try for a baby, I mean. That's the first image that came to me when I saw Nigel."

"*Nigel*? That's not much of a name for a gigolo, it has to be said."

"You're right. It isn't. Patrick is a much nicer name. I'm sorry, Patrick. Let's start again?"

"Okay," he said, kissing her hand. "We'll start again. We'll make a brand new start. Now, will we take down the paintings and put them away before the viewings begin?"

"What?"

"Brenda Brown's paintings? I read in the paper that art can be stolen when houses are being viewed. Especially smaller-sized pieces that are easy to conceal. People stick all sorts up their jumpers, apparently. We don't want to take any chances. I know how much those pictures mean to you."

"Oh! Patrick . . . I've only just realized . . . we're not going to have to sell the house after all! Thank God you weren't able to answer the door that day or else we'd be halfway through the whole rigmarole right now. Those paintings will be our salvation! Even though I adore each and every one of them. Even though I love them almost as much as I love you. But how fitting that they should be able to save us now!"

"How will they? They were only a couple of hundred pounds each. Or have you been fibbing about the cost of them?"

"No, I have not been fibbing, you eejit! The prices were there in the catalogue, for Jesus' sake! Yes, but they've gone up in value. Do you see? By an awful lot. I was talking to Aurora the other day and she told me Brenda had been over to Los Angeles with her husband, the lovely Sean. They were having a show of her work there. And would you believe it? Nicolas Cage, the actor, he turned up and he bought one of her paintings! I forgot to tell you. It was so exciting to have someone from Redstone mentioned in the national news. You didn't see it?"

"No, I've been too worried about money to bother with the news recently."

"Well, anyway, after Nicolas Cage bought the seascape, there was a scramble amongst the other guests to buy up the rest of the show."

"Nicolas Cage? Would he be a big name, now? What would he have been in recently?"

"Oh, Patrick! You really do need to get out more. He's just about the biggest star in the whole wide world today. Even bigger than Brad Pitt or Johnny Depp or Jake Gyllenhaal."

"Jake who?"

"Will you shut up and listen to me, you hopeless man. And so, Brenda sold everything and now her prices have gone up to around five thousand Euro each, and that's for the smaller pieces. And we've got *nineteen* of them. Oh my God, we're going to be fine, Patrick."

"Nineteen times five is ninety-five thousand. Ninety-five thousand Euro! And you wouldn't mind selling them all? If we needed to sell them all? I mean, obviously it depends on how much we can get for each one . . . But I feel very bad about asking you to do this, Miriam. That collection means everything to you."

"Of course it does, but not as much as you mean to me. You clueless eejit! God help me! If I had any sense, I'd grab the lot of them off the walls and run up the road and never come back. But anyway, we've got to be logical now. The paintings are worth serious money and we need money, plenty of it. We could keep one or two, as an investment. We shouldn't sell them all at once anyway. Oh, whatever, we can ask Brenda and Sean for their advice. They might even help us to stage another show somewhere?"

"Jesus be praised. I think I'm going to have another dizzy spell . . ."

"No, you'll be fine, and we're *saved*. Now we can get straight to work on you."

"What do you mean? I need a lie-down, that's what I need right now."

"Oh, no, you don't! There'll be no more dizzy spells and lying down for you, Patrick Gormley. I'm going to drag you back into the land of the living if it's the last thing I do. Put your hat and coat on right this minute."

"Miriam, please!"

"Don't argue with me. All this avoidance is getting you nowhere, darling. You've got to tackle it head-on from this day forwards. You've got to try, for my sake and for your own. If Ethan Reilly was good enough to get himself nearly killed to save you from the fire that night, the least you can do is try and get back to normal. I'm not asking you to go to the guards and plead guilty to arson. I'm not asking you to go before the courts again and make a clean breast of it. What's done is done, and I don't want to be left homeless, in any case. They'd take the house off us for sure. Never mind the credit card companies. The insurance people would take the house, and we'd have to sell my collection to pay the credit-card debts, and we'd be left without a crumb. Our names in the mud, for all time. Plus, you might end up behind bars."

"Oh God, I never thought of that! I can't go to prison, Miriam. I can't. That's my worst nightmare. I'd go mad in ten minutes," Patrick said, his face white with fear.

"Yes, well, you won't have to go to prison if we keep our mouths shut. But I'll tell you what! We will have to give Ethan Reilly whatever we have left after the debt is paid. I promise you that. Now, come on. We're going to Aurora's for coffee to celebrate our salvation from the poorhouse. And you're going to sit in that café for thirty minutes and not a second less. We'll make a start on the exposure therapy today."

"No way, I'm not setting one foot out of this house today," he said firmly, going into the sitting room and perching on the edge of one of the comfy white sofas.

"But you promised me you would really try, Patrick," she said gently. "You said you would really try this time."

"Yes, and I will try. But it's not the agoraphobia that's keeping me indoors today. It's the paintings. I'm not leaving these paintings unattended until they're all sold, or at least safely stored off the premises, my darling. I mean, they're not even insured . . ."

30

Every Day I Write The Book

It was the first day of May. Aurora had been jumpy all morning. She'd put a little notice in the window of The Last Chapter a few days earlier announcing the inaugural meeting of her new, improved book club here in Redstone. Business in the bookshop had been quite good in recent months and she had also introduced a little sideline in unusual greeting cards. She had about fifty regular customers that she knew by name. Hopefully at least ten of them would turn up this afternoon. She had enough seating for twelve around the three tiny tables in the café area, and four tall barstools tucked in at the counter. Possibly, another dozen people could dot themselves around the shop, if need be. She had a big bowl of sweets beside the cash register, and some fresh coffee brewing, and a stack of paper cups at the ready. But no official membership cards and no silly platform for herself to stand on. And no delusions of grandeur, either. This book club was going to be about friendship, and books, and nothing else. She dimmed the lights slightly, just in case any of her potential bookworms were extra-shy, and she waited. Her dark-green painted store had never looked more inviting.

And Aurora herself was looking quite different today, too. She'd had a bit of a makeover in honour of the occasion. Gemma had persuaded her to have her long hair cropped right off and dyed a warm honey-blonde. And the old-fashioned skirts and shoes had been swapped for wide-leg trousers, modern wedges and a slim-fitting polo-neck. Heck, she was even wearing bright red lipstick. The old Aurora was barely recognisable. She polished the counter for the tenth time that morning, gave the glass in the window another rub and checked the bathroom for loo paper and soap. Even though she'd already checked it ten times that day.

At one o'clock, the first curious potential members began drifting in the door or walking up and down the promenade, checking out the lie of the land. Gemma and Victoria came in to support her, as did Miriam and Patrick. Though Patrick did remain standing resolutely by the door and he kept checking his watch. But at least he was *in* the shop and that was the main thing. Sarah and Ethan came too, though Ethan was on his lunch break from the garage and would soon have to go back, he said. When everyone had arrived, Aurora counted a perfect fifteen new faces, and the meeting was declared open. There was a light smattering of applause as the coffee and sweets were handed out, and then Aurora spoke very briefly from behind her little counter and the list of suggested reading was announced, with the titles on offer at a discounted price. She said they could vote for the book they would have to read for the following week's club.

Much chatter ensued as the voting got under way, and just as Aurora was about to begin reading a sample chapter to get things started, the door of the shop rattled open and there stood . . . David Cropper himself.

In full-on Victorian-dandy mode. Wasp-waisted black frock coat and a white linen shirt complete with silky white necktie. His hair an elegant bouffant sweep and his shoes gleaming like black glass. He carried a silver-topped walking stick in his left hand. He came right into the shop, smiling from ear to ear, and bowed to them all with an extravagant wave of his hand.

And then he noticed that he was the only one in costume.

You could have heard a pin drop.

"Oh dear," he began. "I was given to believe that the Brontë Bunch had risen from the ashes. Is this not the case?"

No one answered him.

Aurora, with her newly cropped hair, had not yet registered on David's panorama. She was temporarily paralysed with equal amounts of desire and rage. Oh, he did look ravishing in that coat, she thought wistfully. He'd even perfected the quick, light-footed walk to go with it. And if she'd been on her own in the shop, she might have given in to temptation. Swept the bowl of Raspberry Ruffles off the counter and divested him of his trousers there and then. But she wasn't alone. She was surrounded by her new crop of bookworms and she didn't want to become a laughing stock for a second time.

"Everyone, this is my friend David Cropper," she began, and they all looked from David to Aurora and back again. "Can you just chat amongst yourselves for a moment? Thank you."

He scuttled through the tables and chairs towards her.

"Aurora? But my darling, what on earth have you *done* to your hair?" he said quietly, his forehead wrinkling with disappointment. "Are you wearing – make-up? What is going on here?"

"David, we'll get to that. First of all, how did you find out about the new book club?"

"I saw a notice for it on the Internet."

"I didn't advertise it on the Internet."

"No, well, somebody mentioned it on their weekly blog about Redstone," he admitted, sounding slightly embarrassed.

"Have you been googling Redstone?"

"Perhaps I have had a brief perusal. From time to time."

"Oh, David. Why do you bother?"

"Because I love you," he said, bowing his head slightly in homage to her. The assembled crowd were all ears, straining to hear every word. Whoever said book clubs were boring?

"Right, that's enough silliness for one day," Aurora told him, coughing loudly. "I have a book club to run here. Please leave now, David, or I'll think of some way to punish you for gate-crashing my little get-together."

"I am going nowhere," he said politely, striking up a defiant pose by the cash register.

"Fair enough, you've asked for this," she whispered.

She turned to face her expectant bookworms, to make an important announcement.

"My learned friend has kindly offered to take over from myself as reader today," she said, clapping her hands together with a little flourish. David's cheeks began to redden. Now, Aurora thought to herself, now he'll be off out the door like a shot. For surely he wouldn't hang around The Last Chapter, reading aloud to a small group of housewives and farmers wearing puffy anoraks and jeans?

But she was sadly mistaken. For David wasn't going anywhere, and he definitely wasn't giving up on their reconciliation so easily.

"Ahem," he faltered. "Very well, if you insist. Good afternoon, ladies and gentlemen. I have here with me, in my pocket, a selection of poems by Lord –"

"Oh no, I've already chosen a piece, thank you. Everyone, I give you *Dangerous Kiss* by Jackie Collins. Read by my very dear friend Mr David Cropper. Take it away, David!"

Applause filled the shop. It was surprisingly loud.

Aurora handed David his copy of *Dangerous Kiss* and sat down behind her counter. She poured herself a coffee and winked at him. She was going to enjoy this. Oh wow, was she going to enjoy this! David's face was turning purple with shame and humiliation. She was giggling already.

31

Hold onto Your Friends

And so, June crept around at last. The summer had finally elbowed its way into Redstone village and the rest of the country, drying up the countless spots of mildew and damp that had formed in various domestic nooks and crannies over the previous long and wintry months. The sun was shining, high up in the sky. A rare enough day in Ireland, with not a single cloud to drift across its golden, pulsating shimmer. Day-trippers were arriving in merry, horn-tooting convoys from Galway and the surrounding towns, spilling onto the beach with heavy picnic hampers and soft tartan blankets. Sandcastles were being built and the ice-cream machine at the newsagent's was working overtime. The B&B signs were going up outside freshly pastel-painted bungalows along the coast road. And Sarah was moving out of Rose Cottage. Just as the roses in the backyard were coming into bloom.

She'd decided to take Ethan up on his generous offer to

move in with him, to share with him his little home overlooking the bay. A tiny two-bedroom affair with doll's-house windows and only space for one two-seater sofa in the sitting room. The house was bare and empty now, with white walls and stripped floorboards, but Sarah knew she could work her magic on it with her various bits and pieces, collected over the years and stored in her old attic room in Islington. The house needed a woman's touch, Ethan had said. And she'd told him she'd be willing to give it a go. Just a light and harmless little exchange of words, like that, and it was settled. No serious declarations of love and marriage and children. Those things would come in time, they both knew it. The love part was there already.

Sarah had already spent several nights in Ethan's pine double bed. Sleeping in his arms, listening to the restful sound of his breathing, mingling with the sound of the waves breaking endlessly on the rocks below. He'd given her a key to the house and she'd slipped it onto her green apple key-chain. They'd not got around to moving her bed out beside the picture-window but never mind, because Ethan's bedroom had amazing sea views.

They were holding a party tonight, however, before she handed the big brown key to Rose Cottage back to Mrs Casey. A goodbye party for the pink house, for the next tenant would be moving in shortly.

"Do you want this ice in the basin now?" Ethan asked, coming back from the shop with six packets of ice cubes in a cooler-bag.

"Might as well," she told him. "It'll never fit in the mini-freezer. God, I hope this party isn't going to be a disaster. I'm nervous as anything."

"It'll be fine," he assured her, and his smile was wider than ever. "I told you, we're easy-going folks around here. We'll make our own fun, don't worry."

"Well, we've done the best we can with this room," Sarah said, viewing the blue and white streamers criss-crossed on the ceiling, the bunches of iris and sunflowers in jars and tins on the windowsills and the coffee table groaning under stacks of nibbles and treats, some of which she'd made herself, though most of the fancier ones had been made by Miriam and brought across earlier in the car by Patrick.

Sarah was wearing black flared trousers and a simple red vest, with her hair up in a high ponytail. She just had time to check her make-up in the mirror before the guests began to arrive.

First in the door were Gemma and Victoria, Gemma looking vampish in a tight black dress, kitten heels and with a tiny silk rose clipped to her combed-back fringe. Victoria wore a pair of faded blue jeans and a sequinned bolero jacket, and her hair had been straightened with irons and sleeked down with serum. She'd gained a few pounds and the haunted look was finally gone from her face. They handed Sarah two good bottles of wine and a big box of chocolates and said hello to Ethan.

"Wow, you both look fantastic!" Sarah cried. "You're showing me up, totally," she scolded.

"Stop it, you're gorgeous," said Gemma, laughing. "You're so tall, you'd look good in anything. And that red lipstick really suits you."

"Aw, thanks. I'm really glad you could both make it."

"Try stopping us. Now, we've come a little bit early, Sarah, because I wanted to tell you my good news. I've been offered a job on a big magazine."

"No way! What one?"

Gemma pulled the latest edition out of her handbag and held it up for Sarah to see. It was one of the UK nationals, an inch thick and very expensive looking.

Sarah's eyes were pools of good-natured jealousy. "Congratulations. You *cow*!"

"Isn't it brilliant?" Gemma laughed. "And I'll get four entire pages to fill every month, on my own, with whatever I want to write about. And the money is *fantastic*. I might even give up writing novels, if it works out. They're far too much like hard work! And I'll get a modest expenses allowance. And some freebies, they said. Whatever the editor doesn't want gets divided between the sub-editors and the columnists, and so on."

"Oh, Gemma, I'm so pleased for you." Sarah gave her friend a huge hug. "Congratulations! Oh, well done!"

"You'll never believe how I got the gig," Gemma laughed.

"How?"

"Mike! At my old paper! He put my name forward to the editor, told her I was far too good for a tabloid. Isn't that a miracle? After what I said to him the day we went to New York. I was in shock all day yesterday. Then I sent him some flowers. I guess he wasn't such a bad old stick after all. They bumped into each other at a media dinner in Dublin."

"That's really good news, Gemma. You deserve it, really. Though it was very good of Mike to remember you like that," Sarah said, pouring Gemma and Victoria very small glasses of wine. (They were both new recruits to the cult of healthy eating, these days.) Gemma then ushered Sarah into the kitchen and told her that she'd been asked out on a date by one of the people she'd spoken to on the phone at the magazine.

"He was lovely, Sarah. Really lovely," Gemma said happily.

"What did you say?"

"I said I couldn't possibly."

"Gemma!"

"No, I said I had to spend some time with my daughter. I mean, she'll only be with me for a year or two longer, Sarah. And then, she'll be off again on her travels. Perhaps for good, this time. I think she's learned her lesson, truly. If she gets into any more trouble, it won't be her fault. Poor sweetheart. I love her so much, Sarah. I want to spend every spare minute with her from now on, and then I'll have no regrets when she does fly the nest."

"You're a great mum, Gemma. But don't cut romance out of your life for good," Sarah said thoughtfully.

"I won't," Gemma said, slipping the magazine back into her bag. "It's only for a little while. And the best part is, I can go over to London, if I have to, by boat and train!"

Then Victoria came into the kitchen, looking for a fork so she could sample the cheesecake and the conversation about potential romancing was closed. They could hear the front door being opened, and then Aurora and David came shyly into the room. Looking very bizarre in normal, up-to-date clothes. David in baggy, beige slacks and a toffee-coloured crew-neck sweater. And Aurora in a fitted white summer-dress and peep-toe shoes. They'd brought a big basket of strawberries and a pot of double cream to the party.

"Thanks so much for this," Sarah said, hugging her friend and shaking hands formally with David. They hadn't reached the hugging stage yet because David was still working in Belfast during the week and driving down to Redstone at weekends. But that suited Aurora, because she said David was "still on probation".

"You look lovely, the pair of you," Gemma trilled, still on a high from her new job offer.

"Oh, we'll do, I suppose," Aurora laughed. "I'm still getting used to this new hairstyle of mine. It's a lot more bother than a bun. But anyway, I like it."

"It really suits you," all the women said automatically.

Aurora shrugged modestly.

No need to tell the world she'd not got round to throwing out her corset and bonnet yet. And that sometime soon, she might feel inclined to put them on again. But only for David's delectation, this time . . . She felt bad about wearing such symbols of female oppression in bed. But then again, that frock coat of his really did get her going in that department.

Miriam and Patrick were next in the door, Miriam dressed like a Christmas tree in a green dress with a red glittery shawl draped round her shoulders, a red handbag and shoes and several red bangles on each wrist. Patrick was still very uncomfortable at parties but they found him a seat near the door and assured him he wouldn't be missed if he wanted to nip home early, but that they'd love to see him still there at the end of the night. If he thought he could stick it out. He said he would give it a go, definitely. And he blew his wife a kiss as she twirled round the floor, displaying her new outfit.

"How did the sale go?" Sarah asked them.

"Is it that obvious? We sold ten!" Miriam said, her eyes shining with delight.

"Get away," Sarah gasped.

"Yes. Brenda said not to put the full collection all on sale at once, for fear of destabilizing the market, so we put ten up for sale in that gallery in Dublin, and they all went on the first day. We've paid off the bills, and everything's hunky-dory."

"Oh, Miriam, that's such good news," Gemma sighed. She'd been praying for years that Miriam and Patrick would do something about their problems.

"Yes, and I'm going to work in the newsagent's, and Patrick's going to do two days a week in the garden centre outside Galway, aren't you, Patrick?"

He nodded shyly. He was going to give it a go, anyway.

"You got the shop job?" Sarah asked then.

"Yes, they said you'd changed your mind," Miriam replied. "I wouldn't have taken it otherwise. But they said you didn't need it now so they offered it to me. Oh, don't say you're leaving us, Sarah? Is that why you're having a party?"

"I'm not leaving the village, no. The thing is, everyone, I've a little announcement of my own to make! They're going to publish my seaside-theme diary!" Sarah said breathlessly.

"Hooray!" they all cheered, and Ethan opened a bottle of champagne.

"Sarah, you should have told us," Gemma said, wagging her finger in admonishment. "We would have bought you a card."

"I only heard two days ago," she told them all. "I couldn't take it in, at first. But anyway, they're going to bring out a bigger-size diary for 2009 and it's going to have all my photos in it and lots of quotes from celebrities about their childhood holiday memories as well. The money isn't princely but it's not bad, at the same time. And there might well be royalties, if it sells well. The upshot is, I'll be able to go on freelancing for another while. And I'm also going to do some food shots for my old place, while their current lead photographer is off on sabbatical. I guess the novelty must have worn off pretty quickly for him."

"Well, isn't that glorious news altogether?" Aurora said. "You must give me the name of the publisher. I want first call on the Redstone delivery! I'll set up a special display in the window."

Then the door opened again and Mrs Casey came in, with her four daughters and their families, and the Callaghans from the pub, all of Ethan's mates from the garage and even the chippy girls, with whom Sarah was now on first-name terms. Ethan put some sophisticated background music on his portable stereo and the party was under way. Towards the end of the night, Miriam tried to make Ethan accept a cheque from herself and Patrick, to thank him for what he had done that night ten years ago. But Ethan refused to even consider taking the money.

"I told Patrick at the time, I didn't want any money. It wasn't his fault I got hurt. He told me to get out, to save myself. But I wasn't going to leave him there, was I? I would have done the same thing for anyone else, Miriam. So thank you, but really, no."

"I thought you might say that," Miriam said, smiling at him. "Patrick told me you wouldn't want to know. Well, in that case, will you take this painting? Please? It's only a little one, the smallest canvas we have. But funnily enough, it's the one that always meant the most to me. And now, Patrick and myself have sorted out quite a lot of things, and we're both very grateful to you for what you did. The sacrifice you made. And I want you to have this. Please take it? And I promise you, this is the last you'll hear from either of us on the subject. It's time we left all this business in the past."

She handed him the canvas, and he took it and thanked her.

"Isn't it lovely?" Miriam said. "It's called *Seabirds*."

32

Love is a Wonderful Colour

On the morning of her wedding to Mackenzie, Abigail answered the door in a flurry of excitement, expecting it to be her bouquet arriving from the florist. But it wasn't the bouquet, just yet. It was a small parcel that she had to sign for. A cardboard box, wrapped in thick, brown paper and tied up with old-fashioned white string. Abigail was intrigued. The postmark was Irish. Who could be sending her a wedding gift from Ireland? It could only be Sarah. Yes, there was Sarah's name on the back.

She hadn't told a lot of people about this wedding. Just a few of the girls. Eliza had sent her a lovely pair of bedroom slippers. She couldn't make it to the wedding, she said, because she was off to New York to style a photo-shoot for her magazine. Some hot new actor called Nigel-something had just won a role in a major movie set in a bakery, and she was going over there to cover him in flour and take some black-

and-white shots of him lying on the counter wearing nothing but an apron . . .

Abigail took her parcel to the kitchen to carefully remove the string with a pair of sharp scissors.

"What've you got there?" asked Millicent, feeding the dogs and giving them fresh water.

After the wedding, she'd be moving into one of the newly renovated cottages near the village. She was looking forward to putting her feet up, she said. And she was, in a way. But mostly, she was determined to give her son and his new wife some space, both for them and for the twins. It was early days, of course. Abigail was only three months into her pregnancy. But still. Abigail was the lady of the house now and it was only fitting that Millicent step aside and give the happy couple breathing space. And besides, the new cottages were gorgeous inside! All mod cons. And best of all, they would be warm as toast in the winter. Oh, what a joy it would be to wake up each morning and put her feet out of bed and onto that lovely soft carpet instead of draughty wooden boards. Bliss. And of course, Donal's father was going to be living next door. Dishy sort of man, she thought happily. The father of Abigail's late boyfriend. And a widower, too. Abigail had offered to rent him one of the cottages, and he'd moved up from London the week before, saying how it was a dream come true for him and that he'd always loved the Scottish countryside. He was going to the wedding today. Maybe he'd give her a dance at the party afterwards . . .

"A parcel from Sarah."

Abigail had the paper off the parcel now and she was lifting something small and flat out of the box and unwrapping it from some sheets of tissue paper.

"Oh, I think it's a picture frame," Millicent said, pleased Sarah had sent a gift.

"I don't know if it is a picture frame, it's very light," said Abigail. "Wait, I think it's a painting. It is a painting! Of two seabirds. Look, Millicent. It's beautiful, isn't it?"

"Gorgeous little thing. How lovely of Sarah! What a lovely gesture."

"I know. The painting is by Brenda Brown, I see. Isn't she quite famous these days? There was something about her on the news recently. She lives in Redstone, actually. I hope she didn't spend a lot of money on this painting . . . Oh, here's a note."

Dear Abigail,

There's a long story attached to this painting. And it's not up to me to tell it, now or ever. But it was given to a dear friend of mine, Ethan, in recognition of a favour he did some time ago. And Ethan gave the painting to me. You might as well know, we're an item! And now, I'm giving it to you both, as a wedding gift. I just wanted to say how much I will miss you and that you were the best friend a girl ever had. I'm going to stay here in Redstone, and I've got photography work coming in so I won't have to be selling ice-cream after all – remember how I used to joke about that! Anyway, I hope you have a wonderful day today, Abigail, and that Mackenzie and yourself have many, many happy years together.

Lots of love always, God bless,
Sarah.

"Well, now, wasn't that lovely of her?" Millicent said, wiping a tear from her eye.

"Yes, indeed it was," Abigail replied.

It was a goodbye letter. She would never see Sarah again. She felt like sobbing, but she couldn't possibly do that. She'd ruin her make-up and Mackenzie would be waiting for her in the church by now. And there wasn't time to do it all again.

The front doorbell rang again and Millicent scuttled to answer it.

"It's the flowers," she called. "And the wedding car. Are you ready?"

"I'm coming," Abigail said, gazing at the painting for another few precious seconds. The two seabirds circling each other in the hazy, blue sky. Each one beautiful on its own, but somehow even more perfect together, sweeping their wings across the cotton-wool clouds, forming a perfect circle.

"I'm coming," she said, hoping her red velvet gown wasn't going a bit too far for Glenallon. She wrapped the picture in its tissue paper again and set it down reverently on the kitchen table. She'd decide where to hang it when she came back from the church. They weren't going away on honeymoon after the wedding. They just wanted to take it easy because of Abigail's pregnancy.

"Abigail?" Millicent was worried about the time getting on. "Don't want to rush you but we shouldn't keep Mackenzie waiting much longer. I've got the bouquet in the car for you and all. Are you ready?"

Abigail lifted her shawl from the back of the chair and draped it around her shoulders.

"Goodbye, Sarah, and good luck, and thank you," she said, as she walked out of Thistledown for the last time as a single girl.

THE END

324

If you enjoyed *It Must Be Love*,
don't miss out on
The Trouble with Weddings

Here is a sneak preview of Chapter one . . .

The Trouble with Weddings

SHARON OWENS

1

Dream Weddings
November 2006

H<small>I, THERE.</small>
Oh, wait a minute.

Just had another text in from Julie.

Fifth one today from Julie, that is.

She needn't worry – I can manage on my own for a few days.

Yes, I did warn the violinists they'll have to wear full-length brown fur coats to the Patterson wedding. And yes, I have hired brown fur coats for all seven of them, in the correct sizes, yes, to be delivered from London in good time for the occasion. And yes, I have checked the coats will be security-tagged and fully insured for their little trip to Carrickfergus.

And, send.

God love those poor guys, they don't know what they've let themselves in for. They'll be sweltered playing

Tchaikovsky up to their eyeballs in mink but Narnia is huge at the moment, theme-wise. Huge as anything, I just can't tell you. At least they won't have to turn up in beaver costumes or appear as wicked elves with long pointy boots on their feet. Both of those ideas were mooted by the bride's mother but Julie put her foot down. She likes a laugh, does Julie, but we always have the reputation of Dream Weddings to think of. The bride is dressing as the Snow Queen in palest blue fur. With a two-foot-tall delicate silver crown attached to the top of her head with extra-strong elastic. And the groom is going to surprise her with a sleigh on wheels when they come out of the church after the ceremony. Obviously if it actually snows real snow on the day, we're laughing. And it might just do that 'cos the wedding's on Christmas Eve. But if Mother Nature lets us down, we're going to fill the carpark with three tons of rice-paper flakes. No expense is being spared – the bride's family owns an international haulage company. Well, I have to admit Miss Patterson does look exquisite in that blue fur and, you know what they say, you can't take it with you. (And the Pattersons do give a lot of money to charity so that's okay.) We're even going to make it 'snow' inside the ballroom at the end of the night. Nothing in this business surprises me any more. Wait a minute, now Julie's texting me about the rice paper. Yes, I have obtained permission from the hotelier to shake bags of paper flakes from the rafters in the ballroom. We've lined up three game teenagers who're going to be dressed as snow-clouds.

And, send.

Julie's in New York this week, would you believe? I say

this week but really it's only for four days and then she's flying on to Los Angeles with Henri. Henri's a financial whizz and big-time deal-fixer and also Julie's new boyfriend. He's cultured and polite and extremely good-looking. Eyes so dark you'd think they were made of black glass. And muscles! Well, forget about it. Even his muscles have muscles. When I first met Henri I thought he was gay, his clothes were that perfect. But Julie assured me he definitely didn't play for the other side.

"He's only French," she said.

I'm sure he has a flaw of some kind but we're still waiting to see what it is. Henri's in New York to set up some meetings with an elite group of arthouse film directors and an even more elite group of serious actors (darling), and Julie's there to attend one of the biggest bridal fairs in the developed world.

Oh! There's the phone again.

"Hello. Dream Weddings, can I help you? Our brochure? Of course, if you just give me your address? I'll pop one in the post. Yes, we are very busy at the moment. Fully booked for the next two years, to tell you the truth. Yes, really we are! Yes, you can book now for November 2008 if you forward our little holding fee – it's all there in the brochure. Okay? Lovely. Thank you so much. Cheerio."

I told Julie, don't come back to Belfast with a load of frilly white dresses and traditional veils and posies because we are so getting into the fantasy wedding market these days, it's not funny. Ever since that rock-star wedding we did a few months ago, Dream Weddings has been absolutely inundated with calls. I mean hundreds and hundreds of phone calls and e-mail enquiries from prospective brides and grooms. And even married couples wanting to renew their vows and have another party because they feel they missed the boat, style-wise, first time round. Honestly! The women all wanting Gothic gowns and fairytale capes, and kitsch pink limousines and pink champagne, and Victorian black bouquets and I don't know what else. And the guys are binning the top hat and tails and going for snazzy tailoring. And super-short ceremonies are the order of the day now, with no embarrassing speeches or the endless reading out of dreary telegrams at the reception afterwards. Most of the men we've met would rather die than attempt public speaking so we have a professional speechmaker on our books and he's getting gigs right, left and centre. I'm telling you, it's definitely the end of the white wedding as we know it. Goodbye to the blushing bride and all that.

Today's woman knows what she's getting on the honeymoon. And a good thing too. As Julie always says to me (and only to me, mind you), what's the big deal about white weddings anyway? I mean, no woman would dream of buying a car without taking it for a test-drive first. Julie's words, not mine. So why on earth would she throw in her lot with any guy before she's made certain-sure he can treat her tenderly when the lights go out?

And Julie should know. When it comes to men and weddings, Julie Sultana wrote the book. And that's why Julie will never get married herself. Ever. I mean, she says she won't but I hope she will, one day. But for now, Julie says she's still looking for Mr Right and she's having a lot of fun doing it and you can't blame her for that.

Oh, my name is Margaret Grimsdale.

Mags, for short.

I'm Julie's PA at Dream Weddings.

Author interview with Sharon Owens

1. Have you always written or is it a new discovery?

ANS: I have always loved reading but I only began writing in 2001. I had just finished reading a novel and I remember saying to my husband Dermot that I was really hoping the heroine would have done something differently, that I was disappointed by the ending. And he asked me why I didn't write a book myself. Of course I thought he was joking but the following week he bought me a desk and a computer (and showed me how to use it) and I've never looked back.

Until then I thought writers were special people who were born with a gift. But the truth is anyone can do it if they're prepared to work day and night for about a year. If they've lived at all, and had their ups and downs, and can use a dictionary, then they can write a book.

2. Tell us about your writing process; where do you write? When? Are you a planner or "ride-the-wave" writer?

ANS: I'd like to be able to write only when the muse strikes. But I have to keep to strict deadlines these days. I also write a weekly column and a weekly book review for the Belfast Telegraph. I have a house to keep tidy and a husband and a teenage daughter (Alice) to look after and the worst PMS in the world. So I can't afford to lie about watching telly and thinking about the universe and everything.

I have a very small desk in the corner of our bedroom, and a big comfy chair. I like a small desk because it's impossible to mess it up with clutter and old cups of tea. Our bedroom is painted a coffee colour and is also very tidy. I'm a typical Belfast housewife: everything has to be spotless, all the time.

So I'm up at 7am to get my darlings out to work and school (Dermot is an IT manager and Alice is in fifth year at an all-girls' Grammar in Belfast) and then I load the dishwasher, load the washing machine and go up to my desk with a cuppa. I rarely eat or get dressed before lunchtime. I like writing in my PJs, bare feet and fluffy dressing gown for some reason, though it is rather embarrassing when I have to answer the door to a Tesco delivery or the Post Office van or the electric meter man and so on... (I always say I'm in bed with a cold.) I write from 8am until 12 noon and then I get showered, dressed and made-up and go for a good long walk and buy the paper.

I read the paper in the afternoon, tidy the house and begin cooking dinner at 4pm. At about 7pm I get into bed and read novels until 10pm. Dermot and Alice sometimes come in and bring me tea and sit on the bed and we all have a chat. That's my favourite time of the day. I rarely watch TV any more: just my Seinfeld collection on DVD at weekends.

3. Since your first novel *The Tea House on Mulberry Street* was published in 2003 has your life changed much?

ANS: Indeed it has. I'm not a millionaire but I'm not as poor as a church mouse any more either. I passed my A levels in 1986, gaining the highest marks in NI that year for Art. Then I dropped out of Manchester Art College due to a lack of money and spent two years working in pubs and shops before going to UU Belfast (Art College) to get my degree in book design. I married Dermot at 24 and had Alice when I was 25: I spent the entire pregnancy bedridden with chronic nausea and weight loss amounting to 42 pounds. Thankfully Alice was born a healthy 9 pounds by C-section after I fell unconscious after 6 hours of labour, bringing my final post-baby weight down to just over 7 stone. Which for my height of 5.8 was a shocking sight to behold. I wasn't fully recovered for years afterwards. Needless to say I was in no hurry to get back to work so I spent eight wonderful years as a full-time mum to Alice. She is the light of our lives.

All in all, from the time I left home at 18 in 1986 until I got my first publishing deal in 2003, I was flat broke. I wore the same coat for 13 years: it never wore out and I just forgot to buy a new one. So when Teahouse became a best seller in Ireland and was then bought by Penguin UK for a six-figure sum, I went a bit mad! I set aside enough to cover my fees and taxes and I spent the rest in three weeks.

I paid off our mortgage: it wasn't that big as the house was bought at 1992 prices. I bought a new bathroom with a lovely shower, a new kitchen, a new car for Dermot, new clothes for the three of us, a new shed and new lawnmower to go in it, and lots of new shoes for my size 9 feet. I love DMs so I bought four pairs. It was a wild, crazy three weeks. I gave my sister some money to move to a better flat in London and I began sponsoring a child through World Vision. Then I became sensible again. Now I stick to a relatively normal budget.

4. Do you have a favourite character in the novel?

ANS: No, I love them all. Some of my characters are based on myself, such as Mags in The Trouble with Weddings. She's a 40-year old who still loves her husband, and also loud rock music. The other characters are composites of people I know and people I've read about. But none of them are exactly based on real people: that wouldn't be fair.

5. What character & scene was most difficult to write?

ANS: Again, I wouldn't say writing is hard for me. When I'm at my computer the story just flows and it's as if I'm reading a book to myself. Even I'm surprised by what my characters get up to. I suppose if there was one scene that was hard, it was when Mags' father dies in The Trouble with Weddings. Because she has mixed feelings about his death. And for me that was an expression of how some people can become obsessed by politics, for example, and neglect their own children as a result. It must be very sad when you lose a loved one, yet feel you never really knew them.

6. Who are your favourite authors and favourite novels and why (worldwide and Irish based authors)?

ANS: My favourite Irish author was the late Brian Moore. I love all his books though The Lonely Passion of Judith Hearne, An Answer from Limbo and The Feast of Lupercal are my favourites. My favourite living writers are Anne Dunlop and Claire Allan: because they are both natives of Northern Ireland and they understand what it's like to come from this No Man's Land that we all love, but it's a very complicated and demanding love.

I think the Northern Ireland sense of humour is different from other areas in the British Isles. It's lightning-quick because it has to be, because we are always scanning the room to make sure nobody is going to take offence and start a riot! I didn't grow up only caring about shoes and hairstyles and discos: I had to look out for bombs and potential trouble and unattended packages on the Courthouse steps. I was close to two major bombs when they went off in the 1980s but back then it wasn't something anyone talked about. You just got your hearing checked out at the doctor's and carried on. So my sense of humour is more dark than girly, I daresay. I don't care what I look like or if my hair's like a yard brush, as long as my loved ones are safe and sound.

Worldwide, I would have to say I prefer British authors such as Jenny Éclair and JK Rowling. Jenny is hilarious and very dark indeed, and JK is gothic and every detail is keenly observed. At Art College I had an idea to design a book that looked old and tattered like a spell book, but JK beat me to it with her tales of Beadle the Bard. I'm so, so jealous of that book and I've not even read it yet.

I don't usually like to read books set in faraway places as the cultural references can be so different but these days I am deliberately reading a much wider range for my book review page in the Belfast Telegraph. I've just started re-reading the complete works of my late great-uncle Dr Benedict Kiely, who was a Saoi of Aosdana.

7. Tell us a bit about your next book – have you started writing it yet?

ANS: My next book is called The Seven Secrets of Happiness, and I'm 200 pages in. It's a love story between the beautiful Ruby O'Neill, a widow, and Martin Lavery, a reclusive widower. And the seven secrets are seven little stories that are scattered throughout the novel: each one starts off with the sale of a handbag from Ruby's shop. I'm hoping this will be my biggest book yet, it's the one book I have really slaved over. It's going to be 400 pages long and my most emotional writing ever.

8. **Style, description and fashion seem to be an integral part of your novels - woven with such emotion and beauty in all your writing. Do you consciously focus on the visual impact of your novels?**

ANS: Yes, thank-you very much for noticing. I do love beauty and beautiful things because real life can be drab and grey and unpredictable and heartbreaking. Yes, it can be fun too. But beauty is always there, isn't it? Even when it begins to fade and weather. I am inexplicably drawn to Victorian and Gothic things: funeral coats, expensive marble fountain pens, wrought-iron gates and bone china teapots. I think I may have lived before, in Victorian times, as I love lighting a coal fire and wax candles, and I'd rather walk than drive, and read a letter than an email. I also love hats, gloves, umbrellas and my husband's high cheekbones and Roman nose. I think Nicolas Cage is absolutely gorgeous, and so is Helena Bonham Carter. I like a lived-in look; a bit dusty here and there. My beauty no-no is fake tan, fake bosoms and American veneers. I don't dye my hair as I'm rather looking forward to seeing it turn silver.

9. **Have you always been creative? What other creative outlets are you passionate about?**

ANS: I love painting and drawing. Whenever I have time, which is about once a year these days, I'll line up about 10 canvasses and fill them all in, in one day. I like to paint portraits in black and white, mostly. I sell them in a little gallery in Portstewart or give them away to friends. I also love sketching with an ink pen in gorgeous little hardback notebooks with marbled inlay pages.

I also love decorating fresh Christmas trees and I'll spend hours getting every fairy light exactly right and every glass bauble equally spaced and dangling nicely. Dermot and Alice sometimes move one single decoration to see if I'll notice, and I *always* do. I have a photographic eye for detail in inanimate objects, but often I'll not recognise one of the neighbours if they stop to give me a lift home from the shops. I can also memorise poems very quickly but I'm hopeless with maths and have never learned to drive.

Perhaps my mind is wired up the wrong way! I never cry at funerals but if someone is trying hard to achieve something, even just having a little bake sale to raise funds for charity, I suddenly feel very emotional and tearful. I do laugh a lot, at Seinfeld, for example but I rarely get over-excited. Even when I got my first major publishing deal in 2003, I was straight onto the Yellow Pages, saying to myself, "What great news: now I must get that awful bathroom fixed up at long last. And tiled as well. Let's have some lovely new stone tiles." I didn't have a glass of Champagne until about six months later.